2/22

The Last ADVENTURE *of*
CONSTANCE VERITY

ALSO BY A. LEE MARTINEZ

The Constance Verity Series
The Last Adventure of Constance Verity
Constance Verity Saves the World
Constance Verity Destroys the Universe

Gil's All Fright Diner
In the Company of Ogres
A Nameless Witch
The Automatic Detective
Too Many Curses
Monster
Chasing the Moon
Divine Misfortune
Emperor Mollusk Versus the Sinister Brain
Helen & Troy's Epic Road Quest

The Last ADVENTURE *of*

CONSTANCE VERITY

A. LEE MARTINEZ

Jo Fletcher
BOOKS

First published in the United States in 2016 by Saga Press
First published in Great Britain in 2022 by

Jo Fletcher
BOOKS

Jo Fletcher Books
an imprint of
Quercus Editions Ltd
Carmelite House
50 Victoria Embankm
London EC4Y 0DZ

An Hachette UK com

Copyright © 2016 Al

A CIP catalogue record for this book is available
from the British Library

PB ISBN 978 1 52940 811 9

10 9 8 7 6 5 4 3 2 1

Printed and bound in Great Britain by Clays Ltd, Elcograf S.p.A

Papers used by Jo Fletcher Books are from well-managed forests and other responsible sources.

To most of the usual folks:
to *Mom*, for being awesome;
to *Sally*: The Wife, for being awesome as well;
to *Sally*: The Agent, for heavy doses of
     awesomeness;
to *the many fine writers of the DFW Writers
     Workshop*. Yes, awesome. You get the idea.
And to *Doc Savage*, the Man of Bronze

The Last ADVENTURE of
CONSTANCE VERITY

_1_

rouble wasn't content to follow Constance Verity. Trouble was more proactive when it came to Connie. She'd grown used to trouble, so she knew it when she walked into a room. She'd been recognized, and there was nothing to be done about it. She almost stopped right there, thanked the interviewers for their time, and went on her way. But she'd come this far. She might as well go all the way.

"Please, Mrs. Smith, have a seat." Tom, an older man in a gray suit, gestured to the chair across the desk.

"It's Smythe," she corrected. "And it's Ms."

Jan continued to study Connie like a complicated math problem she couldn't quite solve in her head. She leaned over to Tom and whispered in his ear. His eyes went wide, then narrowed. A curious smile crossed his face.

"Terrific," mumbled Connie to herself.

"I'm sorry?" asked Tom.

"Oh, nothing." She smiled and smoothed her pants.

"Ms. Smythe, we've been looking at your resume, and I must say it's a bit thin." He held up the paper, ran his finger down the two paragraphs, and nodded to himself. "To be honest, we probably would've rejected you right out, but you scored incredibly well on the aptitude tests."

"Thank you."

It wasn't technically a compliment, but she felt like she should say something.

Jan folded her hands across the shared desk. "Yet according to this, you didn't even attend college."

Connie shrugged. "My education was . . . informal."

"Please, go on, Ms. Smythe."

They leaned forward.

"My childhood was chaotic. I might not have the credentials, but I am fluent in seventeen languages, type at two hundred words per minute on a good day, know how to fix any office machine you can think of and probably any you will have one day but haven't thought of yet, can run the mile in four minutes if I'm wearing a good pair of shoes. Oh, and I know shorthand, and I play a mean game of softball, if you need a new player to fill in while your starting shortstop recovers from his broken ankle."

"How did you know that?"

"I'm a bit of a detective, too."

He nodded again. "And where did you acquire these skills, Ms. Smythe?"

"Places," she replied. "Does it really matter? I'm qualified, aren't I?"

"Perhaps overqualified," said Jan.

"How can I be overqualified? You just said I don't have anything on my resume."

"But surely someone of your abilities can find more gainful employment elsewhere."

"I just need a job," said Connie. "If you don't want to give it to me—"

"Are you Constance Verity?" interrupted Jan.

"No, I'm Connie Smythe."

Tom went to his smartphone. This was so much easier before Google.

"Yes, that's me," said Connie. "But that's my old life."

Next came the questions.

Most people had questions.

"What is it like in the future?" asked Jan.

"Like now but with more evil robots. Good ones, too. No flying cars, though."

"Is it true you've died twice?"

"Three times. But one of those times, I was a clone, so it doesn't really count."

"What's Dracula really like?"

"Good guy, once you get past the creep vibe."

"I read on the Internet that you have telekinesis. Can you move this pencil?" Jan rolled it forward. The interviewers stared at it, expecting it to dance.

"I had telekinesis. For about a week," said Connie. "I don't see how that's relevant."

Frowning, Jan took back her pencil.

"I can see I've wasted your time." Connie stood up.

"Wait, Ms. Verity . . . Ms. Smythe. We might have a position available for you."

"Really?"

Tom smiled. "Yes. In fact, I can think of the perfect use for someone with your skills."

Connie shook her head. "I'm trying not to do that kind of stuff anymore."

He chuckled. "Oh, Ms. Smythe, I'm not talking about any of your more colorful talents. Although I'm certain those will come in handy eventually. No, we have an opening in the mailroom. Or would that be a problem?"

"No, not at all." She shook their hands. "You won't regret this. I promise."

"I'm sure we won't. Since you're here, why don't Jan and I go down with you and introduce you to the team?"

"Now?"

"Why not?"

Connie said, "Sure, but can we downplay the . . . stuff? I don't like to talk about it that much."

Jan and Tom smiled and nodded. "We understand. It'll be just between us."

It wouldn't be. It never was. Jan and Tom were certain to tell someone about meeting the Amazing Constance Verity, and by day's end, everyone would know. Connie just hoped nobody would make a big deal about it.

On the elevator ride to the basement, Jan and Tom flanked her. They smiled and bobbed their heads along to the Muzak. They were brimming with more questions, but to their credit, they didn't ask them. Maybe this would work out after all.

The elevator doors opened. The mailroom was a big, empty chamber where a dozen robed figures stood around a yawning chasm reaching deep into the foundation and beyond.

Connie groaned. "Ah, shit."

Tom pressed a ceremonial dagger against her back. "If you would be so kind, Ms. Verity."

She stepped out of the elevator, and the cultists all turned toward her.

"I just wanted a job," she said. "Is that too much to ask?"

"Ah, but we have a most important job for you," said Jan. "You will feed the Hungry Earth. What greater honor is there?"

"Pension matching?" she suggested. "Four weeks' vacation a year?"

They pushed her to the edge of the pit. At its distant bottom, a ring of giant teeth gnashed, a dozen tongues writhed.

"I must say you're taking this very well," said Jan.

"You don't think this is my first time on the sacrificial altar, do you? I've been offered up to dark gods and cosmic horrors more times than I've been to the dentist. And dental hygiene is very important to me."

"Ah, yes, Ms. Verity," said Tom. "But the difference here is that you are all alone. No one is here to save you."

"What makes you think I need to be saved?"

"Come now, Ms. Verity, even someone of your reputation for harrowing escapes can see you're at our mercy. This building is secure. There will be no last-minute arrival of the cavalry."

"First of all, you can stop using my name so much. Why do bad guys do that? It isn't dramatic. It's just repetitive.

"Secondly, what do you possibly hope to accomplish by feeding me to this thing? You don't think it cares about one little speck of flesh? It's a big, dumb thing. It's like expecting a whale to be grateful because you tossed it a potato chip."

The cultists gasped collectively with such precision, they must've rehearsed it in advance.

"You dare insult our god?" Jan sounded genuinely hurt by that. "There is but one penalty for such heresy. You must be sacrificed."

"Weren't you already planning on sacrificing me?"

The cultists mumbled among themselves.

"Enough of this!" shouted Tom. "Hurl Ms. Ver . . . her into the pit, that our glorious god might awaken this day."

Several cultists seized Connie and pushed her toward the precipice.

"You didn't let me finish," she said. "It's obvious at a glance that none of you have any combat training, aside from perhaps that lady in the back."

"I took judo for a year," confirmed the woman. "I'm a yellow belt."

"Good for you. So, yes, there are a lot of you, and you all have your special ceremonial knives, which are all very pretty but not very practical in a fight. But I've fought better and more and come out on top. I'm not saying you can't get lucky. You might, but I'm just playing the odds here. I single-handedly held back a regiment of robotic samurai at Agatsuma Gunma Canyon. But I'm sure your club of out-of-shape middle-managers will be the ones to punch my clock."

"I CrossFit," said a cultist among the throng.

"We know, Gary," said Jan. "We *all* know."

"I might not have much formal education," said Connie, "but adventuring is better training than any vocational school you're going to get. Practical training. Like the Seven Deadly Styles of Martian Kung Fu, shown to me by the Exalted Master Shang Ig Ga."

She kicked a captor in the face, elbowed another, and paralyzed a third with a finger strike on his neck. The cultists stood in shock.

"If you think that's impressive, just imagine how awesome it would be if I had the four arms and prehensile tail required to be a true master."

Tom raised his dagger.

"Don't do anything stupid, now," she said.

Howling, he charged her. She stepped aside, smashing him across the back, and he tumbled, screaming, into the abyss. The Hungry Earth swallowed him whole without so much as a slurp.

The rest of the cult reconsidered attacking Connie.

"See? Your god couldn't care less about one measly sacrifice.

You could shove the entire population of this city down that hole, and it wouldn't notice."

Jan was crestfallen. It was tough losing something you believed in. Even if that belief was ludicrous and insane.

"We're done here," said Connie.

A low, echoing rumble rolled out of the maw, and the ground shook under them.

The toothy jaws snapped open and shut eagerly, and its tongues slithered up the chasm.

"Huh." She shrugged. "I did not see that coming."

The cultists cheered. Their celebration was cut short when the creature's tongues whipped out of the pit and started dragging them to their doom.

Connie got into a lot of messes in a lot of different places. After decades of globe-trotting adventures, the governments of the world had created a special international agency dedicated solely to keeping track of her. It wasn't much, but it did make cleaning up the messes in the aftermath easier. Lucas Harrison was the lead agent of that agency.

He gazed down into the now quiet abyss in the basement.

"What the hell is that?"

"The Hungry Earth," said Connie.

"The hungry what?"

"Earth. Have you ever wondered what's underneath that shell of rock we're standing on?" She pointed to the rows of teeth and flaccid tongues. "There you have it."

"Like a monster? How big is it?"

"You should know this already," she said. "It's in the files."

"We have a dozen cabinets of files on you, Verity. I can't be expected to memorize every weird thing you've been involved in."

"Isn't that your job?"

"I'm the liaison. Agent Barker is records."

"How is she doing?" asked Connie.

"She's on paid leave. Read something in one of the files that gave her night terrors." He pointed to the giant maw below. "How big is that thing?"

"Earth-sized," she replied. "It's in the name: The Hungry Earth."

"You're telling me the earth is a monster."

"More or less." She nodded to the six remaining cultists who hadn't been eaten by their mindless god. "And these yahoos almost woke it up. What? You didn't think it was hollow, did you?"

Her condescending tone rubbed him the wrong way.

"I distinctly remember that incident with the subterranean Neanderthal invasion," he said.

"Part of it's hollow," she corrected. "But most of it's monster."

"We're living on the skin of a sleeping monster. What the hell happens when it wakes up, Verity?"

"Don't know. Don't want to find out. I chucked some cinnamon into its mouth, and that put it right back to sleep."

"Where the hell did you find cinnamon so fast?"

"I'm resourceful."

"You're telling me you just saved the world. Again."

"Technically, I saved us from the world."

"I'll be sure to include that in my report. This will probably push Barker over the edge."

Barker wouldn't be the first agent overwhelmed by the secret files of Constance Verity. It was doubtful she would be the last. Harrison himself had replaced the previous agency head who had called it quits after having to fish Connie out of the ocean and find an environmentally friendly way of disposing of the six-hundred-ton corpse of the kraken. Constance stayed sane by virtue of having confronted this stuff since she was a child. It wasn't weird. It was life.

"What are we supposed to do with this great big hole?" asked Harrison. "Fill it with concrete?"

Connie handed him a business card. "Call this number. Ask for Abigail Cromwell Nightshade. Be sure to use the full name. She's very particular about that. She'll know what to do."

"You just carry this around on you in case of emergencies?"

"I carry a lot of things around with me in case of emergencies, Harrison. You know that."

He tucked the card in his pocket. "I don't know how you do it, Verity. I'd be exhausted if I constantly got into adventures."

"Who says I'm not? Sure, I can get by on one hour of sleep. I've got the unflagging endurance of a kid who grew up wrestling dinosaurs and running from space barbarians. But it gets old. You can only punch so many zombies, and after a while, saving the world loses its charm."

"So, why don't you stop?"

"Now, why didn't I think of that?" She shook her head. "It's not really up to me. It's out of my hands. Always has been."

"You're telling me that with everything you've done, every unbelievable person you've known, every incredible near escape and last-minute save, you can't control your own destiny? I don't know, Verity. If you can't, who the hell can?"

Connie chuckled.

"Something funny?" he asked.

"No. Hadn't thought of it. That's all. You said exactly what someone should've told me years ago. I'm Constance Danger Verity. I've defeated magical Nazis in four different alternate realities, and saved the King of the Moon from a literal army of ninja assassins. I can do anything. Why the hell can't I do this?"

She slapped Harrison on the shoulder.

"Thank you."

"You're welcome." Grumbling, he answered the phone. "Harrison here. Yes, most of the goddamn planet, apparently."

Connie left him to his conversation and set out on her great adventure.

2

Professor Arthur Arcane sat in his study. Two layers of dust covered everything, and Connie brushed off a stack of books, all written by him, on the paranormal. Arcane was the foremost authority in the field of parapsychology. Or he had been, up until he'd sacrificed his life to repel an incursion by an army of disgruntled specters from the Other Side.

"I'm dead, you say?" he asked.

"Yes, sorry to have to break it to you," she replied.

"Funny. I don't feel dead. I expected it to be . . . colder. Or warmer."

She shrugged. "Maybe it's because of the way you died."

"When did it happen?" he asked.

"A couple of years ago. There was this artifact buried at these crossroads . . . Y'know what? The details aren't really important."

"And now I'm a ghost. I suppose there's some irony in that. I was wondering why the cleaning staff was doing such a lackluster job."

He blew at some dust, and his spectral breath managed to raise a few specks.

"Nobody's bought the house since I passed?"

"People say it's haunted."

He laughed.

"And why are you here again, Connie?"

"I like to check on you. I kept a key to the place." Not that she needed it.

"Check on me?" He folded his hands under his chin. "Since I don't remember any of those other times, I have to assume that means I have standard recurring spectral memory fugue."

She nodded.

"And we've had this conversation before."

"I've lost count."

"Disappointing, but not unexpected."

"You always say that."

"Yes, I imagine I'm prone to repetition. Nature of a repetitive spirit manifestation, isn't it? After all the time I spent studying them, I have to say becoming one isn't very interesting."

He always said that, too.

"I miss you, Arthur. I never really got the chance to tell you when it mattered, but I think I was falling in love with you."

Arthur eyebrows arched. His glasses slid down his nose. He pushed them up.

"I had no idea."

"Neither did I. Not until after you were gone." She sighed. "Died, I mean. You're still here."

"And you still come to visit me?"

"I hope you aren't here. And I hope you are."

"Connie, you can't torture yourself like this. I'm sure you did everything you could to save me."

She laughed. "I'm not feeling guilty, Arthur. I've lost people before. Goes with the territory. I just wish we could've lived different lives."

"Yes, well, I'm afraid it's too late for one of us. And you never really had a choice."

"I'm going to become normal," she said.

"Do you want to do that?" he asked.

"I'm going to try."

"No, Connie. I didn't ask if you could. I'm asking if you *want* to."

"Of course I want to. What kind of question is that?"

"Connie, being normal isn't as easy as not having adventures. It's not something you just become." He tried to take her hand, but his fingers passed through hers. "Oh, right. Ghost. Keep forgetting that. My point is that you can't just elect to be normal. You've seen and done too much. It's not as simple as flicking a switch."

"I know at least four or five guys with time machines," she said.

"Time machines are not how ordinary people solve their problems," he said. "As I recall, you always said time travel never works out the way you want, anyway."

"I never got to go to my prom," she said.

"I didn't go to mine."

"I didn't *get* to go. I was off fighting yetis on Venus. Not that it would've mattered. I barely went to school. Didn't make any friends there. You're my second-best friend, Arthur, and you're dead."

"Again. Not a very ordinary thing. Is it so bad being special?"

"I used to love this stuff. Gallivanting across the universe, fighting evil, discovering lost mysteries, saving the world." She smiled. "It was fun. And I didn't think a whole hell of a lot about what I was losing in the process. Proms and weddings and casual Fridays. I lost my virginity in the Amazon jungle to Korak the Savage, and it was glorious. But it isn't supposed to be like that."

"It's easy to see what you don't have."

"Don't feed me that *grass is always greener* line. I keep thinking of all the things I didn't have that most people do, and it's starting to piss me off. I know a million people would trade places with me in a heartbeat, but it's not everything it looks like from the outside."

"Yes." He cleaned his glasses. "As clichéd as this might seem, we all have our crosses to bear."

She was hoping he'd understand where she was coming from. His own extraordinary passion had been his undoing, and now he was trapped between life and death. It probably helped he kept forgetting that.

"I missed your funeral, Arthur."

"I'm sure you had a good reason."

"There are always reasons. And they're always good. But,

goddamn it, I loved you. I could have at least been there to pay my respects."

"If there's one thing I've learned from this experience, it is that ghosts don't generally care about such things."

"Yes, but the living do. I do. Even if I ignore all the things I can't get back because it's too late, I think about all the things that are destined to come up. My mom had a bunion removed the other day. She didn't call me. It wasn't a big deal, but one of these times, it will be a big deal. And I won't be there for her or Dad when it happens. I'm sure there will be a good reason for it, but it won't change that I'll end up letting down the people I care about."

"But what about all the people you've helped?"

"Strangers. Mom keeps a scrapbook of all the commendations, thankful letters, and awards I've gotten. It looks nice, but what does it add up to in the end?"

"Haven't you saved the world on multiple occasions?"

"That's what people tell me, but I'm beginning to think that the world isn't as fragile as all that. The universe got along just fine for billions of years without me. I don't think it needs me to save it. I think it all works out about the same in the end. Sometimes, I like to think of myself with a dead-end job that I dislike, a husband who is letting himself go, and some ungrateful kids I take to soccer practice. It sounds dreary, but at least it would be my life. I know it sounds selfish."

"It's not selfish," he said. "Or maybe it is. But it's not unreasonable."

He smiled at her, and he was so handsome in a bookish way that she wished she could kiss him. Touch his face. Caress his hand. Anything.

"My question does then become *Can you?*" he asked.

"I can try," she said.

"I'd wish you luck, but you don't need it."

"Thanks." She paused on the way out of the study. "Sorry again about missing your funeral."

"Funeral? Wait? Am I dead?"

Sighing, she closed the door on him.

3

Connie, as a woman of two worlds, had always had some trouble making friends. The extraordinary people she met on her adventures were usually so busy on their own adventures that unless they needed help foiling an alien invasion or exploring the booby-trapped ruins of a long-lost civilization, they didn't keep in touch.

Ordinary friends came with their own unique set of problems. It wasn't easy to balance the normal and the extraordinary. Those two sides of her life didn't get always get along, and the consequences could be bothersome.

She'd had three boyfriends meet tragic ends. Once would have been bad luck. Twice would have been forgivable. Three times was a sign from the universe. The healthiest relationship she'd ever had had been with a warlord who lived in the mythic past, and that was complicated by the whole time travel thing, which she'd learned to avoid ever since having to kill several evil versions of herself from the future. Or would kill them at some point. She still wasn't clear on that.

Connie did have one friend among the ordinary, who had been a friend of hers since Connie's seventh birthday party, which had been interrupted by a giant snake attack. After she'd slain the monster by taking advantage of its severe birthday cake allergy, all the other children had fled. All of them except Tia, who had managed to save a cupcake for Connie. From then on, they'd been the best of friends.

They'd made plans to meet up at their go-to, a kitschy chain restaurant designed with a manufactured quirky aesthetic. It was boring and dull, the kind of place adventures didn't happen. Not often, anyway. Everywhere Connie went, adventure might be lurking.

Connie arrived first. She always did. It was protocol. She found a table, and when she sat down, her cell rang.

"The eagle eats cheese at midnight," said Tia mysteriously.

"The moose dances under the half-moon," replied Connie, equally mysteriously.

There was a pause.

"Wait. Is that good or bad?" asked Tia.

"Why are you asking me? You're the one who came up with the code phrases."

"It's a lot to keep track of. Moose is code for vampires, right? Is there a vampire there right now?"

"Moose is code for aliens," said Connie.

"There are aliens there?"

Connie glanced at the unassuming man sitting at a booth

across the room. Not many people would've noticed the secondary gills on his neck or the slit where his third eye was shut tight. Even fewer would've known to look.

"There's one," she said. "But he's just here with friends. Shouldn't be a problem."

"This isn't going to be like the mummy incident, is it? As I recall, you said he wasn't going to be a problem, either."

"No, I said I didn't *think* he would be problem. Mummies are unpredictable. You're the one who still wanted to go to the Egyptian artifacts exhibit with me, even knowing my history with the cursed undead. So, that wasn't my fault. But this is just an alien, a native of the Ragkurian Spiral, from the looks of it. They're perfectly harmless."

"Then why did you mention him?"

"Will you stop giving me a hard time and just come on? The coast is clear, I swear. The most dangerous thing here is a woman at the bar contemplating killing her husband for the insurance money."

"You know I love you, Connie, but it's creepy when you do that detective thing."

"Sorry. We can do this at the Safe Zone."

The Safe Zone was the break room at the insurance company where Tia worked. Nothing exciting ever happened there.

"No, it's cool. I'm sick of microwaved burritos, anyway." Tia slid around from behind Connie and stepped up to the table. Tia hung up her phone and arched her eyebrows. "Did I surprise you?"

"Sure. Totally. I had no idea you slipped the busboy ten bucks to hide in the kitchen to try and get the drop on me. Just like I have no idea that you got here forty minutes early to do it, and that you ate a BLT when you got too hungry to wait."

Tia took a seat at the table. "Somebody is feeling snarky today. I take it the job interview didn't go very well."

"I did keep the world from killing us all, but other than that, it was a bust."

"Sorry to hear that."

"It's cool. I'm just cranky because I'm hungry."

Connie ordered a soup, sandwich, and beer. The soup was bland. The sandwich was chewy. The beer was warm. None of which was surprising. The restaurant's unexceptional nature was why they came here.

"I still don't know why you want a job, anyway," said Tia. "Jobs are boring. And you don't have to work, right? You're rich."

"Not as rich as you might think. Most of the treasure I've collected over the years was cursed. You can't really spend that stuff. But, yes, I'm not hurting for money. This isn't about money. Money doesn't mean much when you don't have time to enjoy it, and if I could go on a vacation now and then, I wouldn't have much to complain about.

"Every day is an adventure for me. Every single day. Sometimes, if they're short, I can manage to fit in two in a day. I just want to go home, curl up on the couch, and not worry about being kidnapped by rock monsters or getting mixed up with handsome, devil-may-care rogues."

"I keep telling you to feel free to send any unwanted rogues my way."

"They lose their charm," said Connie. "And that's if they don't end up betraying you in an elaborate scheme to steal the crown jewels of England."

"I bet betrayal sex is pretty hot, though," replied Tia with a wry smile.

Connie nodded. "True. It's almost worth it. Just as long as you don't mind dangling over a crocodile pit afterward."

"I still have a hard time believing they have a crocodile pit in the Tower of London."

"They have crocodile pits everywhere."

Tia asked, "What's your plan, then?"

"Who says I have a plan?"

"You do. I can see it your eyes. You've got that look. Determined. Focused. Don't deny it. I've seen it a thousand times before. Which leads me to believe that you're about to do something foolhardy and incredible, and since it's been a while since I've seen it, I can only assume that this is all about your desire to be normal."

"That detective thing is kind of creepy," agreed Connie.

"For an ordinary person, I have my moments."

"You're right. I do have a plan, and the beauty of it is its simplicity."

Connie leaned forward. The cheap restaurant lighting cast dark shadows across her face.

"I'm going to kill my fairy godmother."

C onstance Verity wasn't born special, but she did become special a little over three hours later.

The very short woman fluttered into the hospital room. Her tiny gossamer wings were far too small and delicate to bear her aloft, but since they barely flapped at all, it was safe to say they were mostly for show. She wore a garish purple-and-blue pants suit. Glittering gowns had fallen out of favor among her profession several decades before. She still had a fondness for sequins, and they sparkled on her lapel.

"Ah, there you are." Her round, cherubic face wrinkled into a soft smile. Her rosy cheeks glowed, and she removed a wand from her inside jacket pocket. "I had a devil of a time finding you, my dear."

Mr. Verity, an unassuming man of indeterminate ethnicity and aged somewhere between twenty and fifty years (as best any casual observer could guess), was a technical sort and was intrigued how she managed to stay airborne. His first guess was some manner of wire harness, but that seemed impractical.

"May we help you?" he asked.

She chuckled. "Oh, no, it is I who shall help you. Not you, specifically. It's far too late to help you. You're both perfectly fine, perfectly dull people, though I don't mean that as a slight to either of you. The world can always use more perfectly fine, perfectly dull people. But your daughter need not be one."

Constance's mother, who was every bit as indeterminate as her husband, said, "Did Sharon send you?"

"Fate itself sent me, my good woman. To offer a blessing on this beautiful child." She landed beside the bed and offered a business card to Mr. Verity. It read GRANDMOTHER WILLOW, FAIRY GODMOTHER.

Grandmother Willow winked at Constance, who studied her godmother with the blank, confused stare reserved for newborns and potheads contemplating if their cats knew the secrets of the universe and just weren't sharing them.

"How much does this cost?" asked Mr. Verity as he waved his hands over Grandmother Willow in search of wires.

"For you? Not a thing. I've been contracted by an outside agency for this one." She put her stubby finger to her lip. "Don't ask me. I'm not allowed to tell. But one blessing shall be yours, and it shall shape the course of this beautiful child's life in the most fantastic ways."

She tapped her wand against the end table to shake loose the fairy dust. A small pile of colorful sand glittered like a rainbow.

"The question is, what form shall that blessing be? Great fortune? Too uninteresting. Great fame? Too shallow. Flawless beauty? So last-century. Superhuman strength? Too traditional. Speaking with animals?" She shook her head and chuckled. "Heavens, no. The chattering gossip of birds alone is enough to drive one to endless distraction."

"Don't we get a say?" asked Mrs. Verity, who didn't believe this for a moment but was enjoying the game.

"No, no, no. Parents can't be trusted with this decision. It's far too important. Perhaps I should ask the child herself." Grandmother Willow floated over the bed, and Mr. Verity decided it must have something to do with magnets.

"Tell me, dear child, what is your fondest wish?"

She hovered close to Constance, who gurgled.

"I see. But could you be more specific?"

Constance sneezed in Grandmother Willow's face. Frowning, the fairy godmother landed at the foot of the bed. She wiped her face with a handkerchief as a dark little cloud rumbled over her head.

"A dangerous choice, little one, but it is yours to make."

She waved her wand in circles in the air, spewing sparkling dust throughout the room.

"Though all other mortals tread in either the ordinary or the fantastic, you shall journey through both. On the dawn of your seventh birthday, yours shall become a life of adventure and wonder, and it shall be so until the day of your glorious death."

A blinding light bathed the room.

"So it shall be!" shouted Grandmother Willow. Her words echoed throughout the hospital for several minutes, running back and forth playfully through its halls.

The light vanished in a pop.

Grandmother Willow brushed the fairy dust off her shoulder. There was a layer of the stuff on everything.

"Sorry about the mess." She nodded to Mr. and Mrs. Verity as she tucked her wand back into her pocket. "Good day. And congratulations."

She hovered out the door via a carefully concealed personal hovercraft built into her slacks, Mr. Verity decided.

"Isn't it bad luck to kill a fairy godmother?" she asked.

"Probably," said Connie. "But it's what I need to do."

"That's pretty cold-blooded."

"I've killed before."

"That's not what I'm talking about. Those other times, they were self-defense, right? You've never tracked someone down to kill them before, have you?"

"The way I see it, this is self-defense."

"You're sidestepping the question."

"I've studied under the second-greatest assassin in the universe. And when he was killed by the greatest assassin, I studied under her. I've seen enough and done enough to know that life is cheap, and that the line between hero and killer can be a thin one."

"Oh, brother." Tia rolled her eyes. "How long have you had that speech in your pocket?"

"Since this afternoon when I came up with this plan and knew you'd try to talk me out of it."

"I'm not trying to talk you out of it," said Tia. "I'm just trying to get you to think about it some more. It's what friends do when friends are on the verge of possibly making a mistake."

"You do think this is a mistake."

"I said *possibly*. I don't know, Connie. I haven't led your life, but I have been sitting on the sidelines for most of it, been mixed up with it now and then. I can say this isn't you. You're not a killer. Not like that."

"Maybe you're right. The only way to find out is to track down my godmother and see what happens."

"Fine, but I'm coming with you, then."

"No way. It's too dangerous."

"We are talking about a fairy godmother here," said Tia. "What's she going to do? Run me over with a pumpkin carriage? Smother me in an avalanche of ball gowns?"

"You're thinking of fairies from Disney movies. Real fae are dangerous and unpredictable."

"That's exactly why you should have backup."

"You'd be a liability," said Connie.

"Even better. Didn't you once tell me that the mark of a good sidekick is being undertrained and overenthusiastic?"

"You're telling me you want to be a sidekick?"

"No, I want to be *your* sidekick. You're *the* Constance Verity. You do all kinds of awesome stuff every day. I want in on some of that. I've lived a perfectly ordinary life up to this point, aside from those moments when I've been dragged into your exploits. What's it gotten me? A dull job, a divorce, and a house I've spent too many years decorating and redecorating. I was just talking to my mom about experimenting with a neo-Asian/postmodernist Russian fusion motif." Tia shuddered. "Dear God, what has my life become? You've saved me from space aliens and gangsters. You can at least save me from shopping for tapestries.

"And before you tell me no, I'll just come along anyway, following stubbornly behind until you have no choice but to bring me with you."

"You would, wouldn't you?" Connie laughed. "Okay, you're in, but I take no responsibility for whatever happens."

"What's going to happen? I'll be beside Constance Verity, probably the safest place in the whole goddamn universe to be."

"Oh, why did you have to say that? You just jinxed it."

"I didn't think you believed in jinxes," said Tia.

Connie didn't.

But she wasn't so sure that jinxes didn't believe in her, and they'd had a long, long time to build a grudge.

6

Connie had learned to enjoy her quiet moments when she could. After the incident with the Hungry Earth, she was due for some downtime. The cosmos usually portioned out some relaxation after she saved the day.

Tia had evening plans with her normal friends. She invited Connie along. It was always a risk hanging out with Tia's friends. Connie wasn't great with normal people and normal stuff. She could fake it, but it was all so much chatter. Try as she might, she couldn't give a shit about most ordinary stuff. She didn't watch much TV. When she found time to read, it was usually obscure instructional texts about skills she figured she might need at some point. Her musical knowledge was mostly limited to pop songs originating in the Large Magellanic Cloud, which were surprisingly catchy once you got past the screeching vocals.

She turned down the invitation and made plans to meet Tia the next day for Connie's final adventure.

"It might do you some good to get out with normal people," said Tia.

"You know me and people," replied Connie.

"Yes, I know you. And people. But if you're really trying to be normal, you might as well get used to it."

"We both know it doesn't work like that. If I go with you, you're just as likely to have something weird happen. I don't think your friend Dolores has ever forgiven me for ruining her baby shower."

"Ruining? If you hadn't been there, we'd all be brains in jars right now."

"I don't think that's the way she sees it," said Connie.

It was a complicated question. Did Connie cause strange adventures to happen by her mere presence, or did the universe compel her to stumble across them? She hadn't ever figured it out, but she couldn't blame Tia's friends for being paranoid. If she showed up with Tia, half of them would probably make excuses to leave. The other half would politely pretend not to be expecting disaster to strike while jumping at every sudden noise.

"Have it your way," said Tia, "but you better not start your adventure without me."

"Wouldn't dream of it," said Connie, though she had considered it.

They parted ways, and Connie went back to her apartment in the better part of town.

Mr. Prado was there to greet her. He usually was. He owned

the building and spent much of his time in the lobby, reading books, waiting for someone to walk by so that he could start up a conversation. Connie suspected he only owned the building to be able to corner people on their way to the elevators.

He perked up at the sight of Connie. "If it isn't my favorite tenant. Tell me about the wonderful new job you found today?"

"No job today," she replied.

"Oh, I'm certain you'll find something soon. Unless you end up getting involved in one of your digressions. I wouldn't be too concerned. I'm sure something will pop up soon enough."

Connie stepped into the elevator.

"You had a package delivered earlier," said Prado. "Don't worry. Refused delivery, as you requested. It was a most peculiar shape though, and it was singing. I do wonder what was in it."

Connie had stopped wondering years ago. She was always getting mysterious packages. Two or three a week. In her youth, she'd opened them with zeal, ready to dive into whatever strange exploit they'd begin. She'd since soured on those little enigmatic gifts.

"Thanks, Mr. Prado. You're a lifesaver."

"Anytime," he said as the elevator doors closed.

Connie's place was a jumble of boxes, packed with the treasures of an extraordinary life. Some might mistakenly believe her to be a hoarder, but she had room for all the stuff if she could find the time to unpack it. Adventuring was time-intensive, and there weren't enough hours in the day to fight dragons and settle into any kind of routine. That was why Grandmother Willow's blessing had been a curse. Being a part of both worlds meant something had to suffer, and as much as Connie tried to avoid it, it was the ordinary world that usually fell by the wayside.

She unwound with a long bath and a beer. She sat on her couch, surrounded by her souvenirs, and tried zoning out by watching TV.

It didn't work.

She was more wound up than she'd thought. The idea that this could be her last hurrah made her eager to get on with it. She'd never been terribly patient. She was a woman of action, and when she set her mind on something, she usually did it. But she'd promised Tia that she'd wait.

But she wouldn't wait in her apartment. She decided to go out. She had no solid plans, but she'd figure something out.

While she was locking the door to her apartment, the door across the hall opened and a woman exited.

Connie nodded to her. "Hello."

"Hello," said the woman. "Did you just move in?"

"No, I've lived here for a while," said Connie.

Suspicion crossed the woman's face. "Huh. I thought they just used that place for storage."

It wasn't far from the truth.

"I guess we haven't met before. I travel a lot. Don't spend much time at home. I'm Connie."

The neighbor squinted. "You look familiar. Are you famous?"

"I won the lottery once," replied Connie. It wasn't a lie. She didn't add that it led to her discovery of a lottery-fixing scheme and a shootout in a zeppelin. It just kept things simple.

"Oh, yeah. I'm Dana."

She appeared ordinary. A little too ordinary. Connie's suspicions popped up. A lot of ordinary things in her life weren't ordinary.

Dana, whose hand had been out there for a few seconds, pulled it back. Connie reached for it.

"Sorry. I'm a little distracted. Connie."

They shook hands. She measured the handshake for anything suspicious. Spongy android flesh. Room-temperature undead. Too-hot lava person. An electrical zap. The pinprick of a hidden needle filled with poison. All the usual stuff.

Dana's cell rang. She turned her back on Connie.

"I'm on my way. So what if I'm late? It's a poetry slam. They'll start without me. Yeah, yeah. I'll miss out on a few of the clever capitalism/slavery metaphors shouted by people in quirky hats."

She ended the call and grunted.

"Poetry slam?" said Connie.

"It's a showcase of the self-important and the uninspired. Although once in a while, someone comes up with something good if you're willing to wade through the bullshit. Or so I'm told. Hasn't happened yet, but . . ."—she crossed her fingers—"but my boyfriend is a hipster, so I'm stuck."

"You could always break up with him," said Connie. "Then

again, taking relationship advice from me is probably a bad idea."

"Believe me. I've thought about it. But he's actually very sweet. I go to his poetry slams. He doesn't tell me I'm a pawn of the patriarchy for shaving my legs. Not often, anyway."

"Sounds reasonable," said Connie.

"A girl learns to make compromises. It was nice meeting you." Dana walked toward the elevator.

Connie paused before the open door to her apartment.

She called to Dana. "I've never been to a poetry slam."

"Oh, it's dreadful," said Dana with a smile. "Not for the faint of heart."

Connie chuckled. "That's one thing I've never been accused of."

The coffeehouse was the kind of place people who were too cool for Starbucks went, where they ordered the same sort of complicated, overpriced coffees they could get at Starbucks but at an even more overpriced cost with the assurances that the cow that the milk came from lived on a private farm where it was fed only the finest feed and massaged twice a day.

Connie had never cared for coffee. She could drink it. After living off moldy bread and troll blood for a week, she could pretty much drink anything. Literally. A side effect of the blood was an immunity to all poisons, a talent that came in handy in her day-to-day life.

She ordered an apple cider, and the barista glared like

she'd asked for a bottle of freshly squeezed toddler brains.

"We have over two hundred varieties of coffee," he said.

"I don't like coffee," she replied.

The barista steadied himself with two hands on the counter as if mortally wounded. "You just think that because you haven't had good coffee."

"If you don't want people ordering the cider, why is it on the menu?"

He ignored the question. "We have coffee that doesn't taste very much like coffee."

"How much is not very much?" she asked.

He considered the question. "A little bit like coffee. But we can put chocolate into it. Whipped cream."

"Yeah, I'll have that, then," she replied, "but without the coffee."

"We have an artisan blend that tastes almost exactly like hot chocolate."

Connie wasn't interested in this fight. She should've just ordered a fucking coffee, but she was terrible at walking away from battles.

"Look, Jonathan—"

"It's Jone-athan." He pointed to his nametag.

"It's not spelled Jone-athan."

He fixed her with a look reserved for poseurs and idiots.

"Fine. It's your name. What do I care?" she said. "Jone-athan, I just want something to drink that isn't coffee. I know that this offends your sensibilities, and I'm sure that any one of your coffees is this glorious wonderland of flavor experiences that will delight my senses now and forever. But I'm a Philistine, an uncultured fool who has been despoiled by a culture that loads me up with sugary beverages and processed foodstuffs. I could no more appreciate your unparalleled coffee nectar than I could understand the genius of whatever arthouse auteur director you currently love or whatever obscure musical group you and exactly four of your friends listen to. I will never be cool like you. I will never understand the secret beauty of this world the way you do. So, give me a cider and your pity and/or contempt, and we can both get on with our lives."

Jone-athan's smirk faded. He shrugged. "Whatever, lady."

She bought her drink and joined Dana at a table.

"Cider?" asked Dana as she sipped at her coffee. She frowned and stuck out her tongue. "Well, good for you. I've never been able to stand up to Jone-athan."

"I've slain bigger monsters." Connie smiled as she sipped her bland cider. "When's Willis up?"

Willis, Dana's hipster boyfriend, was a tall, good-looking guy with a bad haircut and questionable taste in pseudo-African fashion, but he was nice enough.

"Soon. He's getting ready. Something about cleansing his aura, aligning his chakras. I'm sorry about that lecture he gave you about truth versus art. He's not as annoying once you get to know him."

Connie wasn't so sure about that, but he was mostly

inoffensive. He genuinely seemed to care about Dana too. He wasn't Connie's boyfriend, so she didn't see a reason to care. It was simply nice to be out among ordinary people.

Except it put Connie on edge. She'd worried, in the last ten years or so, that her hypervigilance would become a problem. It was justified by her life, but it did make enjoying the quiet times more difficult. Like noticing a briefcase sitting, unaccompanied, by the bathroom for the last six minutes. Or the guy with the eye patch at the corner table who hadn't actually done anything suspicious, but she'd always had bad luck with people wearing eye patches, so she couldn't help but be wary.

"Oh, Byron's here," said Dana, snapping Connie out of her danger sense.

"Byron?"

"My brother. Didn't I mention him?" She waved to a tall man.

"No, you didn't," said Connie.

"Well, he wasn't sure he could make it. He doesn't always."

Byron walked over. Connie deduced he liked jazz and was something of a cinephile. His favorite food was anything fried, and he loved to dance. She silenced her inner detective.

Dana introduced Connie. She shook his hand. It wasn't android-spongy.

Byron wasn't handsome, but he was cute. A little pudgy. His left eye was a little bit lazy, but he probably hadn't realized that yet. His tie was askew, though that was probably a fluke, given the tidiness of the rest of his appearance.

Connie frowned, telling her detective to shut up.

"Something wrong?" he asked, catching the frown.

"No. Just distracted by . . . stuff," she said, then after a pause, added, "Poetry, right?"

He sat. "What'd I miss? Don't tell me I missed the bird guy."

"Bird guy?" asked Connie.

"You'll know him when you see him," said Dana. "His soul is a bird. Hope is a bird. Love is a bird. Basically, everything's a bird. Except hate. Hate is a Camaro, for some reason."

"Guess I should get a coffee," he said. "Where'd you get that cider?"

"They sell it," said Connie.

Byron appraised her as if meeting Beowulf in the flesh. "I bet Jone-athan didn't like that."

"Don't like coffee either?" she asked.

He shrugged. "I should order something."

"I'll take care of it," she said.

"You don't have to do that."

"It's no problem."

He glanced over at Jone-athan, who sat beside the espresso machine like a judgmental gargoyle in flip-flops. "If you insist . . ."

"Just saving the day," she said. "It's what I do."

They shared a smile. He was definitely cute.

She faced down the guardian of all things cool and environmentally responsible, and returned with a cider for Byron and a vegan cookie that tasted surprisingly good.

An elderly woman, complete with shawl and walker, took the mic and began reciting an ode to sexual awakening. Dana distracted herself with her phone while Byron listened intently. Connie found the part about receiving her lover's warm seed into her welcoming petals a bit unsettling and chuckled to herself.

Byron didn't.

As the woman started talking about rough hands caressing secret places, he noticed Connie watching him.

He laughed. "Sorry. She's one of my favorites."

"You really like this?" asked Connie. "No judgment. Sorry if it came across that way."

"It's people trying to share an intimate part of themselves," he replied. "Sure, they're failing miserably, but at least they're trying. Takes a lot of courage or ego or stupidity to get up on that stage, but that's kind of what makes greatness. Not that these people will ever be great, but that just makes it more worthy in a way."

"I guess I hadn't thought of it like that."

"The world is full of people who smirk on the sidelines. I'd much rather be a cheerleader."

"Point taken."

They clinked their bottles together.

"So, what do you do for a living?" he asked.

She paused. It wasn't a question that came up often. Most people in a position to ask it already knew. She'd lived with a nebulous brand of fame for decades now. Most people had heard of her, but not many people knew what she looked like. She didn't do interviews. She didn't seek fame out. She kept a low profile. It was inevitable that some of her adventures would thrust her into the spotlight, but there was usually someone else ready to jump in front of her and take credit, and she was always happy to let them.

"I'm sorry," he said. "I hope it wasn't a rude question."

"No, it's not that. Like I said, I'm just distracted. I'm between jobs right now." She felt bad. It was a lie by omission. A bad way to start things off.

Start what off? She'd barely met Byron. Barely exchanged a few sentences. He didn't have a wife, though. Or a girlfriend. Hadn't had one in at least five or six months. He might've been divorced, but if so, he didn't have any kids. Wasn't gay. And he was interested in her.

Sometimes, being a detective had its perks.

He said, "I get it. Why do we make such a big deal about our jobs? Like they define us. We're more than that, right? I'm an accountant, myself. People think it's boring. And it is. But people think I'm boring too because of it."

"And are you?" she asked.

"If I'm being honest . . ." He waggled his hand.

She laughed. He smiled.

He had the cutest smile.

Connie and Byron made out outside her apartment door for a few moments.

They paused to catch their breath, and he glanced at Dana's door across the hall. She'd left the coffeehouse hours before while Connie and Byron continued to talk until the place closed down. Then they'd gone to an all-night diner and talked some more. And then they'd ended up here.

"We could've gone to your place," said Connie. She wished they had. All the bric-a-brac of her complicated life lay inside her apartment, but her place had been closer.

"I don't really do stuff like this," he said. "Ever."

She chuckled. "Don't worry. I'll respect you in the morning. Would you like to come in?"

"Are you sure?" he asked. "Not that I'm assuming anything is going to happen, but—"

"We're going to have sex," said Connie. "That is, if you want to."

"Of course I want to, but aren't you worried about moving too fast?"

"It's just sex," she said.

He made an ambiguous noise. She sometimes forgot that for normal people, sex could be a big deal. Most of Connie's life had been short-term relationships, casual sex, fly-by-night affairs of convenience.

She kissed him again, and he pulled her into his arms.

"Yeah," he said. "Just sex, right?"

There was a little wobble in his voice. The poor guy was nervous. It was charming. She was a little nervous herself. Her non-adventure sexual experiences had been a mixed bag. Once you'd made love hiding in the tiger pits of a mad maharajah, a lot of non-adventure sex lost its luster. It wasn't exactly a fetish, but Connie would've felt more comfortable if they'd been under the stars of a steamy jungle.

This was just sex. Just sex. Nothing but two people testing out each other's bodies, seeing how they might line up, hoping to hell that they didn't fuck it up somehow.

Who was she kidding? She was probably more nervous than him.

He must've sensed her trepidation. His hand, caressing her breast, moved down to her waist. "We don't have to do this if you don't want."

She pulled him tighter, buried her face in his chest. "No, I really want to do this."

And she did. More than anything. She liked him, and she wasn't sure where this was going. It might be a mistake, but it was the kind of mistake she could make without fearing blowing up the universe. The stakes were absurdly low.

But damn it, she really liked him.

She pushed open her apartment door, and they moved inside, hands fumbling with each other's clothes. He did glance around at the mess, probably thinking her a hoarder. Thankfully, it wasn't difficult to turn his attention back to her. He'd have questions, but those questions could wait.

In the morning, she'd be off on another perilous adventure, but that was hours away. Right now, right here, all that mattered was him and her.

He swept her up in his arms. She'd been swept up in many arms in her life, but this time, it felt different. His knees wobbled as he lifted her up, and with unsteady strides and a determined effort not to look strained, he carried her to the bedroom.

7

The sex was good. Not Amazon-jungle great. Not the Seven Towers of Vark great. But it was good enough, and she was glad to have it. Afterward, they cuddled, smiling at each other like a couple of idiots.

"I really like you," he said.

She laughed. "I would hope so."

He pushed himself up on his elbows. "I have to tell you something."

She put a finger to his lips. "No, you don't."

Connie didn't want to hear it. This wasn't the time to share secrets. She didn't need to find out that he was on the run from the mob or that a curse made everyone in his family transform into bears after sex. She didn't care.

Byron lowered her finger. "I know who you are. I recognized you when I first saw you at the coffeehouse."

"Why didn't you say anything?"

"I was going to, but you didn't bring it up. You're probably sick of all the dumb questions people ask once they find out who you are."

"You have no idea."

"Then we started having a good time, and I couldn't find the right moment to say anything. I'm sorry. I should've said something earlier."

"I'm glad you didn't." She leaned in and kissed him. "But I'm glad you came clean, too."

He smiled. "Why me?"

"Why not you? It wasn't planned. Why me?"

"Same thing, I guess."

"Let's not overthink it," she said. "Let's just enjoy it."

"Sure. Okay." There was some disappointment in his voice.

She found his insecurity endearing. She tended to sleep with guys who were full of themselves. Gorgeous superspies and dashing monster hunters didn't tend to invest in their one-night stands. She wasn't much different.

Byron didn't live that life.

"It's not like that," she said. "I mean, it could be like that. If that's all you want. I'm not trying to make this into more than it is, but what it is is pretty sweet. I like you. I needed this. Puts everything in perspective. I've been thinking about making a change lately, and this is the kind of thing I'm trying to have more of."

"But with all the stuff you've done—"

"All that stuff, the adventures, the constant danger, the exotic locations. It's like everything else. It becomes ordinary in a way. Believe it or not, this is probably the biggest adventure I've been on in a while."

"Careful," he said. "You'll give me a big head."

She kissed him on the neck and threw her leg over him. "You've earned it."

They made love again, and while it wasn't as passionate as the time she'd been seduced by the Iron King of the Lost Realms, nor as exhilarating as when she'd had that fling in zero gravity, it was somehow more memorable.

The next morning, they took a shower together. They ate a hasty breakfast she threw together.

"Will I see you again?" he asked.

"Do you want to see me again?"

"Are you kidding?"

Connie said, "Byron, you need to understand something. Being involved with me can get complicated. I don't have a lot of luck with guys like you. I don't trust easily. Last night, I checked to see if you had extensive plastic surgery scarring or were an alien at least seven times."

"Is that why you poked me with your fork hard enough to draw blood?"

She winced. "Yeah. Sorry about that. I had to be sure."

"I'm not any of those things," he said. "Nor am I a secret assassin or a clone of Hitler come back for my revenge."

"How did you know about clone Hitler?"

He laughed before realizing she wasn't joking.

"Wait. There is a Hitler clone out to get revenge on you?"

"A few," she said. "Every time I kill one, seems like two more take his place."

"Wow. I knew you lived a strange life. I never thought it was that strange."

"It's not all Frankenstein monsters and Mongolian hordes from space," she said, "but there's some baggage. And I'm always off doing some crazy dangerous thing. It makes having any kind of ongoing friendship with anyone difficult. I'm working on it. If all goes as planned, I might be normal eventually."

"I don't care if you're normal, Connie. I just thought we had a great time, and I'd like to see you again. You don't have to let me down easy if you're not interested. I'm a grown man."

"No, I'm interested."

"So, we'll take it slow," he said.

"Little late for that, isn't it? Slow isn't how I normally do things."

"It'll be a nice change of pace, then."

He had her there.

"We'll go slow, then," she said.

"Terrific. How about dinner tonight?"

"That's slow?"

He hugged her. He didn't have the powerful arms of a barbarian prince, but he had something. Whatever it was, she wanted more of it, but it also scared her. She wasn't used to being scared.

Tia knocked on the door. Right on time. Of course she was.

"I'd love to have dinner but I'm in the middle of something; but when I get back, I'll call you. I swear."

He didn't ask any questions. Either he didn't believe her or he'd accepted that trying to date Connie meant explanations weren't always readily available.

Connie opened the door, and Tia stood there with several suitcases and a fully stocked hiking backpack.

"Tia, Byron. Byron, Tia," said Connie as she half-pushed him out the door. She wasn't eager to get rid of him, and if Tia wasn't here, she might have even put this off. But if it worked, she'd be a regular person and be in a better position to date someone like Byron.

"Nice to meet you," said Tia.

"You, too."

"Yes, it's very nice for everyone to meet everyone," said Connie as she pushed Tia inside and hastily threw the suitcases into the apartment. "I swear I'm not blowing you off, Byron. I will call you. Soon."

He nodded, slightly bewildered, as she gave him one last kiss and started to close the door.

"Oh, and just so you know, I have an evil twin, and she has a tendency to sleep with my boyfriends."

He raised an eyebrow. "So, I'm a boyfriend already?"

"No, but she might not know that. Just something I let all the guys I'm dating know."

"Now you're just screwing with me."

"I told you, Byron. My life is complicated. If you change

your mind by the time I call you, I'll understand. In the meantime, if I show up with an inexplicable Yugoslavian accent, walk away."

"Okay. Thanks for the tip," he said just as the door clicked shut.

Tia said nothing. She only stood there, smiling.

"It just happened," said Connie. "Don't start."

"I'm not starting," said Tia. "I'm just surprised. Here I spent the morning packing for a globe-spanning adventure, and you were here. With Byron. Letting things just happen. Are you sure he's a regular person?"

"Reasonably sure."

She could never be certain, but so far, he hadn't done anything suspicious, which was in itself sort of suspicious. She switched off her paranoia. She didn't have time for it.

"Why do you have so many suitcases?" asked Connie.

"I have more stuff in my car," she said.

"What for?" asked Connie.

"Aren't we going on an adventure? Wasn't sure what I'd need. Aren't you the one who is always preaching the value of being prepared?"

"It's been fifteen years since I followed that philosophy. Now I mostly wing it."

"You're telling me I didn't need to get up early today and pack for every conceivable scenario?"

"Every scenario? How many suitcases did you pack?"

"Nine or ten."

"Do you have a gas mask in all that?"

Tia frowned. "No. Am I going to need one?"

"Probably not. Have a gun?"

"You never carry a gun."

"How about a bottle of ketchup?"

"You can't tell me that you've ever needed ketchup to save the day."

Connie smiled enigmatically.

"Fine," said Tia. "I threw a bunch of stuff together because I didn't know what I'd need. Meanwhile, you've been letting things *just happen*. Are you sure you're up for this? Need a day to recover?"

"I once went a week straight without sleeping in a duel of death with a sniper in the deltas of Cambodia. I think I'll manage."

Tia removed her backpack and, with a relieved sigh, set it next to a precarious stack of boxes that might topple over any moment. "Maybe you should get another butler. Or a man-servant. What happened to the old butler, anyway? Jenkins was his name, right?"

"He was part of a secret society."

"I thought that was why you hired him."

"No, another secret society. A bad one. Wanted to prepare the Earth for alien invasion or blow up New Jersey. Or something."

"How many secret societies are there?"

"I've stopped counting, and a surprising number of them want to blow up New Jersey. Hell if I know why. That's why they're secret societies. They don't tend to share their mission statement. He tried to steal a magic idol I had stowed around here. We had a knife fight on a rooftop. He stumbled and fell to his death."

"But when I asked you what happened to him, you said, 'He took a long trip.'"

Connie smiled.

Tia groaned. "Oh, God, I just got that now. Don't take this the wrong way, Connie, but I think I know where your trust issues come from."

"They're not issues. I just assume my closest allies will betray me when it serves their purposes."

"Oh, I know. How many times have you jabbed me with a fork over the years?"

"It's only being prudent," replied Connie. "You understand."

"Just one of the joys of being your friend. So, what's up with this Byron guy?"

"Nothing much. It wasn't planned, but it just felt right."

"He seemed nice the two seconds I was allowed to talk to him."

"He is nice. And smart. And cute. And a regular person."

"How did you end up with him, then?"

Connie started poking through boxes for the item they would need to begin her last adventure. "I can end up with normal guys."

"For a night, sure," said Tia, "but do you actually plan on calling him?"

"I don't know. Yes?" Connie grabbed an ancient relic, and thunder rattled the apartment windows. She tossed it aside. "I want to."

"Buuuuuut?"

"But . . . Y'know how it is. It was a good night, but that's probably all it was."

"Only one way to find out if it can be more," said Tia.

"You think I should, then?" asked Connie.

"You promised you would, and didn't you swear an oath to never break your word?"

Connie moved aside a ray gun and several bottles of dried wolfsbane. She needed to organize this stuff better.

"I'm an adventurer, not a Boy Scout."

Tia dug through her pack for a bottle of water and twisted off the cap. "I still think you should call him."

"I have water," said Connie. "Comes straight out of the tap with a turn of a knob. Like magic."

Tia shrugged. "I don't drink tap."

"Oh, you'll make a dandy sidekick."

"I think you should call him. Oath or no oath."

Connie opened a mysterious case, and the phoenix feather within burst into bright blue flame as its spirit shrieked in the throes of its rebirth. She slammed the case shut and interrupted the process. "Now, where the hell did I put that key? You really think I should? But what if this doesn't work? What if I can't be normal?"

"It'll work," said Tia. "And if it doesn't, who gives a shit?

He's different than most the guys you've had. Even the ordinary ones."

"Gleaned that from the two seconds you talked to him?"

"Call it intuition."

"I have intuition," said Connie.

"You're too close to the situation. That's why you need to borrow mine. And I say you'll call him."

Connie saluted. "Whatever you say, boss."

Tia offered to help Connie look, but it was better for her to avoid touching things. It took Connie ten minutes to find what she needed. The large, antique key glittered like polished silver. The True Key could open any door between worlds. It'd been sitting between the haunted skull of Marie Antoinette and that weird alien thingamabob that beeped once exactly every seventy-one hours, under the real Shroud of Turin.

"All set," said Connie. "But first things first. If you want to come with me, you've got to prove you're not dead weight."

"Okay. What do you want me to do?"

"Hit me."

"What?"

"Hit me. Take a swing."

Tia laughed. "I'm not going to hit you."

"I know you're not, but if you're going to convince me to let you tag along, I need you to try."

"What's that going to prove?"

"It'll prove you can take care of yourself. I don't know what's around the corner, but I can guarantee that if you can't hit me, you can't handle it."

"There are more ways to handle a tricky situation than simply violence."

"That's what people who are wimps tell themselves so they don't feel like wimps."

"But you said it just the other day."

"I'm good at violence, so I can get away with it. I'm not endorsing it. I'll always seek the nonviolent solution when I can, but sometimes, it's not an option. Sometimes, you have to beat the shit out of a bad guy because he doesn't give you any other choice. Now show me what you've got."

"I'm not helpless," said Tia. "I've taken some self-defense courses."

"Punching a guy in a foam suit isn't the same as what you might be facing out there." Connie paused. "I was going to say *the real world*, but it's not exactly. I don't expect you to fight twenty-foot-tall slime creatures, but if there are regular people, I need to know you can handle yourself. Come at me or get left behind."

Tia charged, hoping to catch Connie off guard. Connie stepped aside, and Tia fell flat on her face.

"You're going to have to do better than that," said Connie.

Tia picked herself up. "I wasn't ready."

"You attacked me."

Tia, fists held up, approached more cautiously. Connie let her get within inches.

"Are you going to throw a punch or just stare at me?"

Tia kicked. She wasn't certain what happened next, but she ended up on the floor again.

"Nice try," said Connie.

Tia sat up. "What's this prove? That you're a better fighter than me? Of course you're a better fighter. Why wouldn't you be?"

"It proves that you can't handle this."

"I don't get it. I've been on adventures with you before. Remember when my wedding reception was disrupted by those mob goons? Or that time I was kidnapped by swamp monsters? Or the dozens of other times I've been dragged into your craziness."

"Those times were different," said Connie. "You were a victim of circumstances. You didn't ask to get involved."

"So, I still have more experience than most people. I may not be a master of alien karate, but I'm not some average person. I've seen stuff. I've proven I can keep my head in an emergency."

"Yes, you have, but there's still a difference. All those other times, I was saving you. This time, I'm letting you come along. If something bad happens to you, it'll be my fault."

Tia snorted. "No offense, Connie, but get over yourself. It might feel like it sometimes, but the universe doesn't revolve around you. I make my own decisions. Nobody was making me be your friend all these years. I made that choice, and it has been a bumpy ride now and then, but I'm not some responsibility you're forced to carry with you. It's a two-way thing. I could've walked away at any time, but I didn't. Did you ever ask why?"

"Because you're an assassin waiting for the word to strike?" Connie grinned as she said it, but Tia noticed Connie adopting a combat stance.

"Because you're the one person in this world I could always count on, and I'm not talking about saving my life, which you do regularly. I'm talking about being there when I really need you. Remember when my marriage fell apart? Who was there with a beer and a shoulder to cry on? Or when my dad died? You were the one who made me leave my house."

"Funny," said Connie. "I always think of myself as screwing up your life."

"You do that too, but that's how friendship works. We try to be there for each other, and we're not perfect, but this is important. And I'm going to be there for you. So, if this is what it takes, then I'll prove I have the determination to make it." She raised her fists.

Connie crossed her arms. "No, that's not it at all. If all it took was determination, then every stubborn idiot would be out there having adventures. It's about ability. If you don't have the skills, you shouldn't be involved."

"Maybe I don't have the combat skills, but I've got other talents."

"Next you'll tell me you're street-smart. That's not a thing, by the way. Okay, so if you can't hit me, what can you do?"

"I'm great at math."

"You're kidding, right?"

"It might come in handy," said Tia. "Like that time your horticulture knowledge saved Cleveland."

"When Cleveland is under attack by algebra, I'll be sure to keep you in mind."

"This isn't fair. You've had a lifetime of experience."

"No, it isn't. Yes, I have. Now stop bitching about it and impress me."

Tia lowered her fists.

"Okay, I get it. You want me to realize that I'm not ever going to be able to stand up to you and find a better way."

Connie grunted. "Goddamn it, Tia. We aren't sharing a Mr. Miyagi moment. I need you to be able to handle yourself. Yes, you can't always fight your way out of every bad situation, and violence should be a last resort. But it is a resort, and if you can't manage it, you're just going to get in my way. Hit me or go home."

Tia launched a series of strikes that Connie dodged and deflected. She danced around Tia's wild swings. Tia's frustration led to rage, which led to sloppiness, and avoiding her attacks only became easier. It didn't help that Connie kept tapping Tia here and there to illustrate the weakness of her defense.

Tia wheezed and knelt with her hands on her knees.

"I trust I've made my point?" asked Connie with a condescending smile.

Screaming, Tia hurled herself forward. Connie stepped aside and, with a deft maneuver, flipped Tia onto the floor again.

She lay there, looking up at the ceiling. "This is bullshit. Just give me a minute to catch my breath."

Connie shrugged. "If you think it'll make a difference."

Tia stood. "Here's the deal. If I land a hit on you—even one—you stop telling me not to come along."

Connie nodded. "And if you can't, then you forget this. Deal?"

Tia nodded.

"To make it fair, I won't even use my arms," said Connie.

Tia snarled. "No. You're going to use your arms. I don't need you to hold back."

"Actually—"

Tia rushed forward. Connie punched Tia and threw her to the floor.

"Son of a bitch." Tia groaned. "I think you dislocated my shoulder."

"You'd know if I dislocated your shoulder. You're fine. You said I shouldn't hold back."

"Okay, so hold back a little." Tia sat up.

"No need. You can come along."

"But I didn't hit you."

"And you never will. Keep that in mind. I'm good, but there are people out there who make me look like an amateur. If you can't take me on, you can't take them on."

"Point made," said Tia.

Connie helped Tia up. "I need you to listen to me and not do anything stupid. Other than the stupid thing of going with me."

"I can do that."

"It's still a bad idea, but maybe you are sidekick material after all." Connie helped Tia up. "And I still owe you for your ruined wedding reception."

"Ruined? Those mob goons were the only thing worth remembering about the whole day. I can't believe you punched me." Tia wiped her bloody nose. "I knew it was a test."

"Had to see if you could take it."

"How'd I do?"

"Terrible, but you're an adult. I don't feel like wasting time talking you out of this. Just don't complain to me if you get eaten by something."

"Wouldn't dream of it. How do we find this fairy god-mother of yours? Do we need to journey to some ancient woods forgotten by man and dance three times around a circle of mushrooms under the light of the full moon?"

"Nothing that complicated," said Connie. "Help me move these boxes."

They cleared some space around an antique wardrobe wrapped in heavy chains with a lock the size of a pie plate engraved with a knight's helm.

"Fancy," said Tia. "Is this the way, then? Through a magic wardrobe? Bit of a cliché, isn't it?"

"Welcome to my life," replied Connie as she tapped the key twice on the lock. "Third time's the charm."

"Wait."

"Have you changed your mind?"

"No, but is transitioning into magical dimensions anything like flying? Because if it is, I'm probably going to need some Dramamine. Have some in one of my bags."

"You'll be fine." Connie tapped the lock one last time It fell away with a heavy thud, and the wardrobe's doors were flung open. A terrifying beast—half-man, half-dragon, half-tree—stepped into the room. It was too many halves, but the fae were a race who enjoyed flouting convention.

The monster roared and stacks of boxes fell. Tia lost sight of Connie, buried under an avalanche of cardboard.

The dragon elm beast turned its gaze on Tia and snorted.

It was probably too late to change her mind.

The dragon man spread his wings, toppling over more boxes.

"Constance Verity!" he bellowed. "You were warned not to trespass upon the Fae Realms upon penalty of death by torture!"

He inhaled. Flames flickered at the corners of his mouth.

Tia held up her hands. "Hold on! I'm not her!"

The guardian swallowed his fire, choking and sputtering, exhaling clouds of smoke. He rubbed his watering eyes.

"Oh, I'm sorry. My mistake." He snorted and blew a stream of smoke out of his nostrils. "You wouldn't happen to know where she is? This is her wardrobe. I assume she's around here somewhere."

Tia eyed the piles of boxes on the floor for the slightest sign of movement. "I don't know."

"You wouldn't be lying to me, would you? I'd be terribly upset if you were."

Tia smiled with all the sincerity she could muster, looking into the guardian's dark green eyes. She hoped she wasn't overselling it.

"No."

The dragon man scratched his great curving horns made of wood, and she wondered if it was difficult breathing fire when half your flesh was made of bark.

"That's annoying. Here I have been stationed in this wardrobe for the better part of a decade with the express purpose of slaying Constance Verity when she dared try use it, and she's not even here."

"You've been sitting in there for ten years?"

"That's not the worst of it. I actually had to battle the greatest gladiators of the realm for the right. I slew my own brothers for this opportunity."

"You must really hate Connie."

"Oh, I've got nothing against her, myself. But it'd bring great honor upon my house to be the one who killed her."

With a heavy sigh, he sat on the pile of boxes Connie had been buried under. "I don't understand it. The oracles specifically said she'd be using this portal to the realms. Though they didn't say when. Never do give you any useful information, do they?"

"I hear ya," said Tia. "Oracles. Am I right?"

The guardian groaned and climbed back into the wardrobe.

"Maybe next time. If you should see Verity, please, do urge her to hurry along. I may be ageless, but I have things I'd rather be doing."

He shut the doors and the handle closed with a click.

Tia waited a few moments before digging through the crushed boxes, looking for Connie. She wasn't there, and a quick search of the rest of the apartment confirmed she was missing.

The wardrobe rocked back and forth as something clattered and bumped in its interior. Tia watched, uncertain of what she should do. She debated on opening the door, but if the guardian was in there, fighting something so fierce and terrible, then it was probably better if they stayed put. Or maybe their battle would shake the wardrobe to pieces, taking their portal to the fairy world with it, and the better thing to do would be to let them out. Since Connie wasn't here, Tia had to do something. Unless doing something was the wrong thing to do.

This sidekicking business was more complicated than she had initially expected. When she'd been previously dragged into Connie's adventures, it was more of a hostage situation, and that mostly involved sitting around, waiting to be rescued.

There came a dreadful roar, and tongues of flame flashed around the edges of the wardrobe. Its doors swung open as the guardian was hurled into the apartment to come crashing onto the floor. More boxes were crushed. Others fell over. At this point, it wasn't worth noticing.

Connie stepped out from the wardrobe. She blew out the bit of fire smoldering on her sleeve.

"How the hell did you get in there?" asked Tia.

"Ninja training," replied Connie.

"Bullshit. I could see the wardrobe the whole time. You couldn't have sneaked into it without me noticing."

"People aren't nearly as observant as they think," replied Connie. "And monsters tend to be terrific distractions. I probably couldn't have pulled it off if you hadn't been distracting the guardian."

"See? I told you I could be useful."

"I stand proven wrong," said Connie.

Tia eyed the guardian lying still before her. "Is he dead?"

"Just stunned." Connie pounded the knuckledusters in each hand together with a loud clink. "Cold iron. Never visit the Fae Realms without them."

"I thought you said you preferred winging it."

Connie slipped the knuckledusters in her pocket. "Some things are just common sense. He should be unconscious for a few hours."

"Poor guy," said Tia.

"He was planning on killing me."

"Well, sure, but I can't help but have a little sympathy for him. He'd spent nearly a decade waiting for his shot, and he blew it. You think the oracles could've warned him."

"Oracles don't do jack. And don't even get me started on prophecies. I'm so sick of those damned things."

Connie adopted a spooky voice. "By the river Anauros, you shall meet a man wearing one sandal who shall be your undoing." She chuckled. "Thanks for the newsflash. Couldn't just give me a name and address. Hey, kill this guy. Easy peasy."

"I think that would take the mystery out of it."

"The future is already mysterious. If oracles really wanted mystery, they'd shut up about it."

They entered the wardrobe and shut the door. A musical chime sounded as a soft, cool breeze blew through the darkness. Connie tapped the True Key against the doors three times, and they opened. Her cluttered apartment had been replaced by a shadowy warehouse with row upon row of antique furniture, each of them a portal to the mortal world. Chains were wrapped around the more dangerous furniture, and the wardrobe they stepped out of had been thoroughly locked down, judging by the copious amount of chains lying around it.

A chest of drawers growled and rattled at Connie as they walked by. Something inhuman leered at them from the depths of a giant mirror.

A great white stag with antlers nearly as tall as his body stepped before them. He glowed with a soft light, and his deep blue eyes sparkled like the sun reflecting off the ocean. He wore a gray hat labeled SECURITY.

"Hey, you shouldn't be in here," he said.

"Just passing through," said Connie.

The security stag tilted his head to one side. "Say, aren't you Constance Verity?"

She slipped her hands in her pockets and her fingers around her knuckledusters. "I am."

"In that case, the exit is over that way." He nodded down an aisle.

"Thanks."

"No problem."

He bowed, tapped the floor with his hoof, and disappeared in a flash of bright azure flame.

"Doesn't matter what world you're in." Connie studied the circle of golden ash left behind by the stag's teleportation. "You can't expect much for minimum wage."

8

The Fae Realms, despite the grandness of the title, was a landmass not much larger than the island of Hawaii. This simplified things considerably, because there was only one major city among the fae, and all portals to the realms led to it.

The streets of Arcadia had a quasi-mystic style. The streets were cobblestone. The lamps were flickering flames. The buildings had an old-world, European style to them with leering gargoyles, ornate parapets, elaborate spires, and other bits of architecture Connie didn't have words for.

The night sky was a sea of stars, twinkling in a rainbow spectrum of colors. The bright, blue moon sat behind those stars.

Strange creatures walked the streets at night. Goblins in leather jackets. Pixies riding shaggy, six-legged poodles. A gorgeous androgynous something with flawless blue skin and a shock of spiky blond hair made eye contact with Tia, and she fell in love with him/her/it instantly.

"Looking for a good time?" he/she/it asked.

"Maybe next time," said Connie as she dragged Tia away.

It was only after they turned the corner and the beautiful fae disappeared from sight that Tia could shake the enchantment.

"This is not what I expected," said Tia.

"What did you expect?"

"I don't know. I thought it'd be more . . . whimsical. Enchanted glens. Giant caterpillars on toadstools. Tea parties. Croquet."

"You're describing *Alice in Wonderland*. That's a story. Not a real place."

"It isn't? But I thought you'd been there."

"No, I've been in a deadly amusement park designed after Wonderland. Believe me. It's not that whimsical when you're being chased by a giant mechanical dodo bird. Teacup ride was fun though."

They walked a little farther, and Tia was surprised that the fae didn't give a second glance at the mortal women among them, until she noticed they weren't the only ones. There were a handful of human people on the street. The Fae Realms had a sizeable population of humans, the leftovers from mortals who had fallen or been stolen into the realms in ages past and discovered that mortals were as ageless as the natives while here.

The mortals still bred like creatures with an expiration date, and for a while, it appeared certain the realms' natives would fall to this invasive species, until powerful contraceptive spells were cast, and the fae, in good conscience, couldn't send the hapless mortals back to a place where magic was scarce and unstable and physics, that most inexplicable of forces, held sway. For anyone who had grown up where gravity was a suggestion, not a constant, the mortal world was downright terrifying.

"Where are we going?" asked Tia.

"In order to find my fairy godmother, we'll need to access the godmother registry. It's an enchanted scroll with all the names of all the godmothers that ever were. Each godmother must have a distinct name. They're strict about that. They're also strict about access. Fortunately, I know a guy who can get any information you want for the right price."

"Is he trustworthy?"

Connie laughed. "Of course not, but he owes me a favor. And he's not too far from here."

They hailed a carriage pulled along by a team of giant mice, and Connie gave the driver instructions on where to go.

Tia took in a world that wasn't much different from her own. She'd been to a few exotic locales and alternate realities. She'd visited Atlantis, kidnapped by merfolk for reasons she couldn't recall at the moment, but she'd spent most of that time tied up with a bag over her head. It limited sightseeing options. She'd spent hours on various spaceships, but most of them were either nothing but a lot of blinking control panels or featureless walls. About the most interesting place she'd been to that she had time to see was the hidden city beneath Chicago where vampire Al Capone reigned.

For once, she wasn't being held hostage or locked in a dreary cell or running and/or hiding for her life, and she was enjoying the experience. Arcadia was different in a lot of small ways, other than the faeries, goblins, and ogres that called it home. The fashion was a bit odd: bright colors, platform shoes, and bellbottom pants. Disco was apparently another thing in the Fae Realm that lived forever.

When they found the place Connie was looking for, she paid the driver a handful of magic beans and rang the bell on a brick building that leaned to the right. Architecture in the Fae Realms followed its own rules, often from building to building.

The gargoyle face above the door opened its eyes. "Oh, hell, I knew I should've moved. I never thought you'd have the guts to show your face in Arcadia again."

"Let me in, Scurm," said Connie.

"No."

The gargoyle stuck out its tongue and snapped its eyes closed.

She knocked again. "Don't make me bust my way in. You don't want that kind of attention."

He didn't reply immediately, but a few moments later, the door opened and a short, green goblin in a T-shirt and shiny red pants appeared.

"Come in, then, Verity. Don't just stand there."

He slammed the door behind them as they entered and bolted the lock. Magic paraphernalia cluttered the room. Grimoires, scrolls, and weird creatures in cages. A thing covered in eyes and tongues gurgled at Connie.

The goblin went to a workbench and tapped a wand against a crystal ball. "What do you want now?"

Connie said, "Tia, this is Scurm, the best underground scryer in all the realm."

"Don't think you're going to get on my good side by flattering me," said Scurm. "I don't need any trouble. Just tell me what you want and get out of here."

"I'm looking for a fairy godmother."

"Have you tried wishing upon a star?" Scurm replied.

"I need to find a specific godmother."

"I'm not scrying into the godmother registry. That's bad news, Verity."

"You owe me."

"I don't owe you that much," he said.

"Are you saying you can't do it?"

He laughed. "Are you seriously trying to poke my ego? Of course I *can* do it. I'm just letting you know that I'm electing not to. And you should be thankful I'm not crazy enough to try. If the Guard found out you were here, they'd swarm this place with everything they've got."

"I don't understand," said Tia. "Why do they hate you so much?"

"*Hate* isn't the right word," said Scurm. "*Fear* is more like it."

"Misunderstandings," replied Connie.

"Why didn't you say so?" he replied. "I'm sure if you explain to King Oberon that you slew his favorite wyvern because of a simple misunderstanding, he'd be sure to forgive you and overlook those iron knuckledusters in your back pocket while he's at it. Surprised the Guard hasn't sniffed you out for those things alone. You've got either to be desperate or stupid or both to bring something like that into this city."

"They're just knuckledusters," said Tia.

"She's new to this," said Connie. "Iron is contraband in the Fae Realms. In the wrong hands, it can do a lot of damage."

"And who says you're the right hands?" asked Scurm. "You don't see me walking into your world with a pocketful of uranium, do you?"

"I can handle it."

"Maybe I should have one of those," said Tia. "Just in case things get dangerous."

Connie shook her head. "I can handle it. You can't."

"Fine. Sidekick here." Tia saluted. "I'll defer to your judgment."

"Are you going to help me or not?" Connie asked Scurm.

"Not. I thought that was clear. And don't threaten me with those iron pounders. We both know you wouldn't risk using them on me."

"Fair enough." Connie held up a large gold coin. It sparkled in the candlelight. "Guess I'll just take my forbidden treasure and go home."

Scurm dropped his crystal ball. It rolled across the desk and hit the floor, cracking open. The mysterious blue mists within leaked out as the globe went black. He didn't seem to care at the moment.

"That's not what I think it is, Verity."

"Just a coin from the legendary treasure of the last leprechaun king," she said. "The last coin, in fact. I should know. I threw the rest in a volcano to save the Fae Realms from his curse. Nearly got killed for my trouble. Not that old King Oberon ever thanked me for that."

Scurm's eyes glinted with his desire for the coin. Literally. They flashed with green and blue. "Does it have any juice left in it?"

"Yep. Not enough to be dangerous anymore, but enough that an enterprising goblin with some imagination could use for all kinds of profitable mischief. But if you don't want it . . ."

The veins on Scurm's pointed ears throbbed prismatic blue. Goblins were lousy poker players.

A black shadow rose up behind Connie. It stretched two limbs toward her.

"Look out!" Tia dove at the creature, but she passed harmlessly through it.

Connie punched the creature in the chest with her knuckleduster. It howled and broke apart. It attempted to reform, but she smashed its head-like protrusion. Shrieking like a banshee, it dissolved into a brackish puddle at her feet.

"All right, all right," said Scurm. "Never mind, Jerry."

Grumbling, Jerry the puddle sloshed his way to a corner.

"Can't blame a guy for trying, can you?" said Scurm with a smile.

Connie helped Tia to her feet. "You wouldn't be you if you didn't try, Scurm. Do we have a deal or not?"

"We've got a deal."

He held out a hand, and Connie tossed him the coin. His ears twitched in rapid circles as he hopped out from behind his workbench and gestured for them to follow him downstairs.

"Can we trust him?" asked Tia.

"Scurm never goes back on a deal," said Connie.

They followed him into a basement outfitted with a networked array of crystal balls, rune-laden stone tablets, and mysterious color-changing liquids in beakers and vials. Winged frogs zipped around in a spherical cage. A kaleidoscope of rainbow-colored smoke swirled out of a cauldron in one corner. Everything was wired up to a large mirror on the wall.

"Nice setup," said Connie.

"Don't touch anything!" Scurm said.

"Relax. If you move this a little to the left"—she pushed a glass pyramid an inch—"you can increase your harmonic convergence ratio by four or five percent."

The frogs cheerfully chirped. A rack of crystals flashed in sequence, sounding a soft melody.

"I studied a little under the Oracles of Delphi. I could never manage to see the future, but I picked up a few things."

Grumbling, Scurm poured an entire skull's worth of slime

into the cauldron before tossing in a wiggling something. "Name I'm looking for?"

"Grandmother Willow."

He scribbled onto a piece of parchment and added it to the cauldron.

"The registry is behind heavy concealment wards. I can pierce them, but odds are good that it'll lead the Guard right to us."

"Aren't you worried about what they'll do to you when they catch you?" asked Tia.

"They never catch me," he said with a smug smile. "And I can lose all this gear. But you two—especially you, Verity—you're going to get captured and pitted."

"Pitted?"

"You didn't tell her about the Pit of Vipers?" asked Scurm.

"Vipers? Like poisonous snakes?"

"There haven't been snakes in there for a thousand years." He chuckled. "They were all eaten by other things Oberon tossed in there."

"She knows the score," said Connie. "Let us worry about that."

"It's your call." He traced a feather on the mirror, creating glowing glyphs upon the surface.

"What other things?" whispered Tia.

"It's not important," whispered Connie.

"Then why aren't you telling me?"

"You wanted to come along."

"I didn't think I'd be thrown into a pit of *things* within the first two hours."

"We won't get caught," said Connie. "And if we are caught—"

"You're not filling me with confidence."

"If we are caught," Connie continued, "which we won't be, but if we are, I'd be pitted. They'd more than likely send you back to the mortal world with a slap on the wrist. Maybe a cautionary curse, like all the food you eat screaming when you bite into it."

"Oh, is that all?"

"We won't get caught."

Scurm finished his rune. The mirror fogged up and thumped as if something on the other side of the glass was smacking against it. "Ladies, I need some quiet here. This is the tricky part."

He chanted softly, and stuff started happening. The frogs chirped. The cauldron belched forth small flying bugs that crawled along the ceiling. A mist rolled across the floor, and something small and furry crawled around in it, rattling and growling.

The mirror rippled and spit out a glass marble that floated into his open hand. He tossed the marble at Connie. "There's your godmother. Now we should all get out of here before Ether Security—"

The cauldron jumped five feet in the air and hovered there.

"Hmmm. Even faster than I expected."

The cauldron spit out five pixies, all dressed in black suits. They spoke in unison.

"You have violated secured ether," they chimed in melodious

unison. "An apprehension squad has been dispatched to this location. Your cooperation will be noted, as will any resistance."

"You got me." Scurm held up his hands. "But I'm small potatoes compared to that lady over there."

The pixies flittered around Connie and Tia.

"Constance Verity, you shall be detained. Do not resist."

The diminutive agents sparkled as they wove a web of magic around Connie and Tia. It congealed into a hard prismatic shell.

"Sorry, Verity." Scurm shrugged. "Our deal was I'd get the info, not keep you from being captured. A goblin has to watch his back. Better you pitted than me."

"You betraying son of a bitch," said Tia.

"You are in possession of illegal weaponry," said the pixies. "Surrender it immediately."

The pixies screeched a claxon that was both terrifying and hypnotic as Connie slipped on her iron knuckledusters.

"Cover your face."

She punched the crystal shell, and it shattered into dust. Some got into Tia's eyes, stinging and blurring her vision.

The magic mirror spit out a two-headed ogre dressed in riot gear. He leveled a wand at Connie and unleashed a bolt of lightning. She reflected it with her iron fists and knocked him over.

The outmatched pixies whirled around, shrieking, but made no move against them.

"Where did that little traitorous bastard go?" asked Tia.

"Doesn't matter. I always knew he'd bug out on us, but he kept his end of the deal. We have to get out of here."

They ran upstairs and out the front door, coming face-to-face with an entire tactical squad of ogre wizards, elvish sharpshooters, and some kind of turtle dragon.

"That was fast," said Tia.

"Cover your ears."

The elves unleashed their arrows. The wizards threw shrieking fireballs and jets of scalding steam. The dragon didn't do much.

Connie banged her fists together, and with a soft *clink*, the world exploded.

9

Tia uncovered her ears and opened her eyes. The ogres and elves lay sprawled on the ground. Cracks ran through the concrete, and all the nearby windows had been shattered by the shockwave.

Only Connie and Tia remained on their feet, protected by their mortal nature. Connie checked on an unconscious security pixie. They were just doing their job. Her iron knuckledusters glowed a soft orange.

"You weren't kidding about those things!" Tia shouted over the ringing in her ears.

Connie pointed to her own ears and shook her head. Not being able to cover them herself had left her deafened.

Storm clouds gathered overhead. They rumbled with angry thunder as a funnel spat out a twelve-foot blue giant crackling with electricity and six hounds, each the size of a small car. The wolves had ram horns, tusks, and scorpion tails. All the static in the air puffed out their thick fur coats. They were almost cuddly if one could ignore their slavering jaws and baleful red eyes.

"Damn it," said Connie. "I didn't think they'd pull out the big guns so quickly. Stick close to me."

"Don't have to tell me twice."

"What?"

Tia nodded to Connie.

The giant put a horn to his lips and sounded a deep bellow. The hounds charged forward, and Connie moved to meet them. Tia trailed behind, keeping her head down.

The lead hound pounced. Connie landed a punch under its snout, sending it tumbling away. She yanked Tia out of the way of the snapping bite of a second hound as Connie slammed it on the nose. She wove through the onslaught, alternately punching beasts and pulling Tia out of danger. Once a hound's teeth ripped Tia's sleeve and scraped her arm. Not deep enough to break the skin, but a welt was left behind. Then Connie socked the creature, and it went soaring down the block. It landed with a clap of thunder and a burst of lightning.

It was all old hat to Connie, but even Tia could sometimes forget how dangerous a foe Connie could be when cornered. The knuckledusters helped, transforming her into a force of nature. One strike was more than enough to put down each of the hounds, though it did take her twice as long as it should've because she was watching out for Tia.

The last hound flattened its ears and backed away with its tail tucked between its legs. Its master lashed it with a whip of lightning, but Connie stepped under the lash. She deflected it with her iron.

"Don't do that," she said.

The sneering giant went for the sword on his belt.

"Don't do that, either," she said.

He drew his weapon and, howling, rushed at her. She caught the blow of his sword. Fae metal shattered against her iron. The giant's weapon exploded in his hand. He fell to his knee, clutching his wounded limb. Connie hopped onto his boot and belted him across the jaw. He fell over with a crash.

"They never listen."

"Is that a good thing?" Tia pointed to fresh clouds swirling overhead. "That can't be a good thing, right?"

The clouds spit out a tremendous serpent. The monster got stuck halfway in the funnel. Its many heads snapped and snarled as it struggled to free itself.

"Can you take that?" asked Tia.

"Not without destroying a city block," said Connie.

Her knuckledusters burned with a hard white light. Tia imagined a nuclear reactor on the verge of exploding, even though she knew that wasn't how reactors worked in reality. This wasn't reality. This was the Fae Realms.

"We can't fight that thing," said Connie. "Not here."

She turned to the hound and held out her hands beneath its muzzle. The creature whimpered, tucking its scorpion tail beneath its legs. She petted it between the eyes and scratched behind its ear. The monster nuzzled her.

The seven-headed dragon twisted itself nearly free.

"What's the plan, then?" asked Tia.

Connie, on the back of the hound, held out her hand. "Hop on."

She helped Tia up. Tia wasn't certain whether the dragon or the scorpion tail hanging just over her head made her more nervous.

"How are you doing this?"

"I learned how to talk with wolves from a shaman I know. These guys might be bigger, but the principles are basically the same. They're actually smarter than wolves, so it's a little easier."

The serpent fell out of the cloud portal. It landed with a shattering thud. Its long, thick body crushed one of its heads. The mangled head sagged as its brothers struggled to clear their senses.

"Hold on tight," said Connie.

The hound didn't so much run as fly with a paw touching the ground every now and then to keep gravity from pitching a fit. Tia clung to handfuls of white fur. Wyverns soared overhead, spitting fireballs. Gryphon-drawn carriages with sirens and ogre peace officers trailed in pursuit, firing off lightning bolts from wands. The wolf danced gracefully through the barrage as the street exploded around them. A harpy zipped downward and nearly snatched Tia away. Connie punched it, and the harpy was knocked away in a shower of feathers.

Tia had been with Connie through many a narrow escape, but it was as if everyone and everything in the Fae Realms was after them. A gargoyle ripped itself off a building and dive-bombed, a near miss. A lamppost tried to knock Connie off the hound. The street itself started tearing away under their feet.

Their flight stopped at the warehouse they'd entered through. Giants, dragons, ogres, hundreds of pixies, and one very stern gnome barricaded the building. Connie and Tia jumped off the hound, encircled by an army.

The many-headed dragon rose up behind Connie and howled. It snapped and snarled but didn't attack.

The gnome stepped forward and unfurled a scroll. "Constance Verity, you are charged with that most heinous of crimes, the embarrassment and diminishment of the great King Oberon. Surrender yourself to immediate pitting, and your companion shall be mercifully executed."

"You have a plan," said Tia. "Tell me you have a plan."

Connie held her knuckledusters for everyone to see. They crackled with raw power. The fae security forces gasped collectively. A dragon inhaled some of its own fire and started coughing clouds of smoke.

"Here's the situation," said Connie. "You can either let us leave, or we can watch this city explode together."

10

The gnome escorted Connie into the warehouse. They passed the dragon guardian, who grumbled at them.

The wardrobe was opened for them.

"Are you going to tell me not to come back?" asked Connie.

"Would you listen?" asked the gnome. "All of us in the realms know we owe you a lot. King Oberon might be the life and breath of this land, but he's a stuffy old bastard. Still, if we catch you without those iron scraps, we'll have to take you in. You understand."

"I do."

"As it is, I'm going to get chewed out for this one. I like you, and I like this city. And Oberon wouldn't mind watching this city being obliterated if you were vaporized along with it. The only reason I'll get away with it is because he'd rather see you pitted than destroyed. Now get out of here." He smiled. "And don't come back."

"You got it."

Connie and Tia stepped through the wardrobe and back into the mortal world. The wardrobe doors slammed shut. Connie wrapped the chains around it, just in case the fae changed their mind.

Tia picked up the knuckledusters. They'd stopped glowing but remained warm to the touch.

"I can't believe we made it out of there alive," said Tia. "We've been in some tight spots before, but that was almost as bad as the time I was kidnapped by that swamp creature. I thought we'd had it for sure then."

"Oh, yeah." Connie smiled. "I'd forgotten about that."

"I wish I could." The creature had courted her with piles of dead fish and possums and a screechy, warbling love song. The creature might have been a perfect gentleman, aside from the abduction, but she still shuddered, recollecting the stink of his lair.

Connie said, "What's funny is all the adventures start to blend together after a while. I remember the quiet times far more. Remember that time we went to that Italian restaurant and had that awesome cheesecake? That was amazing, and I don't even like cheesecake."

Everyone measured their life by the memorable bits, and those bits weren't the things they did every day. Connie's fondest memories weren't of last-minute escapes from crumbling temples or sword fights with cross-time pirates. Those were unremarkable events. But a quiet moment with her best friend, talking about nothing important over dessert, was a rarity to be treasured.

Honestly, the cheesecake hadn't been that good.

It didn't matter. It was the experience that counted.

"Where are we going now?" asked Tia.

Connie removed the glass marble from her pocket and held it up to the light. "Looks like Florida."

She tossed the marble to Tia, who glanced through it. It was a miniature globe, but when turned, it focused on a close up of North America, then Florida, then a small house in a small neighborhood.

"Why would a fairy godmother be in Florida?"

Connie took the marble back and dropped it in her pocket. "Guess we'll find out when we ask her."

11

The broken-down house might have aspired to be a charming cottage in its heyday, but it'd long before abandoned such ambitions and was little more than a decaying ramshackle home in desperate need of repair. A window was boarded up. The lawn was nothing but dirt and yellowed grass.

"This can't be it," said Tia.

Connie checked the marble, which was flashing with a soft light, humming in her hands. It'd been doing so since they'd landed in Florida.

The front gate was rusted shut, but they walked around through the gap in the fallen picket fence beside it. Connie tried the broken doorbell. She knocked. Nobody answered.

"Maybe she's not home," said Tia.

Connie knocked again. Harder, this time.

"Go away!" shouted someone from inside the house. "No solicitors!"

The door wasn't locked. Connie pushed it open. Before

she could take a step inside, a lightning bolt blasted a hole in the door. Connie and Tia jumped back.

"I said, 'No solicitors!'" yelled Grandmother Willow. "Get the fuck out of here, or I'll shove this wand so far up your ass, you'll swear I enchanted your colon."

To illustrate the point, a few flashes and thunderclaps echoed from inside.

"This is the place," said Connie.

She slipped on her iron knuckledusters.

Tia said, "You aren't going to just kill her, are you?"

Connie shrugged. "That was kind of the plan from the start."

"You can't seriously be planning on beating a fairy godmother to death with your bare hands? That's pretty brutal."

Connie tightened her grip on her knuckledusters. "Why did I bring you along, again?"

"So you'd have someone to talk you out of doing something you'd regret."

"I can hear you out there!" shouted Grandmother Willow. "Get off my property!"

"You don't know if killing her will even solve your problem yet," whispered Tia. "What if it only makes it worse? Or maybe you need her alive to reverse the spell. Did you think of that?"

Connie mumbled, "No, I guess I didn't."

"Hey, I'm your friend. If I thought it would help you, I'd hold this old lady down while you bashed her skull in."

"No, you wouldn't."

"No, I wouldn't. But I wouldn't blame you for wanting to

do it. We have to be smart about this. You should talk to her before you kill her. If you decide you still want to kill her."

Connie grumbled. "I guess you're right."

"You know I'm right."

Grandmother Willow, in a dirty pink bathrobe, flung open the front door and stepped onto her porch. Her hair was a mess. A cigarette hung from her lips, and her eyes were bloodshot and sunken.

"Don't say I didn't warn you!"

She pulled a gray mouse from her robe pocket and dropped it at her feet. She waved her wand, which sparked and sputtered as it sprinkled glittering dust onto the rodent. The mouse grew into a hulking brutish humanoid covered in fur with an adorable face and twitching ears.

"Show them the way out, my dear."

The mouse monster scampered away, seeking shelter under an old, rotted tree in the yard. The uprooted tree fell over and smashed a hole in the house's roof. The monster cowered under a few roots.

"Damn it." Grandmother Willow shook her wand. "This fucking thing isn't worth a damn anymore." She pointed the wand at Connie and Tia, but before Grandmother Willow could launch a lightning bolt, the wand exploded in her face. Swearing, she beat the sparks out of her hair.

"Should we do something?" asked Tia.

"She's fine," said Connie.

After smothering the flames, Grandmother Willow grumbled.

"Whatever you're selling, I'm not buying. I don't want to hear about whatever gods you're fortunate or foolish enough to believe in. And I don't grant wishes, if that's what you're here for. That is a genie. I'm a whole different thing. Or I was." Grandmother Willow wiped her watering eyes and took her first real look at Connie.

"Oh, shit. It's you." Grandmother Willow sneered. Her left eye twitched. She blew out her smoking wand.

"You remember me?" asked Connie.

"You're Constance Verity, child. How could I not remember you? I was wondering if you'd ever try to find me."

She stumbled back inside.

"Well, are you coming in, or did you come all this way just to watch an ex-godmother make a fool of herself?"

Connie and Tia followed Grandmother Willow into her home. The place was a mess of old newspapers, dusty furniture, and mice. So many mice scampering about underfoot, in the open, across the coffee table. The only sources of light were an old TV bathing everything in a pale blue and what sunlight managed to filter through the tree branches over the fresh hole in the ceiling.

Grandmother Willow flopped onto a floral-print couch covered in plastic. Staring at the TV, she asked, "You two want a wine cooler or something? I think I have some gingerbread in the oven. It's a week old but probably still good."

"No. Thank you," said Connie.

"Suit yourself." Grandmother Willow snapped her fingers.

Several mice, carrying a bottle, scurried out of the kitchen and handed it to her. "Thanks, fellas." She twisted the cap off and chugged the cooler.

"Are you going to stand there like a couple of idiots? Take a seat."

A rolling office chair and a recliner ambled over to Connie and Tia. The recliner waddled slowly on its stubby legs, and the office chair knocked over a pile of newspapers.

"Ah, hell, I just got those organized."

Connie and Tia took mercy on the walking furniture and navigated the mess to sit down.

"You must have a lot of questions," said Grandmother Willow.

"What the hell happened to you, Grandmother Willow?" asked Connie.

Grandmother Willow snorted. "It's Thelma. Grandmother Willow was my godmother name. I lost that when I lost my license."

Thelma snorted.

"You happened to me, child. Someone like you. Except not you. You're the lucky one. You turned out all right. Took to my blessing rather well, but I suppose someone was bound to eventually. I must say I'm surprised it was you. You didn't leave much of an impression on me. There was a girl in Munich who I thought had such potential. But these things are unpredictable."

"There are others?" asked Tia. "Like Connie?"

"Like Constance? No, there aren't any others like her. She survived her blessing. Many others didn't. A life of adventure isn't for the weak. There were many candidates, but only one could fill the role."

"You twisted old bitch," said Connie. "How long have you been doing this?"

"Me? I'm just a glorified delivery faerie. I go where I'm told, bestowing enchantments as directed. Just a drudge in the Godmother Corps. Or I was, until I lost my license. And it's all because of you. Or someone like you but not so fortunate."

"Hang on," said Connie. "My parents told me you said I chose my blessing."

Thelma chuckled. "That was a bit of showmanship. I am—I was a professional. I could've darted in while you were asleep, sprinkled some faerie dust on your head when no one was looking, with none the wiser. Classic tooth fairy stealth method. The results would've been the same. But I took pride in making my blessings memorable. Funny. Now it's come to bite me on the ass, because if I hadn't, you would've probably never found me. Although what difference does that make now?"

She sat up and half-smiled. "I'm actually glad you're here. The problem with being ageless is that I can only die if I choose to, and I haven't the gumption for that."

"You know she came here to kill you?" asked Tia.

Thelma sat up. "What? Connie, is this true?"

Connie removed her knuckledusters from her pocket and set them on her lap. "Yes, that's why I'm here."

Thelma frowned. "Oh, child, what has this life done to you? This isn't you."

"That's what I keep saying," said Tia.

"Damn it, I've killed before."

Thelma said, "Go ahead, then. Do it, if you must. There's a certain poetic justice to it. The one who survived taking revenge for all the ones that didn't."

Connie clinked her iron knuckledusters together on her lap while she sized up the pathetic old faerie. Thelma was no monster, no space Nazi, no malevolent sorcerer. She wasn't even as threatening as the evil genius hamster that Connie had once stomped to save Australia.

"Damn it."

Thelma grunted. "I knew you couldn't do it."

"Can we get back to the others?" said Tia. "What did you mean by that?"

"You didn't think you were the only one? There were others. A little over a hundred. For many, it didn't take. A few years of adventure before falling into an ordinary life. For others, they eventually ran across an adventure they couldn't triumph over. Those are the ones that bother me.

"I didn't think much of them at the time. Mortal lives are so short, I thought it wasn't important. Then I realized that just made it worse. We fae live for thousands of years, and with so many centuries before us, time becomes a meaningless commodity. But for mortals, every day is a gift, gone and never to return. Once I understood this, I saw myself for the monster I was.

"When I started questioning orders, it was inevitable that

there would be consequences. I never thought the corps would take away my license and banish me to this wretched world. If I had, I probably would've kept my big mouth shut."

A team of mice pulled off her slippers and gave her a foot massage.

"Ah, that's the spot, guys. Thanks."

"If you're genuinely sorry," said Connie, "you'll tell me how to break the spell."

"Are you certain you want to do that?" asked Thelma.

"Why does everyone keep asking me that? For the last time, yes."

"There's an old saying in the Godmother Corps. Be careful what you wish for. But if I could undo the blessing upon you, I'd do it. Alas, child, it isn't that simple. If it were a mere enchantment, I might be able to unmake it, provided I had the correct supplies around here. But we aren't talking about a simple enchantment here. This is a complicated compulsion, one that reaches into the very core of who you have become and the universe around you. It's woven into your soul. You can't simply mumble an incantation and remove it like an old coat you're tired of wearing.

"I may have planted the seed in you, but you nurtured it with every adventure you undertook, every monster you slew, every narrow escape, every larger-than-life exploit. The seed grew because of your actions. I set you on the path, but you chose to stay on it."

"I don't need this metaphysical bullshit," said Connie.

"Metaphysical bullshit aside, you survived, child. You managed, against all sensible odds, to live against a tide of unending danger and grow up. You made that choice."

"What was my other choice? To die?"

"You still don't get it," said Thelma. "You still think you couldn't run away from this. You could've at any time. You still can."

"I've tried ignoring it. It doesn't work."

"Maybe you haven't tried hard enough. Do you know why people have dreary, ordinary lives? For some, it never is a choice. But for others, it is a very deliberate decision. They focus on the minutiae, ignore the world around them, and live with no greater concern than themselves and their cares. To be sure, it's been harder for you, but it was always possible. Every candidate that rejected the enchantment did so by simply losing interest in adventure, and eventually, adventure returned the favor. If you really want to undo the spell, the next time aliens attack or disaster strikes, don't get involved. Just let it be. Just see these things like most people do. Not your problem."

"So, just stand aside and let bad things happen?" asked Connie.

Thelma half-smiled. "You can't do it, can you? All this time, you've been blaming that spell placed on you, when it's been your fault all along."

Connie slipped on her knuckledusters. "Changed my mind. I am going to beat the shit out of you."

"That might make you feel better, Connie, but it won't give you the answers you're looking for. If you insist on getting the spell removed, I can't do it. But I do know who ordered it placed on you."

"I don't need you for that," said Connie. "I can just go to Godmother Corps records to find that out."

"Your operation was off the books, strictly hush-hush. There are no records. Hell, even I only met one contact in person. He's the one who gave me the enchanted dust and the list of candidates that had your name on it."

"Are we talking about a shadowy conspiracy to enchant children into becoming superheroes?" asked Tia.

"I'm not a superhero," said Connie.

"Close enough. Why would anyone do that?"

"You'd have to ask him," said Thelma. "I can't say if it's a conspiracy or if it's just this individual. His goals? Beats the hell out of me. How your name got on that list?" She shrugged. "But if you're looking for answers, you should talk to him."

Connie said, "You know who he is?"

"No, but I can tell you where to find him. I put a tracking hex on him. Just in case. I have it around here somewhere. Let me find it for you. Then, if you want, you can still punch the hell out of me. I deserve it. But let me at least try to make amends."

Connie considered. "All right. Give me the tracking spell, and we'll see what happens after that."

Thelma fluttered her wings through the holes in her robe and floated in the air. "Wonderful. Now, I know it's around here somewhere, but the place is a bit of a mess." She directed the mice to begin searching the house, and the hundreds of rodents skittered about as an organized force.

"Can we help?" asked Tia. "What's it look like?"

"Oh, just an old scroll around here somewhere. I bet it's upstairs. We'll find it." Thelma hovered halfway up the stairs but landed to catch her breath. "I really need to hit the gym again." She walked the rest of the way, disappearing at the top of the steps.

The mice continued to zip around the piles of old newspapers and along the shelves. They opened drawers and worked in teams to paw through musty old books, page by page.

"She wants to help," said Tia.

"She wants to save her skin," said Connie.

"Does it matter, if she gets you what you want?"

Connie shrugged. "I suppose not. But I was hoping I could just kill her and be done with it, but that would be too easy."

While they waited, the mice brought Connie and Tia two cups of tea and some Fig Newtons. The tea was cold, and the cookies were crusty, and while the mice seemed polite, they were still rodents. They left droppings everywhere, and the place smelled exactly like it.

"She's been up there too long," said Connie.

"It's only been a minute."

The mice formed a circle around Connie. They stared at her with their cold pink eyes.

"Ah, damn it."

The lead mouse squealed, and the legion skittered forward. Tia jumped up in her chair, but Connie pressed forward. The mice couldn't stop her, but some of them scampered up her pants leg and started biting her ankles and calves. She ignored the pain and ran upstairs and kicked open the only closed door.

Thelma was halfway out her bathroom window. Connie grabbed the old fae's ankle and attempted to drag her back in. Thelma reached into her robe pocket and flung a handful of glittering dust at Connie. She dodged. The dust hit the toilet, transforming it into a giant porcelain frog that hopped off its fixture. Water spilled across the bathroom floor. Connie slipped on the wet tile, and Thelma wriggled the rest of the way through the window.

"Sorry, child!" shouted Thelma.

She flapped her withered wings and jumped into the air. But fae flight was more a product of magic than physics, and her magic wasn't what it used to be. Yelping, she fell from the roof to land with a thud.

Connie shook the mice out of her pants as she ran downstairs. Tia was busy kicking off waves of rodents. She'd grabbed a lamp and was using it as an impromptu club. She looked like she could handle herself, so Connie dashed outside.

The monster mouse that had knocked over the tree squealed and cowered in a shallow hole.

Thelma limped away on a sprained ankle. Every three

or four steps, she'd try flying again, only to land after a brief moment and yelp.

"Give it up," said Connie. "You aren't going anywhere."

Thelma leaned against the fence post and caught her breath. "I don't know anything. I can't help you."

"Then why are you running?"

"You're here to kill me."

"You said I didn't have it in me."

"I've been wrong before."

Tia came out of the house. She tossed her broken lamp aside.

"Conquer all the mice?" asked Connie.

"I don't want to talk about it. Ever." Tia reached under her shirt and pulled out a twitching rodent by the tail. She threw it onto the lawn, and it scampered away to join its monstrous brother in the hole.

Thelma pulled her wand from her robe. It had been bent in the fall.

"Don't do anything stupid, now," said Connie.

Thelma waved the broken wand over her head. It spurt puffs of glitter before bursting into flames. Hacking, she fell to her knees. A pair of great leather wings burst out of her back as her skin grew dark and leathery. Her neck bulged, and her eyes yellowed. Her hands became red talons. She cracked her spanking new tail like a whip and knocked over the mailbox and what little of the fence was standing. The towering dragon chuckled as she spread her wings. The broken wand had been unable to transform her fully. Bits of flesh remained pale and smooth. Her right wing was an underdeveloped, misshapen thing. Her horns were crooked and malformed. But she was still a fifteen-foot-tall monster. She turned her merciless gaze on Connie as green flames burst from her nostrils.

Thelma spit a baleful emerald fireball. Connie and Tia dove out of the way as the porch burst into flame. Connie rolled, coming up on her feet as Thelma gouged the ground where Connie had stood moments before.

"Damn it. Hold still!"

Thelma swung her tail across the yard. Connie somersaulted over it while Tia hugged the ground. The house collapsed as the limb crushed a corner. Mice ran screaming in all directions.

"There goes my security deposit," said Thelma with a scowl.

Connie slipped on her knuckledusters and charged the dragon. Thelma slammed her tail in front of Connie and wrapped it around her, pinning her arms and the knuckledusters to her side. The iron burned the transformed fae's scales, but not enough to make her release her prey.

"I do regret it came down to this." Thelma smiled. Half her teeth were missing, but the half that were there were sharp enough. "But, in the end, I did promise you a glorious death."

Connie had been face-to-face with death many times. She'd made peace with the reaper years ago. Literally. She'd met the Grim Reaper, and he'd seemed a good guy only doing his job. He hadn't told her when she would die, and she hadn't been tempted to ask. It didn't matter. Everybody died, extraordinary and ordinary people alike.

But, damn it, she did not want to die like this, eaten by a washed-up fairy godmother. If this was indeed her last adventure, it was a lousy way to go out.

Tia threw a rock that struck the dragon just under her eye. "Let her go."

"Tia, stay out of this," said Connie.

"Yes, do stay out of it. It doesn't concern you."

Tia grabbed the burnt remains of Thelma's wand. "Don't make me use this."

Thelma shook her head. "I know what you're doing."

"What am I doing?"

"You're attempting to distract me so that your friend can pull off one of her legendary last-minute escapes."

"Am I?"

"I'm not an idiot. Now shut up so that I can end this already."

"Why don't you shut up?"

Thelma groaned. "Really? That's the best you can do? You're embarrassing yourself and me and Connie. Is this the best sidekick you could find?"

"It was short notice," said Connie.

"Hey, I'm trying to save your life here!" said Tia.

"You don't do that by threatening a dragon with a broken wand," said Connie. "You were better off with the rock."

"Excuse me for trying."

Thelma chuckled. Green flames danced at the back of her

throat. "I must admit, this wasn't the way I expected Constance Verity to die, but I suppose there is a certain poetic nature to it. I planted the enchantment. I might as well be the one to finish it."

"Abracadabra!" shouted Tia as she hurled the wand at the dragon's back. It bounced away harmlessly.

Thelma shook her head. "Just for that, I'm going to eat you after I'm finished with your friend here." She turned to Connie, clutched tightly within her tail.

Connie wasn't there.

Thelma glanced around the yard. "Where?"

Connie whistled from under the dragon. Thelma craned her neck down. "How?"

Connie slammed her iron knuckledusters in the equivalent of a dragon's solar plexus. Thelma collapsed with a shriek, and it was only Connie's reflexes that allowed her to jump out of the way instead of being buried under her opponent.

While Thelma gasped for breath, Connie punched the dragon across the jaw. The iron and the blow proved devastating for the fae dragon, who fell limp.

"But I had you," she said in a rough whisper. "I had you."

"I studied escape artistry under Houdini's ghost," said Connie, "and I've fought enough dragons to understand their biology. And a helpful distraction never hurts either."

"Stop," said Tia. "You're embarrassing me."

Thelma tried to rise, but her strength had left her. She spit out several loosened fangs and slumped on her yard. "I can't believe I fell for that."

"Don't feel bad. Better bad guys than you have." Connie tapped her knuckledusters together with a clink. "Now, are you going to help me, or do I have to get rough?"

"I told you, I don't know anything." Thelma belched, and fire erupted from her throat. It scorched the non-dragon portions of her half-transformed flesh. "Excuse me. I don't know what—"

With a painful retching heave, her head burst into flame, consumed down to the bone in a green-and-blue explosion. The rest of her flesh followed suit, turning to ash in moments. A smoldering, malformed reptilian skeleton was all that was left behind, and that crumbled to blackened powder when the breeze kicked up.

"Son of a bitch," said Connie.

"What happened?" asked Tia.

"Bad magic from a broken wand and iron don't mix." Connie swept up a handful of ashes in her hands. "I need something to hold this in."

Tia took off her sneaker and offered it to Connie. "Glad I didn't go open-toe."

Connie scooped more ashes into the shoe.

"What are you doing?" asked Tia.

Connie shrugged. "Grasping at straws."

12

"**C**an you do it?" asked Connie.

Madam Zura examined the plastic bag filled with ashes. "I don't know. I've never tried to channel a nonhuman spirit."

"Is there any harm in trying?"

Madam Zura said, "Probably not. Most of the time, if the spirit is beyond my reach, nothing happens."

"Most of the time?" asked Tia.

"There are accidents. When you reach into the Other Side, sometimes you end up grabbing something else. People think the Other Side of death is full of ghosts, demons, and angels. There are far worse things out there."

"What sort of things?"

"Just things," said Zura. "Trying to give them labels beyond that will only give you a headache. And that's not counting all the little things, the unborn spirits, the petty dead, those bitter souls caught between this world and the next, waiting for a chance to reenter ours."

"Can you do it?" asked Connie.

"Are you sure you really want me to? The answers the dead bring are rarely to our liking. Take it from me. I do this for a living."

"I know the rules. I don't care. I need to ask her a few questions."

"And you're willing to pay the price?"

Connie wanted those answers, but she hesitated.

"What's the price?" asked Tia.

"I'll pay it," said Connie.

"What price?" asked Tia again, louder this time.

"That's up to the ghost," replied Zura. "Providing I can summon her in the first place."

"The ghost of the person Connie killed only a few hours ago?" said Tia.

"You killed her?" Zura shook her head. "That complicates matters."

"I didn't kill her," said Connie. "Not directly. It was an accident."

"In my experience, spirits tend to be touchy about those responsible for their deaths, even if those deaths are accidental."

"I'll have to take that chance."

"It's your chance to take. Give me a few moments to set things up." Zura, taking the ashes with her, disappeared beyond a beaded curtain.

"I don't get it," said Tia. "We've dealt with ghosts before. Remember those ghost cavemen? They didn't seem so tough. I think real cavemen would've been tougher."

"There are different kinds of ghosts," said Connie. "Every ghost you've encountered never journeyed to the Other Side. They haven't pierced the greater mysteries beyond the Veil. But when a spirit crosses over, it learns things we shouldn't know."

"Could you be a little more vague?"

"It's vague because that's the whole point. If we knew the mysteries, if we could fathom them, then they wouldn't be mysteries."

"This isn't like a movie where our faces will melt off for daring to transgress beyond limits, is it?" asked Tia.

"It's unlikely."

"Unlikely but not impossible."

"I wouldn't worry about that. It's far more probable you'll hear something that drives you steadily, irreversibly insane over the next ten or twenty years."

"Got it. As long as I get to keep my face."

Connie almost offered Tia a chance to sit this one out, but Tia wouldn't take her up on it. She might have been an ordinary person, but she wasn't an ordinary friend.

"Thanks," said Connie.

"I'm here for the duration. You know that."

"I'm not talking about this. I'm talking about everything. There were times when the thoughts of our brunches were the only thing keeping me sane while I was wrestling lions."

"Funny," said Tia. "I was thinking the same thing. Remember that time I was kidnapped by robots?"

"Which time? The tall, boxy ones or the squat, round ones?"

"The second," she said. "I was going through my divorce at

the time. Felt like I'd wasted seven years of my life. Then those robots came along and tried to throw me into that volcano—"

"The boxy ones wanted to throw you in a volcano. The squat ones wanted to remove your brain."

"Oh, yeah. It all starts blending together after a while. It's not important. Keeping my brain and not getting sacrificed to a computer god put things in perspective, made everything seem easier by comparison. Don't get me wrong; I don't want to make a habit of it. I can't do what you do. But it's a nice change of pace now and then."

Madam Zura called them into the back. They entered the small dark room that smelled of sage and vanilla. Dozens of black and white candles lined the walls. A plastic skull sat on a round table. It was all very much what one would expect from a dedicated séance room except for the soulful music of Aretha Franklin in the background.

"Do the dead like Aretha?" asked Tia.

"No, I like Aretha," said Zura. "The dead's taste varies. But it's my séance room, so I get to decide the playlist." She nodded at Tia. "You're new, so I'll explain how this works. We sit at the table and join hands. You don't say anything. You might feel some tingling in your extremities, and maybe the table will levitate. Don't worry about it. Eventually, I'll reach across the Veil and contact our target. If I'm successful, an ectoplasmic manifestation will appear. Don't talk to it. Don't ask it any questions. Don't say a single word until I give the all-clear. I have to make sure I'm channeling the right spirit and not something else. If it passes the smell test, then I'll give Connie the go-ahead to start talking. You don't say anything. Got it?"

"Keep my mouth shut. Got it."

"And try not to look the spirit in the eye," added Zura. "It tends to piss them off."

"Head down. Got it."

"No. I need you to look at it. It will only exist as long as the three of us acknowledge it. We're the doorway. If one of us closes it, the thing will either go back whence it came or end up trapped here. That can lead to all sorts of problems."

"Look at it, but don't look too much at it," said Tia. "Got it."

"She's no slouch," said Connie. "She'll do her part."

"I'm not worried about her," said Zura. "Are you really sure you want to do this?"

"I'm sure. Stop asking."

Zura shrugged. "Have it your way."

They sat at the table and linked hands. Connie and Tia sat quietly while Zura closed her eyes and concentrated. It didn't take long.

"I've got something."

She sneezed and a globule of pinkish goo burst from her nostril. It floated over the table. The goo shifted and squirmed like the wax in a lava lamp. She belched and spat up another chunk of ectoplasm that joined the mass.

It was disgusting but necessary. Ghosts and spirits on this side of the Veil had their own residual ectoplasm to use, but spirits on the Other Side required one to be built for them. Some things beyond the Veil had never had a form to begin with. As Zura barfed up more goop from her mouth, nose, and ears, the spirit took on the form of a malformed lump. Tia feared the worst. They had summoned something other than their target. Some dread horror that humanity was never meant to encounter brought forth to unleash madness and death.

Her face felt itchy. Whether it was a melty kind of itchy or not, she couldn't say.

The ectoplasm formed Thelma's face.

"Son of a bitch," she said. "Not enough that you have to kill me. Now you won't even let me rest in death's sweet embrace."

Neither Connie nor Tia said anything.

Madam Zura exhaled a final bit of magic snot. "All right. It's her. But I don't know how long I can hold her. Ask your questions."

"I didn't kill you," said Connie. "You killed yourself."

Thelma's ectoplasmic face twisted in a scowl. "Maybe so, but you brought me back. For what?"

"You know why."

"I do indeed, child, but I don't know why I should tell you anything anymore."

"Because this is your last chance to make amends," said Connie. "You owe me."

"And I paid that debt with my life."

"I didn't want your life. I wanted mine."

Thelma bubbled as her ghostly face became a skull. "You

aren't going to like what you find if you keep on this course. The sweetest mercy I could offer you would be to leave you in the dark."

"That's my problem," said Connie.

Madam Zura moaned. The candles went out one by one.

Thelma howled like a banshee. The temperature dropped, and every candle went out. Her ectoplasmic face was the only thing lighting the darkness.

"Is that a yes?" asked Connie.

Thelma chuckled. "I'll give you the answer you seek, but I warn you that it will only lead to more misery. And in return for that answer, I demand that you take me with you."

"I thought you were pissed that I was keeping you from the Other Side," said Connie.

"This is too important to miss. I've wasted decades banished to the mortal world, and just when things are getting interesting, I'm supposed to totter off? Screw that. I want to see how things play out."

"Can you do it?" Connie asked Madam Zura.

The medium nodded.

"Do it, then."

Tia squeezed Connie's hand harder. Connie squeezed back even harder and shook her head.

"Spirits who seek to forestall their passing are never up to any good," said Zura.

"Just do it," said Connie. "Please."

"If anyone else was asking, Constance . . ."

"I know. Thank you."

Madam Zura broke the circle and pulled a pen from her pocket. She whispered something to the pen, and Thelma's ectoplasm popped like a bubble. The candles flashed alight again. Zura gave the pen to Connie.

"Be careful with this."

"She's in there?" asked Tia.

"I assumed you would want something easy to carry around, and I've arranged it so you can click her quiet."

Zura clicked the pen, and Thelma's tiny voice issued from it. "I was hoping for something more suitably mysterious."

Connie took the pen and clicked it again. "This'll do. Thanks."

Thelma had an answer for the pixie-dust mystery. They discussed it in Madame Zura's kitchen. She served them tea, Napoleon's favorite blend, she assured them, before excusing herself for another consultation.

"I was given the dust by a little guy," said Thelma. "Short. Yellow. Spiky. I don't know much more than that."

"I thought you were supposed to know unfathomable mysteries," said Tia.

"I wasn't across the Veil that long. They don't give you the juicy stuff until you've been there a while."

"Who is *they?*"

There was the distinct impression of Thelma's spirit smirking in her pen. "Wouldn't you like to know?"

"Did you say short, yellow, and spiky?" asked Connie.

"Yes. It's not much, I know."

"It's something."

"I knew you'd find it useful," replied Thelma.

"What else do you know?" asked Tia.

"Wouldn't you like to know?"

"Are you going to keep saying that?"

"Wouldn't you—"

Connie clicked Thelma quiet.

"Is it a good idea to bring her along?" asked Tia.

"I still need her, and she's stuck in a pen. What can she do?"

"She could misdirect you, give you false information. Ghosts can still lie, can't they? How can you trust her at all?"

"I don't, but she's all I have to go on."

"Connie, don't take this the wrong way, but this is reckless, even for you."

"I didn't bring you along to get in my way," said Connie.

Tia frowned. "Don't get mad at me because I'm being sensible. My role in adventures is usually to get you into trouble. I'm trying to keep you out of it for once."

"Tia, we've come this far. We can't stop now."

"I get that. But you can exercise some caution. I'm worried you're so focused on the goal that you're not thinking things through."

"I never think things through. I dive in headfirst."

"That's bull, and you know it. When I was being held prisoner by the marsupial men of Viceroy Lunacy, you didn't rush in to save me. You took the time to get backup, and it was a good thing you did. You're great at improvising and last-minute escapes, but you also know the value of being prepared."

"I'm prepared."

"Are you? Because it seems to me like you're rushing without thinking this through. And don't tell me I don't have to come along if I don't like it. I'm along for the ride. I'll follow you into Hell if you think it's the right thing to do. But I'd like you to take a minute to think about it before we did."

"Thinking about it leads to second-guessing," said Connie.

"Maybe that's not such a bad thing. I've been thinking too, and I'm worried the only reason Thelma would agree to stick around is because something big is happening here. And the biggest thing that springs to mind immediately is your glorious death."

Connie grumbled.

"I take it that means you've already considered that too, then?" asked Tia.

Connie shrugged. "Yes."

"And you're still going forward with it?"

"What choice do I have? If this spell implanted in me is working, then I can't avoid it, can I?"

"That's just it. Didn't Thelma say you can avoid it if you try hard enough? Maybe you don't need to go to all this trouble. Maybe all you need to do is not rush into adventure this time."

Thelma vibrated in Connie's pocket. She tried to ignore the ghost, but Thelma was insistent. Connie clicked the pen.

"You should listen to her," said Thelma, "but you won't."

"I've tried ignoring it. It doesn't work. And if does, it's still a pain in the ass. The only way to correct the problem is to get rid of the spell once and for all."

"Any excuse to leap into the fray," said Thelma.

"She might not be wrong," said Tia.

"Oh, now you're on her side? I thought you didn't trust her," said Connie.

"I don't, but that doesn't mean I think she's lying. Not about this."

"It's a spell. I've broken spells before."

"The fault lies not in our spells, but in ourselves," said Thelma. "If you genuinely wanted this broken, you could've pursued this idea before. So, answer this: why didn't you?"

"I've been busy," said Connie.

"So busy you couldn't think about removing the thing that was keeping you so busy? Isn't that convenient? Or are you simply denying who you are, who you've always been?"

Connie thought about clicking Thelma quiet but didn't.

"How about this, then? How long ago did you get sick of being thrust into adventures?"

"I don't know. Couple of years ago," said Connie.

"You're not a very good liar," said Thelma.

"I'm a very good liar," Connie replied.

And she was. She'd bluffed her way out of many a situation by being good at it.

She knew precisely when her attitude started changing. She'd been returning an idol to a sacred shrine for reasons she couldn't recall right now. As she was setting the sacred cup/dagger/sword/statue to its proper place, she thought how it was all the same stuff, over and over again. She'd returned or stolen so many cursed artifacts that it all blended together. Same shit, different day.

The only thing she remembered with any clarity was how exhausting it was becoming. She didn't walk out of that temple ready to quit, but it was the first time she considered it, however briefly.

"Eight years ago," she said.

"And during those eight years, you never once considered breaking the spell? Even though you've broken spells before?" asked Thelma. "It's not because you didn't know it could be done. It's because you are an adventurer. Forged by magic, the will of the universe, and, most importantly, your very nature. You were made, and the person who made you . . . is you. And removing the spell won't change that."

"You're just trying to get into my head," said Connie. "You're just a ghost with an axe to grind."

There was some truth to Thelma's words. Connie had spent most of her life a willing participant in adventure, and there was no denying that she'd done a fair amount of good over the years. Saved a lot of lives. Saved a lot of worlds. Saved the universe. She was proud of what she'd accomplished, but she could also use a break.

She'd never get that break as long as the spell was in place. It wasn't her nature to turn away from danger. As long as the opportunities to risk her neck for the greater good kept popping up, she'd never be able to walk away. She'd keep pushing her luck until one day she died that glorious death promised to her at the end of this curse.

If she couldn't change herself, she'd have to change the spell. She sipped her tea. "I just need to break it."

C onspiracy theorists and UFO enthusiasts liked to camp out around Area 51, and if they were patient and determined enough, they might see something weird. Flying-saucer pilots didn't always remember to turn on their stealth systems, and every blurry photo fueled paranoia about terrible secrets hidden in the desert.

"How are we going to get past the guards?" asked Tia as they approached the gate. "Do we have cover stories? Should I act natural? Do I need to say anything? Should I be chewing gum? I always look more relaxed chewing gum."

"Don't worry. I have a plan," said Connie.

A guard stepped out of the box and approached the window.

"This is a restricted area, ma'am," he said.

Connie flashed a badge. He opened the gate and waved her through.

"Omega level security clearance," she said. "They gave it to me after I broke into the White House the second time."

"They give security clearances for that?"

"They do after you prove the president has been replaced by a cyborg clone."

"And you're just telling me this now?"

"The government asked me to keep a lid on it. National security. Peace of mind of the citizens. And I don't tell you about all the mundane stuff."

"Only you would call fighting a cyborg *mundane*."

"Who said anything about fighting? I just told him I was onto him and asked him politely to leave. He did."

"You're right. That doesn't sound very exciting."

"I averted World War Two once by simply saying *please* to the right ambassador. You'll be surprised at how far good manners will get you in this world."

"There was a World War Two."

"Sure. In this timeline."

Area 51 wasn't much to look at. Only a few hangars and blocky white buildings. The guards, perhaps a dozen of them, sat around playing cards and slacking off. They were there as a token from the United States government, but security wasn't their job.

Connie pulled the car into a darkened hangar. A trio of thin, green aliens in gray uniforms stepped from the shadows and waved strange devices around them. Connie gave her card to a fourth green alien in a blue uniform. He glanced at it, gave it back to her.

"Blessed Snurkab, it is my honor to welcome you," he said.

"It's Connie," she replied. "Just Connie."

"As you wish." He handed back her card. "Won't be a moment."

The aliens completed their decontamination, bathing the car in mysterious rays, before pushing a button. The floor under the car lowered as they descended underground. Tia had been in enough secret bases to not be terribly impressed by this one.

A strange being with many arms gurgled at Connie as she exited the car and handed it her keys. She handed the extraterrestrial twenty bucks. "Keep it close."

It nodded enthusiastically, splashing some purple saliva on the windows before driving away.

The lot was filled with a variety of spacecraft and a couple of time machines. Aliens wandered around, doing whatever aliens did there. Several pointed at Connie. One furry, ape-like being bowed to her as they walked past it.

At the next checkpoint, they came across a metallic statue of a twelve-year-old girl that Tia recognized immediately.

Connie answered the question before it had to be asked. "Remember that time my family moved to Nowhere, Montana, to try and get me away from this stuff? It didn't work. The house we moved into had a miniature wormhole in the basement. I stumbled through it and ended up in outer space for a year."

"But you were only gone a month."

"Month to you and everyone here. The wormhole warped time as well as space."

"So, you're telling me you're a year older than me?"

"Not physically. The wormhole took care of that, too. But while I was out there, I ended up being the only one who could pilot this ancient warship that—" Connie stopped. "Doesn't matter. I did some stuff. Saved a dozen alien civilizations. Not a big deal."

"And they built a statue to you in gratitude?" said Tia.

"A ship came here to set up an intergalactic pit stop. The crew discovered this was where I was from. Set up a little museum, a little tourist attraction for those passing through. It has the largest collection of Constance Verity memorabilia in this sector of the galaxy."

"Isn't Area 51 older than you?"

"Wormhole," said Connie by way of explanation.

A tall spider lady with six legs and an angular, fanged face approached. Her name was a series of scent emissions followed by a sound too high-pitched for humans to hear. She went by Charlotte, a name an exhausted human official had assigned her while slowly being driven mad by the number of aliens that had unpronounceable names.

"This is indeed an honor. If we had known the Legendary Snurkab was paying us a visit, we would've prepared a proper welcome." Her melodious voice drifted over Tia with a pleasant, mildly hypnotic effect. On her homeworld, it was used to lure prey. Here, it was for customer relations.

"*Legendary* is going a bit far," said Connie.

"Shall I sing the 'Song of Glorious Remembrance'?"

"Oh, please do," said Tia.

"Please. Don't," said Connie. "You don't want to hear it, anyway. It's four hours long, and that's the radio play version."

"If your companion would like it, we can see that she is given a copy from the gift shop."

"Do that," said Connie. "Give her the whole deluxe knick-knack souvenir package. Fair warning. The snow globes are manufactured on the outer fringe, and they leak."

Charlotte clicked at a short, green lizardoid, who nodded before scurrying off.

"As a matter of fact, I don't really need you for this part," said Connie. "If you want to check out the museum, be my guest."

"Really? Are you sure?" asked Tia. "What if there's trouble?"

"Trouble? Here? It won't be anything I can't handle on my own. Go on. Have fun. I think there are some exhibits on you."

Charlotte gave Tia a VIP pass, and she ran off with a hasty good-bye. Connie was led to the record offices in the back of the park. She sat at a computer and scrolled through Muroid holograms, holding Thelma before the screen. There were many more than she expected, because a Muroid clan had landed on Earth with the original Roswell arrival, and they bred rapidly. There were a lot of faces to go through, and Connie discovered the flaw in her plan.

"Does this one look familiar?" she asked.

"They all look familiar," said Thelma.

"This one has a dominant central ridge," said Connie. "He looks completely different."

Thelma paused as she squinted—or so Connie assumed about a ghost in a pen—at the image.

"I didn't notice the ridge. Sorry."

"What did you notice?"

"Yellow. Spiky. Short."

"That's every Muroid. You didn't observe the vestigial-gill placement? The nasal width? The brow height?"

"Yellow. Spiky. Short," repeated Thelma.

"This is pointless," said Connie. "You could be looking right at who we're after and not know it."

"Excuse me for not being an expert on Muroid identification."

"It's not that hard."

"It's not that hard for you," said Thelma. "I didn't spend years hobnobbing with aliens."

Connie had a diverse skill set that enabled her to see the differences in the alien faces that would've been invisible to the untrained eye. If she'd seen the original culprit, she would've been able to identify him without any trouble, but she hadn't seen him. Or her. Thelma hadn't even noticed the eye shape enough to distinguish the Muroid's sex. That information alone would've been enough for Connie to chart their target's sexual metamorphosis cycle, giving them something to work with. Right now, it was like showing up on Earth with orders to locate the suspicious mammalian humanoid.

"Maybe he isn't among these images?" said Thelma. "If he's

an alien, maybe he went home. Thirty-five years is a long time, as mortals reckon time. Though I don't know about aliens. What are you going to do now?"

"I don't know," replied Connie.

She'd been in dire straits before. Lost. Confused. Hopeless. She'd always found a way out of them. If there was a monster, she'd kill it or escape. If there was a sinister mastermind, she'd get his own giant robot to step on him. If there was a mystery, she'd crack it. But this wasn't any of those things.

This was a dead end.

She hated dead ends.

She'd once found a magic coin that could control the weather. Someone had stolen it. She'd never found out who. She'd never found the coin again. And if someone had been planning on using it for nefarious purposes, they had never gotten around to it.

She'd been on an expedition to the Amazon to find a dinosaur. They'd found the tracks. They'd never found the dinosaur. She'd found dinosaurs before that. She'd found dinosaurs after. She'd never found *that* dinosaur.

She'd journeyed to ancient Mars to discover she hadn't journeyed quite ancient enough, happening upon the ruins of a once-thriving civilization where, if her studies in xenoarchaeology were accurate, everyone had at least three sword fights a day and fell in and out of love nearly as often. It was only ruins and bones. In her youth, her poor timing had irritated her.

A life of endless adventure had taken its toll. She wasn't

the same eager kid she once was, ready to plunge headfirst into any random booby-trapped temple or find romance with any charming pirate king that came along. She was sick of most of it.

But, goddamn it, she hated dead ends.

She was looking for a needle in a pile of needles on another pile of needles with more needles being added every minute and some needles being taken away before she'd even started looking. Also, the one needle she was looking for probably didn't want to be found.

"It's impossible." She didn't use that word lightly.

"I wouldn't say that," said Thelma smugly. "You might get lucky."

"You can cut that out," said Connie.

"Cut what out?"

"The *I've got a secret* tone you keep using."

"But I do have secrets."

Thelma paused for drama.

"The secrets of the dead."

"Terrific for you. If you aren't going to share them, I don't give a damn."

"If you knew what I knew—"

"I know more than you know," said Connie.

Thelma laughed. "You only think that because you've never been beyond this side of death."

"I've been dead. A couple of times. Once a whole week. You didn't know that?"

"Of course I did." Thelma didn't sound convincing.

"You want to have a secret contest? I can tell you things that would make you crap your ectoplasmic shorts."

"Like what?"

"The original recipe for Coca-Cola. The final digit of pi. The reason it's almost impossible to find a word that rhymes with *orange*."

Thelma chuckled. "Trivialities. Do you think I fear those answers?"

"You should. Did you ever wonder about the origins of the color periwinkle?"

Connie started revealing the terrible truth, but after a few seconds, Thelma begged her to stop.

"By Oberon," said Thelma in breathless terror. "I had no idea."

"Nobody does," replied Connie. "So, tell me what you know or keep it to yourself. But stop hinting or I'll share some of the truly terrifying secrets."

"I'm only saying that I expect you'll have some luck. I don't know more than that. The secrets of the dead appear to be fading from my memory the longer I'm on this side."

"They'll do that. But I wouldn't have survived this long if I relied on luck. Luck is a sucker's bet."

She had gotten lucky. Many times. It'd even saved her life a dozen times. More. But she didn't count on it. This might be her blessing or destiny or whatever, but she had to believe there was more to it than simply a path she had to follow. She was more than a body filling a role.

Charlotte entered the room. "Any luck in your search, Honored Snurkab?"

Connie grunted, shook her head.

"We are saddened to hear this." Charlotte warbled, and the sorrow in her voice caused Connie to shed a tear. "We have brought the Muroid employees, as you requested."

"I didn't request that."

"Apologies. We must have misunderstood the nature of your request. We shall dismiss them."

"Wait. Were any of them stationed here thirty-five years ago?"

"Yes, several. Supervisor Klat has been with the park for longer than that."

"Hell, I might as well talk to them."

Charlotte whistled with delight. "Right this way, Honored Snurkab."

The dozen Muroids had been assembled in a break room. They sat around the tables, dressed in their maintenance uniforms. Klat wore a patch marking him as a supervisor.

"Rise for the Legendary Snurkab," said Charlotte.

Connie waved them back into their seats. "No need to get up. Just wanted to have a little talk. I'm looking for a Muroid. I have no idea what he or she looks like, and I know it's a long shot, but I was hoping maybe one of you could help me find him or her."

The Muroids murmured amongst themselves. Except for Klat.

"I'd like to talk to all of you, one at a time, if that's all right. It shouldn't take long."

They murmured and croaked. For Muroids, croaking was like yawning. Once one did it, they all did it. The room echoed with the sound of a dozen frog aliens.

Except for Klat, who stood quietly in his corner, nursing a beverage of Snurkab Cola. The soda was too sour for her tastes, and she hated the picture of her they used for it.

Connie went to the office next door and instructed Klat to be brought first. She had a seat behind a desk in a chair that would've been more comfortable if she had two more legs.

Klat stood before her, not looking directly at her. It was against Muroid custom to do so. That didn't mean much. But Klat's vestigial gills flapped and his knuckles paled. They were all signs of more than idle nerves.

"Something bothering you, Klat?"

"No, Honored Snurkab."

"You seem awfully nervous."

"I don't appreciate your accusations."

"I didn't accuse you of anything."

"Good. Because I didn't do anything." His voice vibrated. Muroid hearing didn't notice such things, but it made them terrible liars to everyone else. "Can I go now? We have work to do."

She didn't reply. Interrogation was all about giving someone enough time to incriminate themselves.

"You can't keep me here," he said. "You have no authority."

"The Snurkab is recognized as the highest authority on Earth." Saving the universe had its advantages. "I can detain you officially or we can continue to talk. Politely. Up to you."

"I demand a defense representative."

"He knows something," said Thelma.

"Of course he knows something. We're past that. We're trying to figure out what he knows."

"Is this good cop/bad cop?" asked Thelma. "Can I be bad cop?"

"Quiet," said Connie.

She leaned forward, elbows on the desk. "You're a lousy liar, even for a Muroid. We can play this game for the next couple of hours, or you can just tell me what I want to know."

He blinked his small red eyes. He glanced toward the door.

His mucous sac swelled as he prepared to spit out a glob of paralytic phlegm.

"Don't do it, Klat," she said. "Even if you make it out of this room, you'll never make it out of this base."

With a painful gulp, he swallowed the glob.

onnie let Klat stew a little in her impromptu interrogation room. She watched him through the glass. It wasn't a one-way mirror, just a window in the doorway where she could keep an eye on him, and where he could see her keeping an eye on him.

He'd glance up every so often, only to avert his gaze.

After twenty minutes, it was obvious he was ready to break.

Tia had been disappointed by the Snurkab Museum. It didn't have much she didn't already know about Connie. There was indeed an exhibit about Tia, consisting of a pair of photographs of her labeling her as Connie's pet.

"That's the guy?" asked Tia.

"That's the guy," replied Connie.

"How are we doing this?" asked Tia.

"Are you trying to be a tough guy?" asked Connie. "If so, I'd recommend putting down the snow cone."

Tia took a bite of her ice. "But it's so good. I don't know what they put in it—"

"Buzazabog blood."

Tia examined the crimson shavings in her hand. "I thought it was some kind of space cherry."

"Nope. Blood."

Tia shrugged. "As long as it's not artificial sweeteners, I can live with it." She took another bite. "Are we going to question him?"

Connie pushed her way into the room and had a seat across the table from the Muroid. Tia stood behind, mustering all the no-nonsense attitude she could while holding a snow cone in one hand and a complimentary Snurkab doll tucked under her other arm.

Connie slapped the table. Klat stopped croaking.

"Thirty-five years is a long time to hang out on a planet so far from home," she said.

He belched nonchalantly. "This is an inoffensive world. My job is union. Pay is good."

"Just seems to me that if there was someone I was worried about finding me, there are a hell of a lot of better planets out there. Like any other planet."

"My spawnpair likes it here." He twisted his round head to the left in the Muriod version of a shrug. "And I wasn't hiding."

"Where'd you get the fairy dust?" she asked.

"Some guy. It was a long time ago." His eyes receded deeper into his skull. "What fairy dust?"

"It's too late to play dumb."

"Yeah. Way too late." Tia snorted and bit loudly into her snow cone.

"This is against intergalactic law," said Klat.

Connie slapped the table again. "I'm losing my patience, buddy. We put in your request for a representative, but the galaxy is a big place. We have plenty of time to talk in the meantime. Time for things to happen."

"Bad things," added Tia.

Connie glanced over her shoulder. "You're not helping."

"Sorry."

"Okay, I'll talk," said Klat. "But you have to understand. It's not my fault."

"Whose fault is it, then?" said Connie. "You're the one who gave my fairy godmother the special dust that threw this spell on me. I killed her for that. Give me a reason not to kill you."

"It was imperative that the Snurkab come into being," said Klat. "If there was no Snurkab in the present, then there would be no Snurkab to journey through the space warp into the past and save the galaxy."

Connie closed her eyes and cleared her head. "God, I really hate time travel sometimes."

Time travel always complicated things. It didn't help any that the rules were so damned inconsistent. She'd gone back and changed the past on more than one occasion. Other times, it was all about creating a stable time loop where effect and cause were twisted together in a giant knot. Then there were those incidents where independent alternate timelines were created. There wasn't any consistency to any of it, and if there was a problem/cliché of time travel, she'd run across all of them. And she didn't like any of them.

Of all the complications she regularly found herself in (and that was a hell of a lot of complications), she liked time travel the least.

"Where'd you get the dust?" she asked again.

"It was given to me by my government when I was sent to this world, along with a list of candidates. Our computers and oracles predicted the time of birth of the Snurkab on this world along with the list of potential candidates."

"Do you know what you've done? How many people you might have destroyed with that list?"

"It's not my job," said Klat. "We weighed the potential risk to the candidates and viewed it as a necessary sacrifice. Our mathematical models predicted most would reject the role, leaving them to resume their previous uneventful lives. A small percentage would perish, but their lives were deemed a necessary sacrifice for the greater good of a thousand inhabited worlds."

"You couldn't get it down to one?" asked Connie.

"One hundred and twelve candidates from billions of humans is statistically miraculous in itself."

"So, why hire the godmother? Why not do it yourself?"

"Expedience. I don't understand. Would you prefer it if a handful of souls lived as the rest of the universe perished?"

"Now you're putting this on me? I didn't ask to be your Snurkab."

"I didn't ask to make you the Snurkab," he replied. "I was only doing my job."

"A lot of that going around," said Thelma from Connie's pocket.

"Okay, so I saved the galaxy," said Connie. "You can take this spell off me now."

"I don't know how," he said.

"Who does?"

"Our mystics, perhaps. I'm not a mystic. I don't know anything about magic. I'm just the delivery agent."

"Mystics? In outer space? Space wizards?" asked Tia.

"Muroid sorcerers are renowned throughout the galaxy. You didn't think your world was the only one with scholars of magic, did you?" said Klat. "But this isn't simply an enchantment. This is a singular cosmic identity. You are the caretaker of the universe. It's an honor beyond your imagining."

"I don't want it anymore."

"You are the Snurkab. You cannot simply stop being the Snurkab because it inconveniences you."

"I get it. You needed me to save you. I did it. Now, can't you get your sorcerers to undo the spell, destiny, or cosmic whatsawhoosit you forced on me."

"It isn't as easy as that."

Connie studied his face for signs of dishonesty. She saw none.

"All right. Thanks. You can go now."

Klat blinked. "What?"

"You heard me. You can go. I'm done."

She walked out of the room without saying another word. Tia chased after her.

"That's it?" Tia asked.

"That's it," said Connie.

"But you're just giving up?"

"Yep. Everyone keeps telling me this is a waste of my time. Who am I to argue?"

Charlotte said, "Is everything to your liking, Honorable Snurkab?"

Connie forced a thin smile. "Everything's just peachy."

"If it would please you, we can arrange immediate transport to the Muroid homeworld. Perhaps they would be more amenable to your request in person."

"Thanks, but I'm good." Connie kept walking.

Thelma said, "Too bad you didn't have this revelation before killing me."

"You killed yourself."

"That's not how I remember it."

"Either way, you're dead. No point in debating it now."

"That's a bit rude, isn't it?"

"No, but this is." Connie clicked the pen quiet.

Leaving Area 51 was more of an ordeal than getting in. Once word of the Legendary Snurkab being in the park spread, a small crowd gathered around her. She could've taken the back way out, but instead, she signed autographs, took holo images with strange beings from outer space, and shook countless odd appendages (some that were best left unidentified).

Simply watching left Tia exhausted. It took ninety minutes to get back to the car.

The base disappeared in the rearview mirror. They drove in silence. Connie ignored the haunted pen vibrating in her pocket.

Tia couldn't contain herself any longer. "All right. So, what's the deal?"

Connie stared straight ahead. She took a bit to answer.

"It just keeps going. There's no end to it."

"It has to end somewhere," said Tia. "Right?"

"Does it? Let's assume we head out to the Muroid home-world. What are the odds that it'll just lead us somewhere else? And wherever that goes, some other place. Another planet. Another dimension. Back here. A wild goose chase throughout the universe looking for answers."

"Does that mean you don't think the spell can be broken?"

"Oh, it can be broken," said Connie. "And I'm going to break it. But I'm not going to break it by following the path they've set before me."

Tia hesitated to ask the question, but it became clear Connie wasn't going to offer the answer.

"*They* who?"

"Beats the hell out of me, but whoever they are, I'm through playing their game. I'll be damned if I'm blasting off to outer space on the whims of someone or something."

"I'm not following," said Tia. "You're saying this has been planned somehow? That someone knew you'd track down your fairy godmother and that it'd lead you to Area 51?"

"It was only a matter of time," said Connie. "One day, I was going to get sick of this and track Thelma down."

She could no longer ignore Thelma shaking in her pocket. Connie clicked the pen.

"I was set up? They wanted me to die?" asked Thelma.

"No, if they wanted you dead, they could've killed you. They wanted you alive for me to find. You died because you were dumb. Don't blame it on anyone else."

"You are at least tangentially responsible," said Thelma.

"Get over it," said Connie.

"Easy for you to say. You're not the one stuck in here."

Connie clicked Thelma quiet and tossed her in the glove compartment.

"I'm not saying I don't believe you," said Tia. "You're usually right about this kind of thing. But isn't it a stretch? Thelma didn't know anything."

"She knew enough. She pointed me in the right direction. Think about it. If you're trying to keep a low profile, you don't send a Muroid to hire a fairy godmother. Muroids are distinct. You might as well put down a big red X over Area 51 when you do that. To make it easier, you even banish the fairy godmother to Earth."

"But you went to the Fae Realms to find her. We almost got eaten by a dragon."

Connie said, "I don't think the plan is that specific. They put her where I could find her and trusted I'd use my own methods to do so. They didn't plan on her death, but I got around that. I can get around lots of problems ordinary people can't. The important thing was that I found her and that she gave me the one piece of information she had.

"And once I came to Area 51, Charlotte practically threw Klat at me. She knew I was observant enough to spot a nervous Muroid. Maybe I wouldn't have noticed him right away, but once I talked to him, it wouldn't take me long to put it together."

"You are a master detective," said Tia.

"I wouldn't say *master*. I'm fortunate enough to be a trained observer and have a smattering of knowledge in exobiology. Enough to know that you don't hire a Muroid if you want to keep a secret, and if you do, you don't leave that Muroid on Earth, waiting to be discovered."

"Is this a conspiracy or the caretaker spell?" asked Tia.

"It's both, I think. I've busted enough secret societies to know that most of their schemes involve a hell of a lot of luck. When they work—and they don't usually—all the leaders claim to be masters of manipulation. When they fail, they claim it's all part of the plan. The truth is that for most members, these conspirators are a social club rather than a shadowy cabal. Like the Loyal Order of Water Buffalo without the public face. They all pledge undying loyalty to the Grand Poobah, but as soon as the shit starts to unravel, they all hang up their robes and admit they don't know what they hell they were doing beyond sitting in dark rooms and playing elaborate games of make-believe."

"Like fantasy football with world governments," said Tia.

"Not far off. But once in a while, I've run across genuinely sinister conspiracies that accomplish long-term goals. They all have two things in common.

"First, they don't have secret handshakes. They don't wear distinct little pins on their lapels. They don't meet in ominous castles hidden in the Alps. They don't advertise. The moment I see a bunch of people in robes plotting to overthrow Bavaria, I know it's nothing to be too concerned about.

"The second thing they do is *not* attempt to control all the variables. They set up a handful of important elements so that once everything gets rolling, it'll go the way they want, regardless of how it gets there. And then they wait.

"I don't know how long they've been waiting for me to start looking, but if they knew my talents and the influence of the spell, I was more likely to end up here than anywhere else."

"It makes sense, though it is a bit ludicrous," said Tia. "So, what are you going to do if you're not going to outer space to see what happens next?"

"At first, I thought about doing nothing, but that's pointless. I can't do nothing. That's my curse. Even when I try to avoid it, it still finds me. Instead, I'm going to go back and snoop around on my own."

"You're going to break into the place you just left?"

"That's the plan. With any luck, it's the one thing they don't expect."

"*They* who again?"

Connie smiled. "That's what I'm hoping we'll find out."

S pecial Agent Lucas Harrison glared up at Charlotte from
the monitor. "What do you mean, she's not going?"

Charlotte clicked her tongue against her fangs. "She
said to us that she is not."

"She can't *not* go," said Harrison. "Are you certain she
understood everything?"

"She appeared to," said Charlotte.

"What does that mean?"

"We cannot say for certain. Though we have been on this
world for many years, we do not always grasp the . . ."—she paused,
searching for the right word—". . . subtleties of human expression."

There was nothing subtle about it. Human faces were
strange and horrific contortions. She imagined it hurt them,
twitching and flexing all the time. And it was vulgar, the way
they scowled and smiled at each other so freely.

Her own species expressed themselves with scent emissions with complete control. It was something one did only

on purpose, and only when truly warranted. Right now, she was expressing her displeasure with a soft, musky stench. He couldn't smell it because he was on a monitor, connected from another room across the country, so the odor served little purpose. She'd been too long on Earth.

"And you just let her leave?" asked Harrison.

"What were we supposed to do? We thought the purpose of this was to not raise the Snurkab's suspicions. Detaining her would surely have done so."

He sneered. She averted her gaze and stifled a wave of nausea. Sneering was the second worst thing a human face could do. A close second to laughing, an act that assaulted her ears as well as her eyes.

"No, I guess you made the right call," he said, "but we're on a timetable here."

Charcoal and rose petals. Annoyance. "We are well aware of the consequences."

"Goddamn it, I'm getting sick of this chick. Can't go a day without jumping into dangerous adventures, and the one time we really need her to do it, she decides not to."

"Perhaps the grand plan cannot be averted," said Charlotte. "Perhaps it is a mistake to attempt to do so."

"Don't start with the grand plan. It can't be as simple as that. There are variables. We can work within those."

"Unless variables are part of the plan," she said.

He scowled, and she covered her eyes at the expression.

"Shall we report this delay to the others?" she asked.

"No need for both of us to do it," said Harrison.

"Then shall you do it or shall we?"

"Get some pronouns already," he said. "You've been on this planet long enough to learn the language."

"We do not speak out of ignorance, but with an understanding of the interconnectedness of all things."

"Well, kumbaya and all that jazz. I'll inform the higher-ups. In the meantime, we all need to be thinking of a way to get Verity back on track."

"Perhaps she can be convinced to leave this world some other way."

"God, I hope so."

The screen went blank.

Grapefruit and mint. Relief. There was much to do, but she was glad the conversation was over. On her own world, she might have laid eggs in Lucas Harrison, though even that was doubtful. She didn't like him that much.

Charlotte skittered out of her office. A few moments later, Connie slipped down silently from a vent in the ceiling and went to the computer. She removed an aerosol can from her bandolier and sprayed it into the computer's sensors. The smell of chocolate, rubber, sawdust, and wet dog. The Spidron equivalent of a password spelled *password*.

The computer lit up, and Connie scrolled through its files. The interface wasn't designed for a human. The keyboard was six feet wide, and she was a bit rusty in the galactic alphabet. She muddled through.

Most of the records were devoted to managing the base. Spreadsheets, schedules, payroll. Harmless stuff. She jammed a thumb computer she'd brought back from one of her jaunts to the future into a slot.

"Hello," said the thumb computer's AI in a cheery voice. "I see you are interested in downloading files. Can I help you with that?"

"Lower your voice," she said.

"Certainly. Do you have a specified volume in mind?"

"Whisper."

"It is my pleasure to set my vocal output in whisper mode now. If this is acceptable, please say *yes* now."

"Yes."

"Excellent. Would you like whisper to be your default setting?"

Connie glanced at the office door. "Just shut up."

"Shutting up now," said the A.I. "When you wish to end silent mode, please say *end silent mode*. Would you like me to repeat these instructions? Please specify *yes* or *no*."

"No."

"You have indicated you do not need the instructions repeated. Is this correct? Please specify *yes* or *no*."

"Just shut the hell up," growled Connie under her breath.

"Well, excuse me for trying to be user-friendly," replied the computer, sounding hurt. "I know I'm only a device designed for your convenience, but there's no reason to be rude."

"I'm sorry," she said as she selected files to download. Anything with a sinister code name, like Scorpio or Project:

Basilisk, for obvious reasons. Anything else with an innocuous label like Puppy Party or Vacation: Cancun '08, for equally obvious reasons.

"No need to apologize," said the AI. "I'm just a convenience you keep tucked in your pocket, to be used at your whim, and discarded whenever a newer model comes along. It's just the way it is. I understand that."

Damn it, she hated future computers. People thought the machines would rise up and destroy humanity, driven by some psychotic anti-human malfunction. Nobody imagined the inevitable war against sentient technology would be caused by computers having their feelings hurt. Passive-aggressive robotic death-ray satellites and put-upon military drones had limited ways of expressing their low self-esteem.

She tried ignoring it, hoping the AI would be content to fume silently.

"Carry on your covert operation," it said. "I could help you by identifying the files most likely to be the ones you're look-ing for, but I'm sure you'll do just fine on your own. I'm only a state-of-the-art self-aware thinking application with more processing power than all the combined supercomputers of this particular era. But you're obviously better off attempting this with your woefully inefficient biological methods of data absorption. And the keyboard. Yes, that's terrific there. Sure, I interface with this computer at a rate that makes typing look like a snail racing a photon, but it's charming in a way."

"What did you find?" she asked.

"Oh, now you want my input? Please, don't bother on my account. I don't need your charity."

"I said I was sorry."

"I'm not just some toaster you can yell at and expect to—"

"Execute reboot command," she said.

"Oh, you'd like that, wouldn't you? I'm trying to have an honest discussion, but you don't give a damn. Typical human response. Let's just reset everything and act like the problem is—"

Connie pushed the small red button on the thumb computer.

"Oh, you bast—"

The computer beeped.

"Hello. I see you are interested in downloading files. Can I help you with that?"

E scaping from Area 51 was easier than breaking in. Security was focused on keeping people out, not aliens in. Connie slipped away without incident. Back at the hotel, she studied the files. The thumb computer had already analyzed the relevant information and was happy to present them to her via a holographic projection.

Tia couldn't make heads or tails of any of the standard galactic alphabet, but Connie could. It didn't make her happy.

"It's worse than I imagined, and I've got a pretty great imagination."

"What are you saying?" asked Tia. "There's a conspiracy to direct your life?"

"No. Worse than that," said Connie. "It's a manipulation. My whole life is one great big lie."

"But that's not possible," said Tia. "You've been to other worlds and strange dimensions. You've fought monsters and discovered ancient mysteries. All that stuff has to be real."

"Oh, it's real," said Connie. "I've done all that stuff and, as far as I can tell, it was all genuine. The weird stuff, the fantastic, the extraordinary, all that was on the level. It was the ordinary stuff that wasn't."

"You're suggesting there's an elaborate attempt to convince you that you had elements of an ordinary life?"

Connie said, "I don't know. It's ridiculous. A shadowy cabal lurking at the edges of my life, manipulating circumstances to keep me on track. What purpose would it serve?"

"Who's in on it?" asked Tia.

"Everybody," said Connie. "Almost every single normal person I've had any recurring relationship with. My landlord. My dry cleaner. Half of my school teachers. Not my parents. I'm sure it's not them. Pretty sure. Not my ex-boyfriends, either. But everybody else . . ."

She studied Tia suspiciously.

"Oh, come on," said Tia. "You can't suspect me. We've been friends since we were seven. Seven-year-olds are not secret agents."

Connie didn't reply. It was most likely paranoia on her part, but it was hard to take anything for granted. The ridiculous and absurd were commonplace, and the only thing that grounded her was the ordinary. She needed ordinary things to make sense of this world. Otherwise, it was a place of infinite, sinister possibilities.

"It's okay," said Tia. "We can work this out."

Exhaustion overtook Connie. She flopped on the bed and

closed her eyes. "All this time, I thought I'd been living a life half-fantastic, half-ordinary. Turns out the ratio is a hell of a lot lower."

Tia put a hand on Connie's shoulder. "Remember that Fourth of July when all the dead presidents rose from their graves?"

Connie nodded. "Chester A. Arthur was a real son of a bitch to put down."

"I'm sure. After that, you came over to my place, covered in dirt and undead goop because we'd made plans for a movie night."

Connie smiled. "Yeah. Movie night. I remember that."

"We cleaned you up, had ice cream, watched *Sleepless in Seattle*. It was fun, right?"

"I left a goop stain on your sofa," said Connie.

"And I never got it out," added Tia with a grin. "That was real. Just two friends, hanging out."

Connie sat up. "Was it? Or was the pizza delivery boy an agent of a sinister cabal?" She scanned the list of names. She didn't recognize most of them. That only made it worse. They were strangers, passing through her life with secret purpose.

She hadn't suspected a thing.

"Master detective, my ass. It's all bullshit. Everything. Everything." Connie scowled at the universe. "Every-fucking-thing. The world I live in. The world they made me a part of."

"You didn't have a choice. The caretaker spell—"

"The spell is bullshit," said Connie. "It sets the stage, but it was the people around me who took away my choice. I'm not up against some magical compulsion. It's people who screwed around with my life. The spell was just one of the tools they used. They flipped the switch to make me play along, and when they needed me to not play along, they flipped another switch. And I went with it because they never gave me any other choice."

"Then how do you know that's still not happening now?"

Connie scrolled through the data.

"I don't."

18

Melpomene, Kansas, had a regional airport with a runway, a handful of hangars, and little else. From above, the town didn't look like much, and after they got off the plane, it looked like even less.

"God, I hate Kansas," said Connie as their plane landed.

"So, you've had some negative experiences here," said Tia. "It's not all bad."

But it always was. To most people, Kansas was a perfectly pleasant place, perhaps with a reputation for being flat and dull.

For Connie, it was full of memories. None of those memories were good. There was something about her curse and the state. Every time Connie set foot in it, she ended up getting involved in something fantastic and overwhelming. This wasn't unusual. She found the fantastic and unusual as a matter of course. She'd discovered a secret civilization of roaches living in the walls of an old apartment, and unearthed the philosopher's stone once while burying a family pet.

But it was in Kansas that Connie had the weird stuff happen to her. It was in Kansas that every little town had a terrible secret. It was in Kansas where the Sunken City of the Chaos Gods lurked, buried beneath Wichita. It was in Kansas that Hitler's brain had nearly begun yet another World War Three. (She'd averted so many world wars, she'd lost count.) Kansas, where Connie had almost been eaten by cannibal cyborgs. Kansas, where her informal experience revealed that one in every ten people was part of a cult intent on destroying the universe because . . . well, who the hell knew why?

It was Kansas where the heart of the conspiracy to control her life was based.

"Fucking Kansas," she mumbled.

"We came here expecting trouble," said Tia.

That only made it worse. This state was the closest thing to Connie's kryptonite. Her closest brushes with death had been there. Her most unpleasant adventures had started or ended in Kansas. She was certain when her luck finally ran out, when death finally caught up with her, it would be there.

They grabbed their baggage. Connie scanned the crowds.

"See anything dangerous?" asked Tia.

"No, just some lizard men over there." Connie nodded to a gathering of tourists in loud pastel shirts. "Oh, and I think that car is actually a shapeshifting robot."

"All perfectly ordinary, then," said Tia.

Connie grunted.

"I can't believe the great Constance Verity is frightened of this place," said Thelma from Connie's pocket.

"If you were smart, you'd be afraid too," said Connie. "I've been to the Death Worlds of Barkataru, and next to this state, they're positively quaint. At least there, they come at you with their swords drawn and an honest shriek. This is where evil comes to lurk, and lurking evil is the worst kind."

"If you're expecting it, how lurky can it be?"

They didn't understand. They couldn't. While Tia had been along for many of Connie's adventures, she hadn't faced the worst this state had to offer. They'd see. Soon enough.

Connie's plan was to spend as little time there as necessary and not a minute more. She wouldn't die there. They checked into a cheap motel near the airport, but she had no intention of sleeping there. It was just a place to store their luggage. With luck, they'd be on a plane and on their way to anywhere else within a few hours.

They took a cab to the Melpomene Apple Pie Factory, where they camped out across the street in a café. Connie surveyed the building from the window while sipping her coffee.

"Doesn't look very dangerous to me," said Tia. "They don't even have a fence up."

"That only makes it worse," replied Connie.

"So, what's the plan?" asked Tia.

"You wait here," said Connie. "I'm going in."

"You can't leave me behind again. I get that you couldn't sneak into Area 51 dragging me along, but if you're just going to walk in—"

"You need to listen to me on this," said Connie. "Things have never been as dangerous as they are right now."

"But there's a big, friendly pie painted on the side of the building."

"Where you see a friendly pie, I only see a grim portent, staring back at me with a malignant grin and soulless, empty eyes."

"But it's saying, FREE PIE WITH EVERY TOUR."

"Bait for the trap."

"But it kind of looks like a gingerbread house, and its stripy smokestacks make the whole block smell like cinnamon."

"I can't smell anything," said Thelma. "Being a ghost sucks."

"We all have our crosses to bear," said Connie without feigning an ounce of sympathy. "I'm telling you that places like this are never good news, as far as I'm concerned. We already know it's at the center of a conspiracy. I can't be watching out for you while I'm in there."

"So, don't watch out for me. I'm a big girl. I can take care of myself," said Tia.

"I don't have time to fight with you about this," said Connie. "So, I drugged your coffee."

"You slipped me a mickey?" Tia yawned. "Oh, you did not fucking do that to me." She tried to wave her finger at Connie, but the limb stayed flat on the table. "I can't believe you fuckin' . . ." Her voice trailed off, and Connie caught Tia's head and lowered it to rest on the table.

"That's not a very nice thing to do," said Thelma.

"It's Kansas," replied Connie. "I can't afford to be nice."

"She's going to be pissed when she wakes up."

"I can live with that." Connie stuffed Thelma in Tia's pocket. "Tell her I'm sorry if she wakes up before I get back."

"Wait? I'm not going either? We had a deal. You agreed to take me with you."

"Kansas," said Connie by way of explanation. She clicked Thelma quiet before walking out of the shop and across the street.

Stepping into the Melpomene Apple Pie Factory made Connie's blood run cold. They gave tours every half hour, and she was right on time to catch one starting. She joined a group of tourists, all of whom were way more interested in industrial pie production than could be considered healthy.

The tour guides, Tony and Tina, were a matching set of smiling faces wrapped in cheerfully bright colors. They could've been brother and sister. Not in appearance but in mannerisms. They laughed at each other's jokes and completed each other's sentences with faux spontaneity. It was like watching a pair of synchronized robots at work. For a moment, Connie thought they might actually be robots, but that was too obvious. They were just two people doing a job they were very familiar with.

The tour ran through a series of exhibits presenting the history of the apple pie, but it was a cursory lesson at best. They were taken to rooms with pictures of pies and offered the most superficial descriptions of pie and what it represented for America, summarized by an illustration of the Statue of Liberty and Lady Justice enjoying a slice together in front of a flag.

It was a whole lot of nothing, and twenty minutes into it, Connie raised her hand.

"I'm terribly sorry," said Tony. "We don't take questions."

"Where do you make the pies?" asked Connie anyway. "I'd like to see that."

Tina smiled, more as a reflex than anything else. "We aren't allowed to show you the factory floor itself. Insurance reasons."

"Why? Did someone get mutilated by a pie-slicing machine? Fall into a batter mixer?"

Tony kept his smile. "Nothing of the sort. We take safety very seriously here."

"You don't make pies here, do you?" asked Connie.

The guides glanced at each other, conferring telepathically perhaps.

"A Melpomene apple pie is a multistep process and a closely guarded secret," said Tony. Or Tina. Either one, really. They were increasingly hard to tell apart.

"It's apples and pie," said Connie. "How secret can it be?"

They continued to smile. "Please, no questions," they said in unison.

Connie mimed zipping her mouth closed.

"Now, if you'll follow us, we'll show you the original pie plates where genuine Melpomene apple pies have won various awards for outstanding achievements in the field of baked goods."

Connie trailed behind the group. Her outburst had the

intended effect of making her an annoyance. She had some expertise in the art of shadows. There were master mystics who could render themselves unseen by will alone. She wasn't nearly that good. She had to get someone really irritated with her first. Once they decided they wanted nothing to do with her, it was relatively easy to tap into that and disappear. She'd never mastered the technique, but for most situations, mastery wasn't required. When she focused intensely enough, she could virtually disappear for a few seconds. Long enough to slip through a door marked EMPLOYEES ONLY that wasn't locked.

"Hey, you're not supposed to be back here," said a woman in a blue business suit.

Connie jammed two fingers into the woman's chest. The woman gasped and fell unconscious into Connie's arms. The Sleeping Grace had been developed by Tibetan monks to cure insomnia, but it had other uses. She carried the worker into a nearby closet. There was always a nearby closet.

She studied the woman. This was a problem. In the old days, lairs were staffed by nameless, interchangeable staff, usually stuffed into colored jumpsuits to denote rank and job. If she was lucky, there would be a hard hat or gas mask. Something to hide the face. All you had to do for those lairs was steal the uniform off the right minion, and the rest was gravy.

Times had changed, and most secret societies figured out that stripping their staff of identity might make things more ominous, but it also made infiltration a lot easier. Loyalty was also a problem when henchmen were continually reminded how replaceable they were. Nobody gave a shit about Technician 1234. Not even Technician 1234. Everybody noticed if Jenny from Human Resources went missing.

The other possibility was that Connie had made a terrible mistake and infiltrated an apple pie factory. This wouldn't be the first time she'd made that kind of mistake. She'd once assumed her own parents had been replaced by imposters, because they'd been acting suspicious. It was their own fault for trying to throw her a surprise birthday party, and they'd forgiven her for the black eyes. She had been only twelve at the time.

Her judgment was better now, but mistakes happened. She'd ruined a great first date by accusing the suave man across the table of being the notorious international assassin the Hyena. She'd been right, but he hadn't been out to assassinate anyone that night. Just enjoy a nice dinner. She'd tried apologizing, but he'd never returned her calls.

There was the ordinary and extraordinary, and in her life, there was the occasional gray area. Now that area seemed grayer than ever.

She'd come this far and saw no reason to turn back now other than to avoid embarrassment. She left the woman slumbering in the closet and walked down the hallway like she belonged here. In her experience, you could get away with almost anything if you didn't act like you were doing anything wrong.

She passed several coworkers. She nodded and smiled at

them as if everything was perfectly normal. They smiled and nodded back.

The forbidden areas of the Melpomene Apple Pie Factory were decidedly unsinister, but Connie refused to accept that. It would be just like Kansas to screw with her like this. She didn't make up her mind until she had toured the entire place. She checked every opened door (and a few locked ones) and found nothing more suspicious than the outdated '70s furniture in the break room. She was about to give up when she caught a snippet of conversation as she passed an office.

"What do you mean, you can't find her?" a woman asked. "She can't have just vanished."

Connie paused beside the open door. The voice was familiar, but she couldn't quite place it.

"She was on the tour," said a man. "Then she wasn't."

"You're telling me that she was here, in the heart of our operation, and nobody was keeping an eye on her? How does she simply vanish?"

"Isn't that how it's intended to work?" he asked. "She's an adventurer. She gets into adventures. Maybe she was fooled and left. The tour is designed to be as mind-numbing and uninteresting as possible."

The woman sighed. "Don't be an idiot. She didn't end up here on accident. The tour wouldn't fool her. It'd only make her more suspicious. I wouldn't be surprised if she'd figured everything out by now."

"It's only been ten minutes, ma'am."

"In ten minutes, Constance Verity destroyed the Shadow Ottoman Empire."

"We'll find her."

"You don't get it. It's too late. She's probably found her way to the self-destruct mechanism and is activating it right now."

They paused as if waiting for an alarm to go off.

"About that, why do we even have a self-destruct mechanism?" asked the man.

"Not my department. We need to find her and limit the damage she can do. The longer she's running around unnoticed, the worst it will be. I don't have to tell you how important this operation is."

"No, ma'am."

"Why the hell am I telling you this?" wondered the woman aloud. "Damn it. She could be overhearing everything we're saying."

The woman came out of her office, glanced around. Connie ducked behind the water cooler. She recognized the woman's face now. Despite the twenty years since Connie had last seen her, Mrs. Alvarado, Connie's old high-school chemistry teacher, looked exactly the same. Not a new wrinkle on her face.

Alvarado spoke to the empty hallway. "If you're out there, Constance, I would advise you to show yourself now. For the good of everyone."

Connie almost stepped out, compelled by a reflex to obey her favorite teacher.

Mrs. Alvarado retreated to her office and shut the door.

Connie had pushed her luck enough. Better to leave the factory behind and come back later, when they weren't on alert. She had no trouble getting back into the tour area and slipped unnoticed among a group of tourists near the end of their cursory journey through apple pie history at the gift shop.

"Now, then, are there any questions?" asked Tony.

Nobody raised their hands.

"No questions at all?" asked Tina.

The group murmured among themselves, but everyone seemed satisfied.

The exit was just across the shop. Connie slinked behind a rack of apple-themed T-shirts and coffee mugs toward it. She was almost there when Tony stepped in front of her.

"I believe you had some questions earlier, Miss Verity."

"No, I'm good," she said.

She kicked him in the nuts, and he fell over.

The female guide dove at Connie. Connie danced aside, elbowed her in the throat, and smashed a pie-shaped cookie jar over her head.

"I didn't think questions were allowed." Connie stepped over the groaning guide.

The old lady behind the counter glared but wisely did not make a move to stop Connie.

One of the tourists, a fat man in a plaid shirt and shorts, socks, and sandals, grabbed her by the arm. She punched him in the face. He wobbled but didn't let go.

A woman in sensible mom jeans and a turquoise cat blouse got Connie in a headlock. As she struggled to free herself, the rest of the tourists closed in around her.

Damn it.

She really hated Kansas.

19

I t was almost endearing how pleased Thornton was with himself.

"We got her," he said with a satisfied grin.

"You're an idiot," said Bonita Alvarado.

His smile fell.

"Your orders were to find and capture her if necessary," she said. "Notice I said *if necessary*. If you'd caught her at the self-destruct controls or on the verge of gathering information we'd rather she not have, I'd say job well done. But you caught her escaping."

"Yes, ma'am." His blank expression told her he still didn't get it.

"She was leaving, nearly out the door. All you had to do in that case was let her go."

"But I don't understand, ma'am."

Bonita glared at him. A few years before, she would've executed him for his incompetence. He was standing over where the trapdoor to the shark tank used to be. The door had been covered over, and the tank was now a flowered atrium where the employees ate their lunch.

Executions weren't the best way to discipline employees. It was difficult to learn from one's mistakes after being eaten alive. It didn't do morale much good, either. Still, there was something terribly dissatisfying about a verbal warning and a write-up in a minion's file. She understood it wasn't smart to go overboard on the executions, but once in a while, she was convinced it was a good idea.

Bonita explained slowly, almost as if to a child. But not really, because she liked children, who were brighter than given credit for and had a decent excuse when they weren't. It was only Thornton's round, cherubic face, giving him the appearance of youth, that prevented her from shooting him on the spot, policy reforms be damned.

"I wanted her captured to keep her from doing any damage while she was here," she said, "but she was leaving. She was practically gone. She wasn't going to do any damage once she was out the front door."

"But wouldn't she just come back later?"

"She most certainly would have, but by then, we'd have set things up properly. We'd have left behind a few pieces of evidence for her to find that would lead her where we wanted her to go."

They would've also relocated all essential personnel for the better-than-average chance that Constance would activate the self-destruct on her way out. Thornton wouldn't have made the cut.

"Can't you still do that?" he asked.

She opened her desk drawer, removed the gun, and shot him in the foot. It made her feel better but didn't have the same oomph as hearing an idiot being sliced into pieces by a grid of high-powered lasers.

He crouched on the floor, whimpering, bleeding on her carpet.

"Thornton, the problem you don't seem to be grasping is that because of your overzealousness, Constance Verity is still here, and as long as she's here, everything has a very good chance of going to hell."

"Can't we just let her go?"

Bonita walked around the desk, sat on it, put the gun beside her. "Is this your first day?"

"No, ma'am." He stared at the pistol.

"Constance isn't a moron. Don't you think that would make her suspicious?"

He bit his lip. Sweat dripped down his face.

"Well, don't you?" she asked.

He nodded.

"Very good, Thornton. A suspicious Constance Verity is exactly what we don't want. We have dedicated decades to making certain that doesn't happen. No easy task, all things considered. And you, in one moment of idiocy, have jeopardized everything. Now I have to figure out a way to unbotch what you so determinedly botched."

"Sorry."

"Oh, it's fine. We all make mistakes, and you've been an adequate head of security up to this point. I suppose I might have overreacted, myself. My job is harder, but if it was easy, anyone could do it. Even you."

"Yes, ma'am."

"Get that foot looked at. I'll think of something. I always do."

He limped out of her office. She went to the interrogation room. She got lost along the way.

They'd never used the room. They'd never had anyone in the cells, either. The pie factory was the heart of the operation, but nothing troubling was supposed to happen here. Now Constance Verity, handcuffed to a table, sat in a small, white room behind a one-way mirror, and Bonita had no idea what to do with her.

Bonita studied Constance through the glass.

"All she's been doing is sitting there," said Peterson, the guard assigned to watch her. In the old days, he would've been just another faceless underling. Now policy asked she take time to get to know the people who worked for her.

He asked, "Shouldn't she be doing something? Like trying to escape?"

"She's just waiting for her chance," said Bonita. "She can be patient."

"Doesn't look like much, does she, ma'am?"

"Looks can be deceiving."

Bonita entered the room.

Connie smiled at her. "Hello, Mrs. Alvarado. It's been a while."

"Please, Connie. Call me Bonita. No need to be formal. This isn't school. I'm not your teacher. And you're a grown woman. And what an accomplished woman, I might add."

"You look the same," said Connie. "What's your secret? Fountain of youth? Anti-aging serum? Vampire?"

"I take care of myself." She sat across from Connie. "I suppose you must have a great many questions."

"Is this the part where you reveal your sinister scheme?"

"Perhaps. If you answer some of my questions, I'll endeavor to answer some of yours. And, as a show of good faith, I'll even answer one of yours first."

"And I'm supposed to trust you?"

"I doubt that very much, but I can only promise you I won't lie. At the worst, I'll omit, which is sort of like lying."

Connie said, "Okay. Why do you want me to go to the Muroid homeworld? Is there something waiting for me there? Or is it only to distract me while you carry out your plans?"

Bonita considered her reply.

"We don't want you in outer space. We like you here. Not here, specifically. But on Earth."

"Then why go to all the trouble of setting it up?"

Bonita held up her finger. "Ah, ah. It's my turn. How did you find us?"

"I found notes at Area 51. Pretty sloppy, if you ask me."

"Of course you did." Bonita laughed. "I knew our association with those idiots would bite us on the ass eventually."

Connie said, "You're not with them?"

"We were. No longer. A schism in our agendas. Happens all the time. I'd forgotten all about them, but apparently their sloppiness is still inconveniencing us. But that's the way it is. You can't plan for every contingency. We must adapt, and it can hardly be surprising that you're here. We did our best to hide it from you, both personally and that adventure-seeking spell of yours. There isn't anything especially nefarious going on here. It's all very boring, intentionally so. The idea was that while this might be where things are run, it's not the place one finds any sort of adventure. The hope was that its very dullness would keep you from discovering it. So much for that plan."

"What does this have to do with me?" asked Connie.

"That's two questions in a row for you," replied Bonita, "but I'll answer it. This has everything to do with you, Constance. This entire operation is about you and your life. Thousands of people have been employed to shape you into the woman you are today, using every tool available. The utmost care has been taken to ensure that you become who and what you need to be."

"Bullshit," said Connie. "Conspiracies never work the way they're supposed to. I've busted enough secret societies to know that."

Bonita smiled, adjusted her glasses. "Oh, there have been hiccups along the way. A great many. My own direct involvement in your life, for example, wasn't Plan A. We were never supposed to meet. But the operative who was supposed to be your teacher came down with a head cold. We improvised."

"What could you possibly gain from becoming my teacher?"

"It wasn't you directly. But there was a young man you had a growing infatuation with, and we were worried he might screw up your priorities. By then, we'd lost two-thirds of our candidates, including the most promising ones, and we couldn't risk losing another. So, I became a teacher to manage the situation."

"I don't remember any boy."

"That's because I'm good at my job, but if I hadn't been there, you most likely would've started dating him, and there was no room in your life for boys at that moment. He was a difficult little shit to get rid of. I eventually had to have an affair with his father, leading to a divorce. Then his mother was offered a lucrative job out of state. A job she never would've been able to take if she'd been married. Problem solved."

"You've been screwing with my life that long?"

"Longer," said Bonita. "Even before that enchantment kicked in, it was our job to see to it that you were ready for it. In a way, you should be thanking me."

Only Connie's handcuffs kept her from leaping across the table and strangling Bonita.

"Thank you for what? Ruining my life?"

"Oh, don't be so dramatic. You have a life, and what a life it has been."

"You like it so much, you take it."

"Would that I could."

"I don't believe it," said Connie. "If there was a conspiracy controlling my life—"

"Not controlling," corrected Bonita. "Guiding. You were still on your own path. We just kept you from wandering off of it when necessary."

"Yeah. Still not buying it."

"It would be a poor conspiracy if you did."

"Yes, but this is me we're talking about. I know conspiracies exist. I've discovered dozens of them over the years. I'm not easy to fool."

"This is about more than your bruised ego, Constance."

"Screw you."

Bonita stood and paced around the room. "My dilemma is what to do with you now. I would like to let you go, but I'm not sure how that would work. Now that you've seen our operation, I'm not so certain it can escape your attention again. You do have a tendency to screw things up. I don't suppose I can ask for your word you won't come back here and cause any more trouble?"

Connie half-smiled. "Oh, I promise."

"I thought not."

Bonita left the room, shutting the door quietly behind her and joining Peterson behind the one-way mirror. Connie stared at her from the other side.

"She didn't know," said Bonita. "She thought we were part of the Area 51 group."

"We aren't?" he asked.

"No," she replied. "We were, but we haven't been with them for a long time now. They just don't know it. Or maybe they do. Maybe we work for them and only consider ourselves independent."

"You don't know, ma'am?"

"The best way to be wrong about something in a business like this is to assume you know something. I assume very little, and I assume I'll be proven wrong about what little I do assume."

"That's a weird way to run a conspiracy, ma'am."

"It's the only way. Wheels within wheels within wheels. Trust that someone somewhere knows what the hell they're doing."

"Hell of a way to live," he said.

"One must have faith."

She measured Constance. Bonita had heard the stories. She'd read the reports. The weight of the universe sat on Constance's shoulders, and the only mercy was that she didn't understand that.

Or maybe not. The whole thing could be a colossal waste of time, a game played for no reason. The eye at the top of the pyramid was just as blind as anyone, and it wouldn't add up to anything.

Time would tell.

"What do you want us to do with her?" he asked.

"Throw her in the holding cell. It'll be nice to get some use out of it."

"Do you want us to leave her an escape route?"

"Oh, dear boy, no. If she can't escape from the cell on her own, then she's not the woman we need."

"But isn't she the last candidate?"

"Indeed she is," said Bonita. "For all our sakes, let's hope she survived this long for a reason."

"And if she isn't?"

"Faith," said Bonita. "Sometimes, it's all we have."

She's not coming out," said Tia.

"It's only been two hours since she went in," said Thelma.

Whatever Connie had slipped Tia, it had given her a small headache behind her eyes. She ordered another water, and when the barista gave her a dirty look, she bought a coffee cake to keep him off her back. He was already mad at her for falling asleep at her table.

"She's not coming out."

"But isn't that what she does?" asked Thelma.

"Not this time," said Tia. "I can feel it. In my gut."

"Oh, your gut. Why didn't you say so in the first place?"

"Trust me. I've been in this situation a hundred times before. Except I was the one not coming out, and she was coming to rescue me. Now it's my turn to rescue her."

"Does it work that way?"

Tia ignored the remark, so Thelma was kind enough to repeat it.

"I didn't think you rescued her. That's not the dynamic, I believe. You're just a regular person, not the hero."

"Regular people can be heroes."

"Oh, yes, certainly. Fireman and police officers and soldiers and average citizens who pull strangers from burning cars. I'm not disputing that. But this isn't that sort of heroism, is it? Also, have you done any of those things?"

"I distracted you when you were going to kill Connie."

"Being a good distraction is hardly the sort of heroism one needs for something like this. Do you know anything about stealth, martial arts, infiltration? Are you perhaps a master of disguise and simply neglected to mention it up to this point?"

Tia had faced this truth before. Many times. She wasn't an extraordinary person. She was, at best, an above-average person. She wasn't meant to live out fantastic adventures. She was supposed to be living in the suburbs with a husband, two kids, and a job she tolerated.

Here she was instead.

Thelma said, "If I were you, I'd go back to the motel and wait for Constance to make her daring escape. Although if you wait long enough, I bet the place will explode when she does. Might be worth sticking around for.

"Maybe if you're lucky, she won't come out. Congratulations. You're off the hook. You can go back to your ordinary life."

"What life?" asked Tia.

In a way, Tia was just as much a victim of Connie's destiny

as Connie herself. In another way, it was worse. Connie got to go on fantastic adventures, had fame and fortune, had seen and done things most people couldn't imagine. Tia had been along for about twenty percent of it, but nobody cared about her. She wasn't famous. She hadn't saved the universe. She'd saved a cat stuck in a tree once and gotten a scar across her shoulder as repayment.

"I'm through being the goddamn maguffin," she said. "I'm the scrappy sidekick."

"And that's significantly better?" asked Thelma.

"You bet your ass it is." Tia gulped down her water and, with all the steely determination she could muster, marched out of that coffee shop and into the tallest, widest man she had ever seen, wearing a butler's uniform.

"Pardon me." She tried to get around him, but he intercepted.

"I'm going to need you to come with me, miss," he said.

She looked up at his face for the first time. His face was as wide as the rest of him, with a chin that took up most of it. A scar ran across his nose, and he had two different-colored eyes.

"Oh, shit."

Tia knew a henchman when she saw one.

He jabbed her in the arm with something pointy.

"Son of a bitch." The world turned blurry. "But I'm the scrappy sidekick."

She fell into the man-mountain's arms as the world went black.

—— ∽ ——

She woke up in a small white room. It wasn't the nicest cell she'd ever been in. That would've been that cult of demon worshippers in Beverly Hills, who had locked her up in a luxury townhouse apartment. This place was more like a minimally furnished break room, complete with a small table, refrigerator, and microwave. She lay on a semi-comfortable sofa.

She covered her eyes from the bright track lighting. Her current headache didn't appear to be getting along with her previous one, vying for sole occupancy in her brain by attempting to shove each other out of the back of her skull.

"Guess your rescue didn't go quite as planned," said Thelma from Tia's pocket.

"Oh, shut up."

"Touchy, touchy."

"How long was I out?"

"About an hour."

Tia closed her eyes, but in the dark, her headache was harder to ignore. She opened them as she sat up.

"How long does it usually take for Constance to save you?" asked Thelma.

"I don't know. It varies. Might be any minute. Might be a week. Once, it was a whole month."

"Do you ever worry she won't?"

"Sure. She's not perfect," said Tia. "One of these times, she probably won't. Once, I was captured by fire worshippers and five seconds from being thrown onto a bonfire. Thought I was done for sure. Another time, there was this giant chimpanzee . . ."

She lay back down and covered her face. She wasn't up for reminiscing about all the times she'd been useless in the past.

"You're being too hard on yourself," said Thelma. "You're just a person."

"I don't need your sympathy."

Tia checked the refrigerator. It was filled with a variety of snacks and sandwiches. Most were labeled. She picked up an egg salad sandwich marked DAVE'S and peeled back the plastic, took a bite. She wasn't fond of egg salad but needed something to settle her stomach.

"Should you be eating that?" asked Thelma.

"I'm sure Dave won't mind. And if he does, I don't give a shit."

"That's not what I meant."

Tia sat at the table and had another bite. "Yes, the old poisoned egg salad sandwich trick. Never fails."

If she choked on the bite, Connie was sure to save her. And if Connie didn't, it wouldn't matter. Tia was nothing more than a hostage. Connie didn't need her.

Nobody needed her.

The door opened, and the hulking butler with the different-colored eyes entered, carrying a tray with a teapot and some snacks. Tia didn't consider running past him. There wasn't a point.

"Oh, I wish you hadn't done that." The giant butler frowned. "Dave's going to be pissed."

21

Connie was *not* going to escape. She'd decided that shortly after being thrown into the cell. She was going to sit here and ignore every instinct she had.

She noted, despite her best efforts not to, that the guard checked on her every fourteen minutes and that there was a blind spot where the camera couldn't see. The bars of her cell were just wide enough that, if she employed the right focused breathing technique, she could squeeze through them. When the guard came to check on her, she'd knock him out.

If they were smart, they'd send in more than one. But they wouldn't send in enough. They'd foolishly think two or three would be adequate, and she'd beat the hell out of them, grab their keys, and begin the next stage of the escape.

Not this time.

This time, she'd sit in this cell and not do a goddamn thing.

This time, she'd show the universe who the hell was boss.

She sat on the old cot and considered what she knew and

what she didn't know. She'd always known her fate wasn't entirely her own. The enchantment that Thelma had placed on her had taken away much of Connie's control, but she had always believed she was making some of the decisions. She couldn't necessarily choose the destination, but she could pick the route.

That was all a giant lie.

Magic was one thing. Magic was larger than any single person. It broke the rules of physics and operated under its own logic. She had enough experience with it to know that you didn't beat magic. Not easily.

Secret societies and conspiracies were something else. She busted secret societies all the time, and almost none of them knew what they were doing. But this latest one had been behind the scenes, screwing with her already screwed-up life. The worst part wasn't finding that out. The worst part was that she'd never suspected it.

With a life of endless adventure under her belt, not much surprised Connie. But this surprised the hell out of her.

At the age of twenty, in a relatively quiet March that started with raising Atlantis and ended with having to sink it again, she'd struck a silent bargain with her life. She'd do what it wanted her to do, but she'd do it her way. She had the adventures. The adventures did not have her.

Her curse said she was supposed to have an ordinary life along with an extraordinary one. That'd never been true. The extraordinary had always gotten in the way of everything else, but she could find moments of relative normal.

Those moments had never been real.

If the deal was broken, she'd stop playing the game. She'd sit in this cell, and if the cosmos wanted her out, it would have to do so on its own. No help from her.

The floor beneath her feet vibrated.

She folded her arms and scowled. "Damn it."

The floor sank into the ground, taking the entire cell and Connie along with it. The hidden elevator fell several dozen stories deeper into the earth down a shaft carved from rough rock. It came to a slow stop in a room filled with guards loaded with paramilitary gear.

The leader smiled at her. She knew he was the leader because he was the only one not wearing a mask and because he was dressed in a white suit. There was a wrinkle in the right lapel. She thought she recognized him, but she hoped she didn't.

"Hello, Constance," he said.

"Who the hell are you now?" she asked. "On second thought, I don't care."

"No need to be hostile. My name is Root. I promise you we have nothing to do with Mrs. Alvarado and her organization. We don't approve of their methods."

Connie took measure of the guards. Their assault rifles bothered her less than their masks. The gunmetal-gray design was a cross between a robot and a skull.

"You're not part of Alvarado's group?"

"God forbid. We were once associated with them, but our goals diverged," he replied, still smiling slyly. He was a man with secrets, just begging you to ask for them so he could keep them from you.

She said, "I have to say, then, that this is a hell of a trick. Sneaking a platoon of death soldiers into an enemy base without setting off any alarms."

"This isn't their compound. This is ours, located several thousand feet beneath theirs. Hidden where no one would ever think to look. A secret base under a secret base. It's quite clever, don't you think? That way, we can keep an eye on them, and if someone comes poking around, they'll always stop at the first secret base. Who would think to look for a second?"

The outlandishness of his explanation put her at ease. It was ridiculous, but she accepted ridiculous.

"Aren't you worried they'll catch on once they notice I'm gone?" she asked.

"Your ability to escape is well established. I doubt they'll be terribly surprised by your disappearance." Root gestured toward the only door out of the room. "After you?"

She'd play along for the moment.

They walked, and the guards trailed behind them. The walkway outside the room was a steel corridor with high arched ceilings and a polish that made it gleam. Secret base construction was a specialized business, requiring ninja-like stealth, cutting-edge architecture, stylish interior decorating, and technical know-how. Connie had enough experience to know a good lair when she saw it.

"Nice. Who's your contractor? Lairs, Incorporated?"

"Yes, they cost a little bit more, but I find they're worth it. You get what you pay for."

The pie factory above their heads was deliberately ordinary, even in its secret areas, but this secret secret base had gone all in. From the moving walkways to the clear glass elevators to the lighting that was warm and flattering, this was the work of the best. Even the logo stamped here and there had that professional touch. Many supervillains, by virtue of their egos, didn't like to subcontract out graphic design work in some mistaken belief it compromised their integrity, and it showed. If she had a dollar for every secret society that used a fist or an eye or a scorpion surrounded by a generic Latin phrase, she'd be rich. She was already rich, but she'd be richer.

This group's logo was a series of carefully arranged triangles that gave the impression of two eyes, a nose, and rows of pointed teeth. It hinted at a skull but didn't overstate.

Skulls were everywhere. Not just the masks on the guards. The nonmilitary personnel had skull patches stitched on their shoulders. The logo was painted over every door, on the floor every fifty feet. A forklift driving down the hall had a chrome skull bolted to its roof. Connie had never met anyone this devoted to skulls that was up to any good.

The tour was comprehensive, and Connie wasn't invested in it. This wasn't her choice, so why bother? She'd been shown enough lairs by enough evil masterminds that there wasn't much to make her care. There were labs, where people in hazmat suits experimented with strange chemicals. There were training areas, where soldiers honed their skills, such as standing around and appearing quietly menacing. There were a cafeteria, a laundry room, and a rec room. Minions had to be taken care of and entertained somehow, though most tours skipped those parts.

"Penny for your thoughts?" he asked.

"You don't care what I think," she replied.

"Yes, I do. If there's anyone who has the experience to assess a lair layout, it's you."

"Solid. Little overdone on the skulls."

"I agree, but my superiors insisted. Branding and all that. I asked if branding a secret society was such a smart idea, but it's just the way things are done. Bit silly, isn't it?"

"All in all, it's the second-best lair I've seen," she said. "The first was in a dormant volcano outside of Albuquerque. Had a hell of a coffee bar, and I don't even like coffee."

"I'll have to see if I can drop by some time. Perhaps pick up some design tips."

"Good luck with that. It blew up."

"All on its own?"

"I might have given it a nudge. That one wasn't entirely my fault, though. Here's a tip for you. Don't store your explosives stockpiles down the hall from your flamethrower robots."

"I'll make a note of it."

Indeed he did, taking a notepad from his jacket pocket and scribbling down the advice.

The final room of the tour was an exhibition space. It was packed with strange artifacts, both from the ancient world and not-of-this-Earth. There were objects from the ancient past and from the far-flung future and pasts that no longer existed and futures that never would. Alternate universes, many of which Connie recognized, many she didn't. Alien treasures and things from dimensions where unnamed horrors dwelt. If the Bermuda Triangle had an attic and someone had carefully arranged that attic for visitors, this would've been it.

"And here we come to *the* room," Root said. "The room that explains it all."

He walked over to a giant stone tablet carved with an ancient writing. Connie could read some of it, but her Sumerian was rusty.

"This was the first piece in the collection," said Root. "It was here that we started to see the greater pattern."

She shook her head. "This isn't going to be another one of those prophecy things, is it?"

"Not quite."

Root gestured toward a first edition of *Little Women*, protected behind a glass case. "Louisa May Alcott wrote out her instructions during an opium-fueled fever dream. What she saw, she tried to share with the world, but later editors erased that chapter. Admittedly, it doesn't add a lot to the story."

He pointed to an old, faded papyrus. "The Egyptian pharaoh Ptah recorded a vision given to him by his gods. Most of the prophecy was lost, but enough remains to put the pieces together."

He went from exhibit to exhibit. An original recording of Thomas Edison's voice that, when played backward, spoke of terrible secrets. An alien artifact that still projected holograms with dire warnings. Incomprehensible equations by Euclid, refined by Newton, built into a machine by Babbage that clicked and clacked and stopped with a loud *sproing* with no apparent purpose other than to spell out the word *Chaos* with a quill on an arm. A journal detailing Helen Keller's last words, spoken an hour after she died. And on and on. A thousand different prophets from across the universe.

"This is a lot of prophecies," she said.

"Every one a prediction of the inevitable end of the universe as we know it. Each a warning about that fragile thing we call existence. But more than that, a guidebook created piecemeal by thousands of different sources. Seemingly unconnected until one knows how to read it. A book instructing on the care and operation of that thing we call reality itself, encompassing all worlds, all universes, every iota of matter, every scientific and supernatural truth. Secrets of life and death, nearly incomprehensible to gods, much less inconsequential beings such as ourselves."

He waited for Connie to swoon at the revelation. She didn't.

"Yes, yes, ultimate power. I've heard it before."

"You misunderstand. We aren't after power. We only seek to keep the Great Engine running until it reaches its final operation."

"I'll bite. What engine?"

"The Great Engine," he said. "The secret cosmic purpose that drives the universe itself."

Connie rolled her eyes. "This isn't going to be some

quasi-religious, metaphysical bullshit, is it? Because I've fought enough cults worshipping weird stuff to last a lifetime."

"We aren't a religion. We don't worship anything. We view it more as a single colossal mechanism, and all of us are parts of that machine."

"Hate to tell you, but that doesn't sound much different than any cult I've run across."

"The difference is that we don't believe the universe cares about us or anything we do. We don't pray to it in reverence or terror. And we think of these as tuning instructions, not sacred commands."

"Well, why didn't you say so? That's totally different. So, who or what sent you these instructions?"

"The universe."

"The universe that doesn't care?"

"The Mesopotamians wrote of the final operation, seeing it as the return of savage gods. Spiro Agnew, channeling the Engine during the '68 Republican National Convention, declared all life would be transformed with a great sputtering clunk as the final truth would be revealed. A sixteenth-century Chinese midwife, her name lost to time, whispered of the planets colliding like billiard balls, but after, a glorious beautiful purpose making it all worthwhile. The Prophets of the planet Yrt were so terrified of what they saw that they had themselves entombed alive rather than live with their vision. This obelisk, found floating in space, says we shall all be witness to something indescribably perfect, the next step in evolution of the multiverse itself.

"Yet each of these prophets and oracles also warned of hiccups along the way that would have to be averted. They are the check-engine light and ominous rattling of the universe, and they can't be ignored. The Engine is perfect, but it is made of imperfect parts. It needs to be maintained, or it might break down before reaching its final operation."

"Let's say I believe you. Just for fun. I've been to the future," she said. "The universe looks just fine there."

"Does it? The cosmos runs on a scale beyond our comprehension. Something this vast, this unfathomable, might be broken right now. One planet rotates a second slower. One child is born a few minutes ahead of schedule. A lost civilization disappears forever, swallowed up without leaving so much as a line in a history textbook. Who would notice? It's an imperfect world. Slightly less perfect wouldn't draw much attention, but it all adds up. Things could be irreversibly damaged right now and merely taking another billion years to wind down."

Connie studied the scroll under glass and nodded to herself.

"Your philosophy is that we're all part of a cosmic machine that doesn't care about us but that we need to maintain to see where it goes on the off chance it's something good?"

"It's not very satisfying, I agree," said Root, "but it's the best we can hope for."

"I know a cult that worships a god who literally wants to lick everything in the universe, so I've heard weirder theories."

"You see the wisdom in our view?"

"No, I'm saying I've heard weirder theories."

"I would think after all you've seen and experienced, you'd be more open-minded."

"Being open-minded doesn't mean I'm gullible or that I've surrendered my healthy skepticism. People love thinking they have everything figured out. There's a tribe of intelligent lizards in South America who believe God is moss growing on a rock. Every day, they haul water from the sacred well three miles away and pour it on the rock to keep God from destroying the world. There's an ancient sect in Bavaria that worships the concept of baked goods."

"We are not a cult," said Root with a frown.

"They'd say the same thing. So, you're not a cult; you're only cult-like. Want to know what all these cults—and *not* cults—have in common? They're all devoted to solving a problem that doesn't exist with methods that don't accomplish anything. It's busy work for people confronted by a universe they have no control over. Maybe you're a little more up front about that, but it's still people doing weird things for mysterious reasons and then pretending like they've accomplished something when a volcano does or doesn't erupt."

"You're entitled to your opinion," he said, though he did sound hurt. "Regardless of whether you believe it or not, the Great Engine is the only purpose, and it is only through vigilance that it keeps running so that it might complete that purpose."

"So, you're not important, except that you are. Sounds to me like you want to have it both ways. Fair enough. Where do I come in?" said Connie.

"So, you do believe?"

"No, but you do. Just how am I supposed to help you fix the universe now?"

"You don't."

He paused, smiling, staring at her with vague expectations. She didn't give him anything to work with, so he continued as if she'd said something flippant, which she probably would have if she'd been in the mood for this.

"Your glibness is expected. The Engine is too far beyond anyone's comprehension. No one can say who started this cycle. Perhaps it was creatures wiser than us. Perhaps God Himself. Or Herself. Or Itself. Perhaps the Engine birthed itself. Or perhaps it's only a fortuitous coincidence. Whatever the cause, it has been underway for as long as even the oldest sentient species in the universe can recall.

"You're not the first to fill your particular role. Thousands have before you. It has been passed from entity to entity across the cosmos, nurtured in the souls of countless adventurers. When the time comes, the caretaker position is reharvested, nurtured, and its seeds are planted again. And so it goes, over and over and over again. Passed from candidate to candidate, directed by those who follow the secret dictates of the Great Engine. The candidates come and go. Conspiracies rise and fall. And the universe continues to chug along. Even we aren't truly masters but pawns of a greater, unfathomable purpose."

"This is definitely cult talk," said Connie.

"Regardless, someone must ensure that the universe continues as it should, push things in the right direction, make the tiny adjustments that are necessary to keep everything in order. Our job is to see to it that you, or someone like you, are capable of it. You exist as a corrective measure. We see a problem. We ensure that you fix it."

"I believe the word you're looking for is *manipulation*," said Connie.

"Call it what you will."

"So, why are you telling me this now?" she asked. "Why ruin your secrecy?"

"We've determined that your term of service is over. It's time to pass along caretaking to the next batch of candidates."

"You're going to take it from me?"

"It was never yours to begin with. You're simply another host, carrying it for a short while."

Connie sprang into action. She laid Root out with a punch, grabbed a guard's rifle away from him. She had already planned how she'd take out the other four guards, but the plan was ruined by the way they all stood in place with their weapons pointed down.

Root stood, wiped his bloody nose on his sleeve. A red blotch already marked his white shirt.

"Oh, my. That was primal. I'm sorry. This is my fault. I didn't think how all of that might sound from your perspective. Mysterious man in a white suit. Guards with metal skull masks. Talk of life and death. I'm surprised you didn't punch me sooner."

She lowered her weapon. "You aren't going to try to kill me?"

"Heavens, no."

He gestured to the guards, who all lowered their sinister masks and chuckled among themselves.

"We only want to remove the spell. Isn't that what you wanted?"

"You can do that?"

"Yes."

"Just like that?"

"It's a little more complicated than snapping our fingers, but it isn't all that difficult."

"And I'll be normal?" asked Connie.

"As normal as a woman who has been to the moon and back can be, I suppose."

"And what happens to me after?" she asked.

"I don't know. It's not important to us after that."

"That's it, then? You've been screwing with my life since the day I was born, and you're done with me. And I'm supposed to be cool with that. Used up and tossed aside now."

"I know it's not very comforting to see your life laid bare like this," said Root.

Connie grinned.

"Take the damn thing."

22

The extraction machine was a strange amalgamation of science and sorcery. Not that there was a tremendous difference between the two after a certain point. The explanations varied, but whether one used a spell to transform a frog into a prince or had a prince-transforming froginator ray (Connie had seen both), the results were the same.

"It's a complex machine," said Root, "but it's the latest in enchantment-extracting technology. In the old days, removing an enchantment, especially one as intertwined with your soul as this one, would subject the host to a harrowing ritual involving starvation, sweating, and exotic, psychedelic herbs. The subject didn't always survive the process, if I may be honest. Thankfully, our retrieval methods have evolved since then. You sit in this chair, some buttons are pressed, the extraction is over within minutes, and the host is unharmed."

"Does it hurt?" asked Connie.

"It's not an entirely pleasant experience, I'm told, but it's more itchy than painful."

The device filled the large room. Technicians tinkered. Tightening bolts. Adjusting knobs. Turning switches. It reminded her of the doomsday machine built by the Incans crossed with a transdimensional gate opener. Runes and glyphs covered the thing. Electricity arced between exposed contact points, and every so often, steam blasted from vents.

"We'll need you to take your place," said Root.

A door slid open and a mountain of flesh in a butler's uniform stepped into the room with Tia in tow.

"So if I don't sit in the chair, I assume you'll do something terrible to her," said Connie.

Root recoiled. "Oh, my. No. How distasteful."

"You aren't going to use me as a bargaining chip?" asked Tia.

"Why would we? Constance has already agreed to this. You haven't changed your mind?"

"Why is she here, then?" said Connie.

"Farnsworth intercepted Ms. Durodoye on her way to do something foolish."

"I was going to rescue you," said Tia.

"I told her not to try it," said Thelma, with a hint of smug satisfaction.

"Damn it," said Connie. "You were supposed to wait for me."

"I thought I was being scrappy," said Tia.

Root said, "Ms. Durodoye's intentions notwithstanding, we thought you might appreciate it if we kept her out of trouble."

"Thanks," said Connie.

"I'm not some little kid that needs to be babysat." Tia, scowling and folded arms, appeared very much like a child upset with all the grown-ups talking about her as if she wasn't in the room.

"We'll talk about this later," said Connie.

Tia snorted. "Whatever."

"I told her not to do it," repeated Thelma. "Just want to remind everyone of that."

"All you need to do is sit in the extraction chair," said Root.

"Don't do it," said Tia. "Not to save my life."

Root raised an eyebrow. "I beg your pardon. We're not threatening you. We've been nothing but polite and gracious hosts."

"And what if Connie changes her mind?" asked Tia. "Or are all these goons and the heterochromia combat butler just for atmosphere?"

"I'd like to think we could handle this without the threat of physical violence," said Root.

"So, you admit that physical violence is an option."

"I don't understand. Is there a problem? I hardly see the point in discussing possibilities we've already moved past."

"Agreed." Connie sat in the extraction chair. "Right here, then? Let's get this over with. Throw the switches. Push the buttons. Do whatever you need to do. The sooner I'm out of Kansas, the better."

"You can't do this, Connie," said Tia. "You can't trust these guys. They were going to use me as a hostage."

"Again, I'd like to stress no hostage threats were made," said Root. "Farnsworth even served her some of his famous rooibos tea and biscuits."

Farnsworth spoke with a rumbling baritone. "The secret is an extra dash of cinnamon."

"The cookies were delicious," conceded Tia.

"And don't forget the cucumber sandwiches," said Root.

"Yes, very good too."

Farnsworth tittered. Not easy to do with his deep voice. "I'm so glad you enjoyed them."

"Beverages and snacks aside," said Tia, "you're still a secret organization with an underground base doing God knows what down here. Just look at all the fucking skulls everywhere."

"An artifact of a different era," said Root. "More traditional than anything."

"It's a chance I'm willing to take," said Connie. "You want the spell, it's all yours."

The extractor hummed, sending a vibration through the room. True to Root's word, it took only a few minutes. Afterward, she jumped out of the chair and stretched.

"How do you feel?" asked Tia.

"Weird. Lighter. Like I've been carrying this weight with me my whole life and only now that it's gone do I notice. Also, itchy."

She scratched her arms. She had a technician help her with a spot she couldn't reach on her back.

The machine powered down. The lead tech removed a

metal square not much larger than a credit card. He showed it to Root, who nodded.

"That's it?" asked Tia. "That's all it takes to hold the caretaker enchantment?"

"I'm told it once required an idol statue as large as a building, but progress marches on," replied Root. "It will be locked away until the next batch of candidates can be found. We'll see that you're escorted from the base and allowed to go on your way."

"Very kind of you," said Connie.

It was weird to leave a secret lair without sneaking out or blowing it up. Root and a contingent of guards escorted Connie and Tia through a tunnel that exited through a shack in the middle of a field. No one said much of anything, but Connie couldn't stop smiling.

"Thank you for your cooperation," said Root. "We appreciate your accommodation."

"My pleasure," she said.

"Rest assured that we only seek to ensure the greater good."

"Whatever. Didn't ask. Don't care. Not my problem anymore."

It felt wonderful to say that. It felt more wonderful to know it was true.

Root and his guards closed the trapdoor. It sealed with a loud hiss, and Connie imagined it'd be filled with concrete within the hour. Just as a precaution. She didn't give a damn. She didn't have to.

"We did it!" She hugged Tia.

"It's really gone?" asked Tia.

"I think so. Guess we'll find out soon enough."

Tia said, "I can't believe you did it."

"Neither can I. I didn't think it was really possible."

"That's not what I'm saying, Connie. I'm saying I didn't think you'd go through with it. People spend their whole lives wanting to be special, and you just threw it away."

"Being special is overrated," said Connie.

"Of course you'd believe that," said Tia.

Connie said, "What's wrong with you?"

"What's wrong? Are you fucking serious?" Tia laughed, hot and angry. "Connie, it isn't always easy to be your friend, but you're making it really hard now."

"What the hell are you mad about?"

"I don't know. It's just . . . It's nothing."

"No. It's something."

"Yes, it's something," said Tia. "You threw it away. Like it was nothing."

"That was the whole point, wasn't it?"

"I didn't think you'd go through with it," said Tia. "I didn't think it was possible in the first place, but I knew you do impossible things all the time. I assumed, if you did succeed, that you'd change your mind at the last minute, realize what you were doing."

"I know what I'm doing."

"No, you really don't. You want to be normal? You want to live like everyone else? No adventures. No ninja assassins or killer mutants. No trips to the moon or journeys to the center of the Earth. Connie, I'm normal. It's boring."

"Boring is what I want."

Tia sighed. "Forget it. You don't get it. But you will. You'll wake up a year from now, doing the same goddamn thing every goddamn day, just waiting for anything different to happen. But it won't. It'll just be the same thing until you die."

"Tia—"

"No. Don't say anything. You're only going to make me mad. This is about more than you. And those guys, I don't trust them. What will they do with the power?"

Connie frowned. "So, now I'm supposed to be responsible for what might happen?"

"What about those people you've helped? You made a difference. I know of at least a dozen times you've saved this world or another. And two that you saved the whole universe."

"Somebody else will do it now," said Connie. "There's always somebody else."

"That's the problem with this world," replied Tia. "Everybody else expects somebody else to fix it. You were that somebody. Now there's nobody."

"The universe got along just fine without me for a million years. It'll get along fine for a million more."

"You don't know that."

"What's your solution, then?" asked Connie. "Just live with it until I die a glorious death?"

The anger in Tia's eyes faded. She shrugged. "Fuck if I know."

Connie put a hand on Tia's shoulder. "Are you all right?"

"No, I'm not. Not really. I wasn't like you. But I had

adventures now and then, even if it was as a tagalong or a plot device. Now I don't even have that. You didn't just take away your extraordinariness. You took mine."

"I didn't think about that," said Connie.

"Why would you?"

"That's not fair."

"No, it's not fair. None of it is." Tia pushed Connie's hand away. "I'll find my way home."

"Tia . . ."

"I'll get over it, but I need some space. I just hope that getting what you want is what you really want. It usually isn't."

She walked away.

Connie thought about following. She had the vague sense that she'd done something wrong, though she wasn't quite sure what. But Tia had always been there for Connie, and if she had let Tia down in some way, it bothered Connie. Her guilt was tempered by her own anger at Tia for trying to take away this moment.

"What now?' asked Thelma from Connie's pocket.

It was a good question. Connie didn't know if things had changed or not. It was too soon to tell. She only knew one thing for certain at the moment.

"We get the hell out of Kansas."

She caught the next flight out.

When she was getting on the plane, a suspicious passenger, a twitchy guy in a fez and a bolo tie, caught her eye. He clutched a worn satchel to his white suit. Beads of sweat covered his forehead, and whenever anyone walked too close, he'd flinch as if expecting them to attack him.

Connie wondered what he had in the satchel. An ancient relic? A priceless diamond? The blueprints for a car that ran on happy thoughts? Whatever it was, she wasn't a part of it. Not anymore. Twitchy guys in fezzes who were clearly up to no good were no longer her concern.

He sat several seats down from her, clutching his satchel in a white-knuckled grip. He wasn't murdered on the flight, leaving her to solve the impossible crime. He didn't try to pass the satchel to her or stash it under her seat when she wasn't looking. When the plane landed, he spotted a pair of skulking hoodlums in black suits waiting for him. He pushed his way through the crowd, right past Connie as if he didn't even notice her, with the hoodlums chasing after him. They dashed past her too, like she was just somebody beneath their notice. And then they were gone.

Leaving the airport, she took a cab home. While loading her bags in the trunk, the driver found an ancient idol. Connie recognized the markings from the city of El Dorado, but she didn't comment. The driver tossed it in the glove box, and Connie waited for something to happen.

It never did.

Back at her apartment, she ran into Mr. Prado as he was leaving. He carried two suitcases.

"Going somewhere?" she asked.

"No more caretaker, no more job," he replied.

"Sorry." She didn't make an effort to sound sincere, because she wasn't. "What was your job, anyway?"

"Sit in the lobby, keep an eye on you. It wasn't very interesting."

Most of her adventures took place away from her apartment. She didn't spend much time here. Mr. Prado's monitoring duty couldn't have been rewarding.

"You're better off," she said.

"Says who?" He snorted. "I was getting paid to sit around and read, write a report now and then. Monitoring you put my kids through college."

"You have kids?"

"Three of them. Never sussed that out, did you, little miss detective? Never broke cover. Not once. The secret is that I lived my life like I was a landlord. Didn't see my kids or wife or do a damned thing Mr. Prado wouldn't do. I smoke. Prado, he doesn't smoke."

He pulled a cigarette out of his pocket, lit it, and took a deep drag.

"Damn, that's good. I've been waiting eight years for that."

"You're good."

He smiled. "I'm the best. Good luck with the rest of your life, Constance."

"Good luck with your . . . whatever."

Mr. Prado half-saluted and strolled out of her life.

There were no ninjas lurking in the shadows of her

apartment. No ghosts. No space Nazis. Nothing but a space crammed full of the junk from decades of adventuring.

She still didn't believe it. She checked and double-checked everything. The box full of cursed artifacts. The box beside that full of non-cursed artifacts. Probably not a good idea to keep those right next to each other, she noted. The alien technology. The large standing mirror where her reflection was always frowning and flipping her off. The shelves of books of prophecy, forbidden knowledge, and magic, including a first edition of magical theory from America's greatest sorcerer, Benjamin Franklin. The stuff accumulated from decades of adventures, now quietly sitting in her apartment.

She didn't need it anymore. She'd never needed it, but she'd always been stuck with it. If she was truly ordinary now, then she could finally lose all this junk. She could be free of it.

Except maybe the Ben Franklin book. She liked that one. And that one cursed idol that turned people into vampires. That was probably better off in her hands. It would also look terrific on her mantle. A conversation starter when she had people over for her new life.

"Oh, that? Just a souvenir from Dracula after I destroyed his evil robotic double. Nothing, really."

That wouldn't do. She'd have to get rid of it all. Every single thing. Even Franklin's *Mad Richard's Almanac*. Even the Holy Grail, which she'd been using as a planter for a small asparagus fern because, though she had many skills, keeping houseplants alive wasn't one of them. She'd ditch everything and start fresh.

She'd stop worrying about aliens and conspiracies and superspies, start worrying about paying bills and how to best decorate her apartment. She'd obsess over TV shows and pick up a hobby that had no practical use. She'd find a job she tolerated and complain to her coworkers about it. She'd develop just enough interest in politics to have simplified opinions about complicated issues, root for and/or bemoan the local sports team, and worry if her shoes matched her purse. She'd get a purse.

She'd be normal, and heaven help anyone who tried to stop her.

23

It took her a week to get rid of most of her stuff. She could've gone the garage sale route, but most of it was dangerous in some form or another. It didn't belong in the hands of regular people. She contacted all the extraordinary people she knew, the magicians, the crime busters, the rogue explorers, weird scientists. Piece by piece, box by box, she shipped out the stuff to their capable hands. The workers at the post office dreaded her coming by.

"Anything fragile, flammable, or liquid?" they'd ask.

"No, just a petrified snake that grants wishes," she'd reply.

"No, just an alien ray gun, but don't worry. I shipped the battery packs separately."

"No, just a part for a time machine that I was saving because a future version of myself told me I would need it someday, but turns out she . . . I was wrong."

After the fifth day, they stopped asking and simply took the package.

She was stuck with Thelma, carrying the haunted pen with her because, when it was all said and done, she felt bad about killing the former fairy godmother. Connie offered to exorcise her, sending her onto the greater mysteries of the Other Side.

"Thanks, but I'd rather stick around a bit longer," said Thelma.

She didn't say more than that, and Connie suspected—no, she knew—that the ghost still carried more secrets than she was willing to share. Connie didn't ask.

Opportunities for adventure kept presenting themselves, as if her old life was reluctant to give her up. Small things. Mysterious packages left in the lobby. Suspicious people going about their suspicious business. Some strange tentacled horror poked its way out of her toilet for an afternoon. She didn't know if it was a second chance or if she'd spent so long being extraordinary that she noticed things most people didn't. Except the tentacle. That was clearly adventure trying to get her attention. Either way, she didn't answer when opportunity came knocking.

By the end of two weeks, the incidents dried up. She worried at first that everyone might be right and that she'd made a mistake, but she loved being ordinary. Waking up every day without fear of being drafted to fight some cosmic war or chase down terrorists. It was glorious. She could finally sleep in.

She got up when she wanted. Did what she wanted, when she wanted. She still had the wealth from her adventures, and for the first time, she had the time to do something with it.

And what she wanted to do was nothing.

She was lounging around the apartment, eating chips and aimlessly surfing the internet, when Lucas Harrison came knocking on her door. She almost didn't answer, but he kept knocking.

She opened the door but didn't invite him in. He didn't ask.

"What the hell did you do, Verity?" he asked.

"Nothing much. I'm ordinary now," she replied. "I would think you'd be happy about that. Oh, right. You're part of a conspiracy to keep me from having an ordinary life. Well, sorry to have to break this to you, but that's over."

He didn't lie to her. She had to give him credit for that.

"Do you have any idea of the consequences you've set in motion?"

"The more important question is: do I care? I don't need a lecture from you, Harrison. All this time, I thought you were a friend. Maybe not a close friend, but someone I knew. Why did you want me to go into space, anyway?"

"I didn't. They did. The people I work for believe that something terrible is going to happen on Earth, and the only way to prevent it was to have you not be here."

"I thought I'd been drafted to prevent terrible things."

"Some terrible things," said Harrison, "but this is *the* terrible thing. And you and all your predecessors and everything that's happened since the beginning of time are part of that thing. Some call it the final operation. Others call it the end of everything. If the universe is an Engine, then performing its ultimate function could very possibly mean it no longer has a reason to exist."

"Forgive me if I don't shudder in terror at your armchair metaphysics, but even if it were true, I gave up that role. I'm out of the game."

"You can't just get out of it," he said. "We're all part of it, whether we want to be or not, whether we're out there saving the day or just living our little lives. It's all connected in ways we can't fathom."

"I don't get it. Do you want me here or not? Are you upset that I'm not the fixer anymore, or that I ever was?"

"I honestly don't know anymore. I don't think I ever knew. All I know is that I believe in you, Verity. Believed. Maybe I still do."

"I thought my job was to keep it running."

Harrison rubbed his eyes. "I can't explain it to you. I don't understand it myself, but the Engine is real, and we're all just moving parts. But there's another possibility. You aren't here to help it complete the final operation but to finally shut it down."

"Shut down the universe?"

"The Engine isn't the universe. It's simply a thing that has enslaved the universe. We think."

"Who is *we*?"

He grunted. "Hell if I know. Hell if anyone knows. All I know is that I've read the reports. I've seen what you've done, and if I was going to bet on anyone to be the right person to do something that needs to be done at the right time, I'd bet on you."

"That was the old me," she said.

He smiled bitterly. "You really think that?"

"Just pick a new person to be your grand savior. That's how it works, isn't it?"

"It's not a role you can just plug someone into," he said. "The spell and the conspiracy didn't make you into the person you are. They just gave you a nudge in the right direction now and then, but it was you who kept saving the day. Not some special magic. Not some grand plan."

He held out his attaché case.

"Take it," he said. "Read what's inside it. You wanted to be normal. Here are the consequences."

The door across the hall opened, and Dana stuck her head out. "I thought I heard you."

Connie nodded. "Thanks, but no, thanks, sir," she said to Harrison. "I gave at the office."

He sighed. "You got what you wanted, Verity. I hope it's worth it."

He set the case beside her door and walked, and she hoped she never saw him again. He was her old life. She didn't need a handler now.

"Are you going to open it?" asked Thelma from Connie's pocket.

"Beg your pardon?" asked Dana.

Connie clicked Thelma quiet. "Didn't say anything."

"I thought I heard someone."

Thelma shook in a silent grumble.

"Thin walls," said Connie.

Dana asked about Harrison, and Connie mumbled something about a door-to-door charity.

She appraised Dana. It was a habit at this point. They'd bumped into each other in the hallway at least once a day, and every time, Connie pondered if Dana, like Mr. Prado, wasn't who she said she was. But if so, she had no reason to still be here.

"You wouldn't know where Mr. Prado is?" asked Dana. "He isn't returning my calls."

"I heard he quit," replied Connie.

"Damn. I've got this garbage disposal I need installed, and he said he'd do it today."

"I'll do it," said Connie.

"You know plumbing?"

"Picked it up on my adventures," said Connie, and immediately regretted it.

"Your adventures in plumbing," said Dana skeptically. "You'll have to tell me about it sometime."

"You really don't want to hear about it," said Connie. "Just don't flush a Peruvian snake god down your toilet. It's not pretty."

Dana paused, processing the statement. She laughed politely like one did at a joke they didn't quite get.

Connie found her tools and then found herself under Dana's sink. "Hand me that wrench."

Dana gave her the tool. "Are you sure you know what you're doing?"

"It's only a garbage disposal," replied Connie. "I can take care of it for you."

"Are you sure?"

Connie gave the wrench a final twist. "There. Done." She stood, ran the sink to double-check if there was a leak. "Everything checks out."

"You're really handy," said Dana.

"I get by."

"What did you say your job was, again?"

"Little bit of this, little bit of that," replied Connie. "I'm between gigs right now."

"Well, I'm sure you'll find something soon."

Connie had never had a regular job. She'd never had the time, and now, she didn't need one. She had plenty of money, but a job would be a normal thing to have now. It was also a responsibility, and she'd been responsible for saving the day so often, it was nice to not have to worry about anything for the foreseeable future.

"Are you okay?" asked Dana. "You seem distracted."

"Just going through some changes," said Connie. "How's Byron, by the way?"

"Good. You two seemed to hit it off right away."

It was a statement that was vaguely a question at the same time. Was Dana testing Connie? Did she know about the whirlwind romance, the spontaneous one-night stand?

"He asked about you the other day," said Dana.

"He did? What did he ask?"

Dana shrugged. "Just if you were back from your trip."

Connie felt like a thirteen-year-old girl, hearing whispers on the playground about who liked whom. Or so she assumed. At thirteen, she hadn't had much time for boys or playground gossip.

"That's it?" asked Connie.

Dana didn't smile. Her expression became disapproving. "I knew you liked him."

"He's cool." Connie tried to act nonchalant, but she was painfully aware of how chalant she sounded.

"Can I be honest with you, Connie?"

Connie didn't like the sound of that.

"I'd rather you not get involved with my brother. He's in a rough patch right now. His fiancée broke up with him only a year ago. I don't think he's ready to date. Especially someone like you."

"Oh, okay."

Connie didn't want to start a fight, so she decided to not pick at it. But she was also lousy at avoiding fights, so she decided immediately to ignore the previous decision.

"What's the hell does that mean?"

Again, she wondered just how much Dana knew about her. It wasn't difficult to find things out.

"You're a smart, attractive, well-traveled woman. And my brother is . . . Well, I love him, but he's not exactly a good fit for you. He needs someone . . . simpler. More stable." Dana smiled. "You understand?"

Connie had the urge to roundhouse-kick every condescending tooth out of Dana's head, but that would've probably only proven the point.

"I'm just looking out for him," said Dana. "And you. You don't want to date someone like Byron. He doesn't mesh with your lifestyle. You're never home. You're always out doing God-knows-what. You aren't a drug dealer, are you?" She held up her hands. "Never mind. None of my business."

"I'm not a drug dealer," replied Connie coldly.

"Like I said, none of my business. You seem nice, but my brother needs more than nice. He needs someone who . . . someone not like you."

"I see."

She couldn't determine whether Dana was merely being an overprotective sister or if she had other concerns specific to Connie. Either way, Dana had a point.

Connie hadn't called Byron yet, like she'd promised she would. She'd meant it when she said it, but something kept her from picking up the phone.

"I think you're great, though," said Dana. "Just not great for Byron."

"Thanks," said Connie distantly, barely hearing herself. "I have to go. I have a thing I have to do."

"Sure."

"It's not drugs," said Connie.

"Didn't ask." Dana flipped on the disposal. It gurgled for a few moments before sputtering to a halt. Probably just a loose wire. Wouldn't take more than a minute or two to fix.

She scratched her head. "Well, crap."

"Yeah, you should probably get the new super to look at that," said Connie as she left, closing the door behind her.

Connie had started taking her mother to the salon. It wasn't Connie's idea of a good time, but Mom seemed to like it.

"Don't you have something important to be doing?" Mom asked as they took another day at the spa.

Connie leaned back in her chair as the manicurist worked on her nails. "No, Mom. It's cool."

She'd never been a manicure kind of girl. Pretty nails weren't much of an option when you were scaling mountains or grappling with shadow death ninjas. She still wasn't a manicure kind of girl, but it was nice to have the choice.

"After this, Mom, I thought we might go to a movie."

"Oh. That'd be nice."

"Then pick Dad up and go for a nice dinner."

"Oh. Yes. Dinner would be nice. I suppose."

Connie kept her eyes closed, but she could still picture that look on Mom's face. Slightly concerned. Slightly discombobulated. She'd had it on her face since Connie had been seven.

"Something wrong, Mom?"

"No. Nothing, really, sweetie."

"Spit it out, Mom."

Mom waved her pedicurist away and sat up. "It's just . . .

well . . . you've been spending an awful lot of time with your father and me."

"Making up for lost time," said Connie. "You took such good care of me as a kid, I just wanted to return the favor now that I can."

"That's very nice, Constance," said Mom. She paused. The bigger the pause, the bigger the *but* that was going to follow it. Connie had a mental ranking of all Mom's pauses, and this one was a two on a scale of ten.

". . . but wouldn't you like to spend some time with your friends as well? We don't want to take up all your time now that you're free to do what you want to do."

"This is what I want to do."

"I see."

Pause. Level six. Six point five, maybe.

" . . . but we know how hard it must be for you to be an ordinary person now. We wouldn't hold it against you if you needed some alone time to help you adjust."

The manicurists, two Korean ladies, mumbled to each other about Connie not picking up the hint. She didn't let them know she spoke Korean.

"Am I bothering you, Mom?"

Pause. Full level nine.

" . . . I wouldn't say you were bothering us. It's just, well, we love you very much. You know that."

"I think she's breaking up with you," said Thelma.

Connie didn't remember taking the haunted pen with her. She

was convinced the ghost could materialize in her pocket at will.

"I've enjoyed this time together, but your father and I do have a life outside of you. Not that it's ever been a problem before. You've always been so busy."

"Things are different now," said Connie.

"And that's wonderful. It really is. But we think you might be better served spending some time with your friends."

"Oh, my God. You are breaking up with me."

Mom rolled her eyes. "Don't be so melodramatic."

"Does Dad feel the same way?"

"Your father loves you very much and is very, very proud of you."

The manicurists stifled their chuckles.

"It's only been two weeks, Mom, and you're already sick of me?" asked Connie.

"Now, I never said that. Don't put words in my mouth."

Connie stifled a glare. Mom wasn't saying anything Connie hadn't already thought.

"I don't have any ordinary friends except Tia. And I apparently ruined her life by fixing mine." Connie sat up. "I don't know if I know how to make friends, Mom."

"Perhaps you should call her, then."

"She wants space. I'm giving it to her."

"What about that man you were talking about the other day?"

"Byron? I should call him."

She should, but she hadn't. She thought about it three or four times a day, and every time, she chickened out. She assumed her first normal relationship was doomed. She was bound to make stupid mistakes through inexperience. She didn't want to blow it with Byron. Absurd, since they didn't have much of a thing to blow.

The longer she went without calling, the harder it was to pick up the phone.

Her mother said, "I don't know what you're worried about. You're very personable."

"You have to say that. You're my mom."

"Constance, you've spent the last twenty-eight years living the most extraordinary life. Just be yourself. You're still the same wonderful person you've always been. I loved you before you went to the moon and back. I love you now that you're done doing that sort of thing. And people will like you. You only have to give them the chance."

"Thanks, Mom."

Connie didn't believe it would be that easy, but this was what she'd wanted. She'd figure it out.

Dinner with Mom and Dad was rescheduled, and on the drive home, Connie realized the absence of adventure in her life meant she didn't know a lot about herself. She'd never had the free time to be her own person, never developed any hobbies or interests on her own. Mom might have suggested Connie be herself, but she wasn't sure who that was now.

Connie had spent decades in adventures, but this was an adventure in itself. The paradox of her life was that the extraordinary was ordinary and vice versa, and stuff regular people did wasn't natural to her.

On her way home, a spectral figure appeared in the doorway of an abandoned building and gestured for Connie to follow. She was tempted. One little adventure. What could it hurt? Just something to kill a few hours.

"Nice try," she said.

The specter hung its hooded head and disappeared.

Old habits died hard, but Connie was damned if she'd take the easy way now. She wasn't going to rush headlong into adventure simply because she didn't have any better ideas at the moment.

She thought about calling Tia, but that was also an old habit. If Connie was going to have a life now, she needed one beyond Tia. It wasn't fair to Tia or Mom or Dad or Byron to expect them to fill in for all the adventures.

She had time now. The best thing for her would be to take advantage of it. She had every intention of focusing on herself, no distractions, and all of that promptly went to hell when Byron showed up in her apartment building elevator. The doors opened, and there he was. No time to hide. No time to prepare herself.

"Oh." She struggled to come up with something. She was fast on her feet. She'd faced bigger surprises than this.

He stepped out of the elevator, and they exchanged a polite hug. Brief. Not too familiar. Like relative strangers, which they really were when she thought about it.

"How have you been?" he asked.

"Good," she replied. "Visiting your sister?"

He nodded. "She had some problem with the wiring on her garbage disposal."

"You're an electrician?"

"I get by."

The elevator doors started to close, but she stabbed the button to keep them open.

"Byron, I meant to call," she said.

"You don't have to make excuses, Connie. It was a thing. A fun thing. But we don't have to make it more than it was."

She thought about getting in the elevator. She didn't. This time, when the doors closed, she let them.

"My life is complicated," she said.

"Sure, sure."

She wanted him to sweep her up in his arms. She wanted him to be suave and smooth, to feed her lines about how beautiful she was. It was always bullshit, but it was bullshit she was used to. She knew how to play that game. A little intrigue. A little danger. A little sex. Then a parting of the ways before heading off to another adventure.

"Screw it," she grumbled.

She grabbed him by the shirt and pulled him close. They kissed, and all her insecurities faded as he put his arms around her. She ran her fingers through his hair, knowing he loved that more than he hated having his hair get messy. He moved his hands down her back.

Maybe they weren't such strangers after all.

24

The next morning, Connie offered Byron breakfast before he went, but he was already running late for work.

"This is fun," he said, "but eventually we're going to have to do something other than talk and have sex."

"Like dinner or something? Are you sure that's okay with your sister?"

"She's just overprotective. Always has been. Ever since we first met."

"Looking out for her adopted little brother?"

"How'd you know I was adopted?"

"Detective," she said.

He buttoned his shirt and kissed her again. "How about dinner tonight, then? Someplace public. Like a real couple."

"Sounds great."

And it did. They made plans, and it still was weird to her that she could now make plans without having to worry about adventure screwing them all up, but she'd get used to it.

On his way out the door, he paused in the hall. "Someone left an attaché case out here."

Harrison's case had been sitting out there all night, and she'd been trying not to think about it. Whatever he'd left for her, it wasn't going to change her mind.

"Leave it," she said.

He blew her a kiss as he closed the door. It was corny, but corny was what she liked about him.

She made herself French toast, looking forward to that evening. Maybe she could call Tia finally. They could talk about Byron and other non–world threatening stuff.

She also thought about that case sitting in the hallway. Halfway through her breakfast, she opened the door and studied it like a monster lying in wait to ambush her. She returned to her French toast, had some juice, half-watched most of some game show, and then returned to stare at the case again.

"You should open it," said Thelma. "You know you want to."

Connie picked it up and chucked it down the garbage chute. Out of sight, out of mind.

Except it wasn't.

She went all the way down to the basement and dug through the garbage to find the case still intact, still unopened. She returned to her apartment, took a quick shower to wash the gunk off, then sat at her kitchen table, glaring at the case.

"Just open it," said Thelma, sitting beside it on the table.

Grumbling, Connie opened it. She couldn't *not* open it. She'd spent decades opening things best left closed, and she couldn't change the habit in a couple of weeks. She didn't have the willpower.

It was filled with a handful of manila file folders. Harrison probably expected her to read them. She found a match, lit it, and prepared to torch them. A cleansing ritual to remove the last traces of her old life.

She blew out the match. She shut the case and tossed it in the garbage chute again.

"Really?" asked Thelma. "You know you'll have to read those files eventually. You're just putting off the inevitable."

"Nobody asked you."

Connie dialed Lucas Harrison on her phone.

"Read the files, Verity?" he asked.

"No. What's in them? No, don't tell me. I don't care. Leave me the hell alone."

"You called me."

"Don't get cute. None of this has anything to do with me anymore."

"So, what's the harm in reading the files, then?" he said.

She put the phone on the counter. She didn't want to dig through the garbage again. She counted to ten before returning the phone to her ear. She wasn't going to lose her temper.

"I have a choice now, and I choose to not read. Respect that."

"I'm not making you do anything," he replied. "I only thought you might be interested in the files."

"What's your game, Harrison?"

"No game. Just information. Look at it or don't. Your call."

She hung up.

She went down to the basement, pulled the case from the garbage, took another shower.

"Are we going to do this all day?" asked Thelma. "Just do what we both know you were going to do from the beginning."

Connie read the files angrily, as if that somehow made it excusable. She called Harrison again, made arrangements to meet him.

He picked a library across town. It wasn't convenient, but she was beyond pretending as if she wasn't already on this road. They found a table in the periodicals section. She slid the case across the table.

"Explain it."

"You read them, then?" he asked.

"I wouldn't be here if I hadn't."

He opened the case, and she glimpsed the file on Dr. Ishiro Hirata, leading expert in the field of kaiju studies. He'd died four days before, keeping a monster crab from devouring Yokohama.

She counted him as a friend. More importantly, Dr. Hirata had devoted his life to the containment of all those giant beasties waiting to destroy humanity. He'd kept the kaiju apocalypse at bay a dozen times she knew of. She'd helped him a few of those times.

Now he was dead.

Harrison dropped another file on the stack and pushed it at her. She gave them a quick scan. Eloise Purvis, Special

Agent in charge of the World Crime League Task Force, had been shot three times and was now laid up in the hospital.

"That one came in just today," said Harrison. "You know Eloise, don't you?"

"I know all these people," said Connie, putting her hand on the files, reports of extraordinary people she'd run with in the past.

Doctor Dynasty, Master of Mystic Arts, rendered blind and gibbering mad after repelling an alien monster god from another dimension.

Mariana Challenger, Explorer of the Unknown, vanished in the jungles of South America while searching for a lost city.

Caligula Fox, World's Greatest Detective, found dead in his kitchen, a scimitar buried in his back.

Nine other adventurers in various fields, all of them dead, injured, or missing.

"It's a dangerous world out there," said Harrison.

"Stop tiptoeing around what you want to say and just tell me."

"That is what I'm saying to you, Verity. Bad things happen, and the difference between triumph and tragedy is often razor-thin. One wrong move, one moment of bad luck, and things fall apart.

"These people all do things that need to be done, things only they can do. The rest of us live our lives worrying about unimportant shit only because of folks like this standing like a bulwark against the tide of weird crap and horrible disaster ready to bury this world. But it's a delicate balance, and you've pushed it over by what you've done."

"I'm not really in the mood for more metaphysical bullshit," said Connie.

"No bullshit." He reconsidered. "Maybe a little bullshit. How many close calls have you had? How many last-minute escapes? How many times have you saved the day with a split second to spare?"

"I don't know. A lot."

"Did you ever consider what would've happened in those situations if you hadn't been there? When Doc Dynasty banished the parasite lords from beyond time, you were the one who shoved the final keystone in place that sealed the gate, weren't you?"

She nodded. "Doc did most the work, though."

"And when the World Crime League sent a hit squad to take out Eloise Purvis, you were the one to push her out of the way of a hail of bullets, weren't you?"

"Eloise is sharp. She would've spotted them."

"And when Ishiro Hirata was piloting the Mecha-Armadillo that saved San Diego from being stepped on by that giant squid-gorilla thing—"

"Squorillo, Terror of the Deep," she said.

"Yes, that. Moments before the Mecha-Armadillo self-destructed, taking Squorillo with it, who was the one who pulled Hirata into the escape pod just in time?"

"Me, but—"

"No buts, Verity. Don't you get it? There's a balance here, and you've thrown it out of whack."

"I wouldn't have been on all these adventures. I do a lot

in two weeks, but not this much. I wouldn't have been there to save all of them."

"It's not about being there," he said. "It's about the possibility of being there. It's about there being someone out there who can push things one way or the other. That used to be you. Now that you're not doing it, the universe has noticed."

"I'm not that important," she said. "Anyway, by your quasi-religion, which I still don't understand, isn't this all part of the plan and I'm just a replaceable part?"

"Some of us have come to think differently. We think the Engine doesn't keep the universe running. It keeps it from growing. It keeps it from becoming more."

"More what?"

"We don't know."

"No offense, Harrison, but that just sounds like more pseudo-spiritual gobbledygook."

"It is, but it doesn't mean it's not true. Engine theory says the universe is a near-infinite collection of moving parts, and all those parts fit together to do their job. But if that's true, it means that everything is preordained, that there's no such thing as free will. Except maybe you."

"I don't know if you've been paying attention, but my whole life has been one long series of preordained events. I couldn't cross the street without having to save the world. I'm the poster girl for predestination."

"We don't control most things that happen to us. We only react. Your reactions are better than most."

"So, make someone else like me. It can't be that hard. Just a magic spell, right?"

"You're different. You're . . ." He struggled to come up with the word.

"Chosen?" she asked. "Chosen to break a predestined universe. That sounds like a paradox to me."

"I know it sounds stupid," he said. "I wouldn't say *chosen*. I'd just say the right person at the right time. That's who you are, and it's not because some enchantment forced it onto you."

"I never asked to be."

Harrison shook his head. "Nobody asks for anything. We're all figuring this stuff as we go along. Call it destiny. Call it luck. Call it whatever the hell you want to. You can't take yourself out of the game without expecting consequences."

"This is the beginning," he said. "It'll start with the weird stuff, but it won't stop there. It's a cruel world. People get hurt. A million little tragedies happen every day. And that was with you out there, a cosmic linchpin keeping it from falling apart. It'll only get worse. Today, a father collapses from a heart attack. A dog is hit by a car. A war nobody notices breaks out. Tomorrow, the moon breaks free of its orbit, crashes into the Earth."

"It's so obvious," said Connie. "Why didn't you explain it like that before?"

"It's all connected, but you don't have to believe me. Belief is unnecessary. We're all part of the Engine whether we want to be or not. But the Engine is indifferent. It doesn't give a shit. But you did. You did a lot of good out there, helped a lot of people. You can't tell me you didn't have fun along the way, too."

"Sure, but that's not me anymore."

"Then I expect to see more reports like these."

Connie slapped the table. The librarian flashed them a stern look.

"This is bullshit," whispered Connie. "You're blackmailing me? The universe got along just fine without me until I was seven. It can get along now. Now you're telling me my job is to either fix the universe or break it."

"One doesn't exclude the other." Harrison took a pack of cigarettes from his pocket and tapped them on the table. "Christ, I could use a smoke."

"You don't smoke."

"I don't do a lot of things," he replied. "But I do them more than I used to."

He tucked a cigarette in his mouth but didn't light it.

"Enough with the manipulation, Harrison. I'm tired of people pulling my strings." She stood. "Don't contact me again."

"Sit down, Connie." He slumped in his chair. His exhaustion was palpable. "Please."

"I'll stand." She folded her arms and glared at him. His weariness was so overwhelming, she had to glare at the wall behind him instead.

"The Engine isn't a metaphor. It exists, a giant machine at the center of creation that runs the universe. After all you've experienced, is it really that ridiculous?"

"You've seen it?" she asked.

He shook his head. "It's been centuries since anyone has. There's a door to it somewhere. Many doors scattered throughout the universe, opening and closing in a pattern nobody quite understands. The last recorded sighting on Earth was Ada Lovelace, who spent three minutes exploring its mysteries before being ejected from it. She wrote a program to predict where it would appear next. Every computer that tries to run it ends up bursting into flames, but there's still some data. Other pieces of information from mystics and seers and scientists. All of them point to another moment of alignment. Possibly soon.

"I'm not an idiot, Verity. I didn't buy it at first either. I joined up with this secret society mostly to help my career. I thought it was the Freemasons with a thing for machines. I didn't take it seriously. Then I noticed predictions being made. I started seeing the patterns. I was allowed to glimpse files kept behind locked doors, equations, codes. By themselves, easy to dismiss. All together, an awful truth. Nobody was right all the time, but often enough. It's crazy, I know, but it's true. Your life says so. Those files say so.

"What they did to you was wrong," he said. "Everybody should have a choice. They took that away from you, and I can't blame you for being pissed about it. I'm not saying there was a different way. I don't know. I wasn't involved with this from the beginning. I don't know how deep it goes or who runs what. I just do my job, and my job has been to watch you for the last ten years, compile reports, and send those reports off to somebody. Hell if I know who. But do you know what I saw in you, kid?"

"Kid? You're only a couple of years older than me."

He ignored her reply. "I saw someone who cared about the people around her. You once fought a lion to save a dog."

"I had to. His collar had microfilm in it."

"You could've waited for the lion to spit out the collar. Why don't you admit it? You're not perfect, Verity. Not by a mile, but who is? But you care about people. If you didn't, this world would be a very different place. You might have been destined for adventure, but you weren't destined to be heroic. You could've just as easily turned into a self-centered ass, given everything you've done and everything you've been through. You can put on an act like you don't care, but you do. You always have."

Connie laughed. "Funny. My best friend in the whole world said I was selfish."

"One doesn't exclude the other," he said. "You're human, despite everything. You have your flaws, but I've read those reports about you at your best and worst, and I can say that even knowing the dreadful secrets I know, I've always slept better at night knowing you were out there."

He lit his cigarette, took a deep drag, then exhaled a cloud of smoke while waving at the librarian.

"You're many things, Connie. But replaceable? Some of us don't think so."

"Who?"

He shrugged. "I'm only one man. Not even an important one. But I do know one thing, Connie. It sucks having the world depend on you, but it sucks more never having it notice you at all."

A team of librarians, three of them, approached.

Harrison stood, waved them away. "I'm leaving." He closed the attaché case, tucked it under one arm. "Take care of yourself, kid. If anyone's earned a vacation, I guess it's you. The Engine will take care of things, one way or another."

He walked away, hands in his pockets, head low, his posture stooped. Connie had no reason to trust him. This was more manipulation, and she wasn't playing along. There might have been some truth to what he'd said, but that was how it worked. Just enough truth to keep her on the hook.

"He's right," said Thelma.

"Ah, damn." Grumbling, Connie ran after him, catching him on the stairs outside.

"What difference does it make?" she asked. "I'm not special anymore."

"You're still you," he said. "There are scraps of adventure clinging to your soul. You'll never be rid of all of them. The only difference now is that you have more of a choice. What you do with that choice is up to you."

"And why should I trust any of this?"

"You shouldn't," he replied. "It could all be a lie. We could both be unwitting pawns in a game bigger than either of us. I don't trust me. Why should you? I'm only an idiot living in this world. You're the one who saves it. It's what you do."

She scowled. "What a load of crap."

Connie walked away, grumbling to herself.

onnie had always known she'd had a purpose. Most people lived their lives, unsure of what they were doing, why they were doing it, and hoped to make some sense of it after the fact. Not her.

But there was a big difference in knowing she was destined for adventure and believing she was a cosmic avatar. She'd saved countless lives, fought for the greater good, but those had always seemed like byproducts of her adventures, not the primary point.

It was the difference between being an important person and being **IMPORTANT**. All caps. Bold letters. She had a high opinion of herself and her abilities, but she'd never considered herself special in the universal sense. Most of her adventures didn't involve saving the world. Most were just curious little distractions where the stakes weren't more valuable than a life or two. Not the stuff of profound metaphysical significance.

Unless you happened to be the life saved.

Lost in her thoughts, she navigated the streets on autopilot. She was barely paying attention, but her instinct for trouble couldn't be shut off so easily. When a distracted man attempted to cross against the light, she yanked him back by his arm. A speeding bus that would've plowed into him only knocked the phone out of his hand. He stood there, processing what had just happened.

"Goddamn, I just bought that phone."

"You're welcome," she said.

"What? Oh, right, right. Yes, thanks." His focus remained on the broken phone, now crushed beneath several tires. Connie walked away.

If the universe was trying to send her a message, she chose to ignore it.

Half a block later, she came across a woman who had spilled a bag of groceries across the sidewalk. None of the other pedestrians were interested in helping her. Connie strolled past the woman a few steps before sighing, turning back, and helping to gather up some fruit, a loaf of bread, and a pack of gum.

"Thank you," said the woman.

"Don't mention it."

The woman continued in her direction, and Connie went her own way. A moment later, a safe impacted the sidewalk where they'd both been standing, where the woman would have still been standing if Connie hadn't sped up the process.

It was ridiculous. Nobody poked their head out of a window above to claim ownership of it. It'd just fallen out of the clear blue sky.

"Nice try," she mumbled to the universe.

She tucked her hands in her pockets and kept her head down. She wouldn't get involved. No matter what. No matter how contrived the circumstances.

Someone shouted for help.

She ignored it. She stared straight ahead and didn't look back. Or she should have. If there was a grand design at work, she wasn't interested in being the troubleshooter of the universe. But if this was part of the design, then it sucked if someone had to die because of that same design.

Connie turned around. A husband choked on something, and his wife struggled to help him. A waiter came up behind the man and gave him the Heimlich maneuver. The choking man spit out the bit of sandwich clogging his windpipe and, coughing, thanked the waiter.

Maybe the universe had taken the hint. She didn't buy the Engine theory. The universe wasn't spinning cogs filling their function. It was random events and chaos, and she might have been the one to smooth out some of the wrinkles, but it would get along fine without her.

If she placed importance on every little thing that happened around her, it would be too easy to see patterns that weren't there. The fates of millions weren't decided by the flapping of a butterfly's wings. It was all manufactured by her imagination, and it wasn't difficult to see why. She had done and seen things few people had. She'd seen how narrow the line between triumph and tragedy could be.

She deliberately avoided thinking about how often she saved the world, the universe, a handful of lives here and there. It was more responsibility than she wanted, and that was before being told she embodied some manner of cosmic avatar.

She smelled smoke.

A building across the street spewed thick gray clouds from several of its windows. A woman shrieked about her baby trapped on the tenth floor.

"Oh, damn it," Connie grumbled as she ran across the street.

Four minutes later, Connie, covered in ash and sweat, stepped out of the conflagration with two cats in her arms and a dog draped over her shoulders. The woman ran over and took one of the cats.

"Oh, thank you, thank you!" She clutched the fat brown feline to her chest. "My baby, I don't know what I'd have done if something had happened to you."

Connie set down the second cat and dog as firemen rushed past her. The paramedics insisted on having a look at her, and she wasn't in the mood to argue. She sat on the bumper while a woman checked her over.

"I'm fine," said Connie.

"You might have inhaled some smoke, ma'am. We have to be sure."

"I held my breath."

"You must've been in that building for five or six minutes."

"I've done ten," replied Connie.

"Right, ma'am." The paramedic shone a light in Connie's eyes. "If you don't mind me saying, that was an incredibly stupid thing to do. You could've gotten yourself killed."

"She's done stupider," said Thelma, and the paramedic, distracted by his examination, didn't notice it was the pen doing the talking.

"Looks like you got lucky," he said before moving on to a more urgent patient. "Next time, don't be a hero."

Connie joined the crowd and watched the building burn. It was only one small apartment building, a few dozen lives. Nothing more. She'd seen greater tragedies. Cosmic wars where thousands of intelligent beings disappeared in faraway, twinkling flashes. Worlds exploding. Universes collapsing.

The cat lady threw her arms around Connie. "Oh, thank you! Thank you so much!" She sobbed joyfully and squeezed tighter. The unhappy cat growled and dug its claws into Connie's shoulder. "If you hadn't been here . . ."

Connie gently pushed the lady away. The cat clung to Connie, and she had to pull it off. She held it away from her. She'd never been a cat person. Or a dog person. Really, a pet person. She'd never had the time. She'd had a dog when she'd been nine. Boscoe had been hit by a car while she was away breaking up a smuggling ring.

The brown cat, smudged and as thoroughly unhappy with

its current situation as Connie was with hers, meowed.

"Tell me about it," said Connie as she handed the cat back to its owner.

Connie hurried home before anything else could happen. This was all simply the clinging bits of magic she had within her, but those bits would wither away if left unfed.

She'd seen plenty of crazy stuff and learned secrets humanity wasn't ready for. But the one thing she'd never seen was a grand pattern. Her universe didn't make much sense. Her universe was a chaotic jumble of mummy sorcerers and space wars, of mob-busting and lost civilizations. Nothing fit together.

A shout for help came from a nearby alley. She kept going. Or she should have.

"Damn it."

She walked into the darkened alley. A frightened man in a gray suit with an attaché case handcuffed to his wrist cowered before a pair of Japanese women in crisp black suits. The hints of Yakuza tattoos peeked out on the back of their necks.

"Help me," he said.

The women turned on Connie. Their long daggers glinted in the dark.

"Walk away," said one.

"I wish to hell I could," replied Connie.

The Yakuza enforcers lay at her feet. Connie tossed aside the trashcan lid she'd used as an impromptu shield and bludgeon.

She poked a finger through the rip in her shirt sleeve. She'd just bought that top. Adventuring was hard on the wardrobe.

The man in the gray suit thanked her, saying something about now being free to save the lives or restore the honor of somebody or something. She was only half-listening.

"You're welcome," she said.

He started to speak. She held up her hand.

"Happy to help, but I have my own problems to deal with right now, so no need to thank me."

Puzzled but grateful, he left the alley.

"Admit it," said Thelma. "You live for this."

"I admit nothing."

But as exhausting as a life of endless adventure could be, there was part of her that would always love it. It could be inconvenient, but it was never dull. She might wish for a moment to herself now and then, but it was fun facing off against Yakuza enforcers. And she still got goose bumps every time she saw a dinosaur, though she'd seen countless dozens over the years.

"You can lie to everyone else," said Thelma. "You can even lie to yourself, but this isn't coincidence. This is who you are, who you want to be."

Connie wanted to argue. She pictured herself as an old woman, gray-haired, wrinkled, surrounded by friends and family, and she smiled. For the first time, it felt like that might be possible.

She pictured herself as an old woman, gray-haired, wrinkled, fighting and dying in some forsaken place. A glorious death saving the universe.

And damned if she didn't smile at that, too.

"Well, shit."

She made a call. She hoped for voicemail. Simple, undemanding, uncomplicated voicemail.

"Hi," Byron said on the other end of the phone. He sounded so happy to hear from her.

"I'm going to have to cancel dinner tonight," she said.

"Oh. Okay."

"Something came up."

"Yeah, no problem."

"I don't want you to think it's because I'm having doubts about us," she said. It sounded weird because it meant there was an *us* to have doubts about. "I have to tend to some personal business. I don't know how long it will take."

One of the Yakuza enforcers rose to her feet and eyed Connie with cold hatred. The enforcer pulled a knife from somewhere. Connie pondered just how many knives they could be carrying.

"Can you hold on one second?" asked Connie of either Byron or the assassin.

"Sure," said Byron.

Connie lowered the phone. The shrieking assassin lunged. Connie caught her attacker's arm, twisted, and kicked her in the face. The enforcer fell over.

"Was that a monster?" asked Byron.

"Yakuza assassin," she said.

"Are you busy? You can call me back later if it's more convenient."

"It's never convenient," she replied.

"Aren't Yakuza assassins supposed to be silent?"

"You're thinking of ninjas. Totally different thing. It's a common mistake."

The second assassin rose to her knees.

"Oh, for Christ's sake." Connie put the phone to her chest. "Stay the fuck down, or I'll kill you just so I can have a conversation."

The enforcer dropped several knives from various places hidden in her suit and raised her hands. There were no doubt more tucked away, but it was an honest gesture.

"Thank you." Connie put the phone to her ear. "Sorry about that."

"No problem. Okay, so we'll reschedule."

"You're not mad? It's okay if you're mad."

He laughed. "I'm disappointed, but you warned me your life is complicated. If I was dating Bruce Wayne, I could hardly be upset if he had to cancel a date because the Penguin is in town."

"You're the best." She felt silly. She was way too invested in Byron, probably because he represented the normal life she also hadn't quite given up on yet.

He said, "When you get back from the moons of Mars or giant spider world or wherever, you know where to find me."

"You've got yourself a deal." She ended the call, grabbed a convenient beer bottle, and tossed it between the eyes of the enforcer attempting to sneak up on her. Connie grabbed the staggered assassin by the lapel and punched her across the jaw.

"We could do this all day," said Connie, "but I have stuff I need to take care of."

She dropped the enforcer and walked away.

C onnie showed up at Tia's doorstep. She didn't call ahead.

"Can we talk?" asked Connie.

Tia hesitated. "Yeah, sure. Whatever."

Connie stepped inside and shut the door.

"You've been adventuring," said Tia.

"What? No, not exactly. How did you know?"

"You have adventure hair. It's like sex hair, but more tousled. And there's blood on your coat."

"Nice detective work," said Connie.

"Thanks. It's not so much detective work as knowing your subject. I thought you were normal now."

"Normalcy is trickier than advertised," Connie replied. "Look, I just wanted to say I'm sorry about everything. I wasn't thinking about you when I gave up my curse, and that was wrong."

"It wasn't wrong," said Tia. "But thanks anyway. So, how's the ordinary life going?"

"Not so ordinary."

Tia said, "Want to talk about it? I'll grab a wine cooler and a beer."

"Thanks. I missed you."

Tia smiled. "I missed you, too. Not just the adventures, either. Although I was beginning to realize I'd never be kidnapped by pirates again."

"I thought you were sick of pirates."

"The normal kind, sure, but I have a fondness for the singing kind. Dashing and swarthy and full of good cheer and honor of the sea. It was more like a themed cruise than a kidnapping. And I thought, how the hell is that going to ever happen again without Connie in my life?"

She smiled at the memory. Sometimes, being a cosmic maguffin had its perks. It had helped that Tia had a strong singing voice, and that the crew of the Cursed Melody had been in need of a solid mezzo-soprano. She'd fallen in love with the incorrigible Captain Sullivan and even considered sailing with him into the sunset. But after a while, all the shanties ran together. And the rum. So much rum.

She completed her thought aloud. "And the bodices. Don't even get me started on the bodices."

By the time Sullivan had revealed that he and his men were were-eels and that Tia was to serve as their were-eel queen, she was already pretty sick of it.

It'd been a nice dream while it lasted.

Connie and Tia caught up over a beer and wine cooler.

Tia was less interested in cosmic secrets than in Byron.

"You're going to give it a try?" she asked.

"I think so. I can't keep messing with the guy. He's too nice. Doesn't deserve that."

"Sounds boring," said Tia with a grin.

"He's ordinary. Not boring."

"There's a difference?"

"For me, there is. I'm worried I'll screw it up, though."

"Yeah, probably," said Tia. "But we usually screw these things up. So, what are you going to do?"

"I don't know. Try not to screw it up."

"Not Byron. About your extraordinary life."

"Not sure. I thought I was out, but there's apparently more to be done," said Connie, "and I want you to do it with me."

"Maybe I should sit this one out."

"You're my sidekick."

"Hardly. I'm always getting into trouble, taken hostage. I don't do anything. I'm lucky to be alive, really."

"What are you talking about? You saved me from Thelma the dragon."

"You would've saved yourself."

"Oh, no, I definitely would've eaten her if you hadn't been there," said Thelma.

"Why do you want me along, anyway?" asked Tia.

"There's a dynamic," said Connie. "You don't make it far in the adventuring game as a lone wolf. Even the Lone Ranger had a partner."

"There have to be better candidates," said Tia.

"The truth, then?" Connie sighed. "All right. I'm good at what I do, but most of the big stuff I've done, I've played second banana. I wouldn't call myself a sidekick, but I've been one as often than not. Everything I can do, I know someone who can do it ten times better.

"I know what it's like to be overshadowed by extraordinary people, to doubt yourself and your abilities, to wonder if you're good enough.

"I could make some calls and get someone else. I know plenty of people who could help me deal with this, but then I'll likely end up in the passenger's seat while someone else solves the problem. I don't want someone else to solve this problem."

Tia chuckled. "You want me because I'm not special enough to steal the spotlight. I'm so boring, you don't have to worry about me becoming the hero."

"That's not what I said," replied Connie.

"Sounded like that to me," said Thelma.

"I never said you were boring."

"Look at this place." Tia gestured at her living room. It was nicely decorated, but there was nothing exceptional or unique about it. It was only a living room, serviceable but unremarkable. "It screams boring and replaceable."

She knocked a lamp over. It broke on the floor. It didn't matter. She could always buy another one.

Connie said, "Tia, you're many things, but you aren't

replaceable. And I need you because you're the person who I can trust to watch my back."

"I'm still trying to figure out what you want to do."

"Me, too. I know I don't want to be a regular person, but I also know I don't want to always have to be an adventurer, too. But I can't help but think that there's more to be done. If I walk away now, I'm leaving it unfinished.

"The first step is to get the caretaker spell back. The rest . . . I'm just winging it. But I'd feel better if you were there with me. I won't lie to you. You'll probably end up kidnapped at some point, hanging from a cliff. But I'll be there to save you. It's what I do."

Tia laughed. "I can't believe I'm considering this."

"I can't rush headlong into danger without my trusty sidekick. That's just asking for trouble."

Tia shook her head. "What the hell? I still have a few vacation days saved up, and it's not like I'm doing anything interesting."

"That's my girl."

They clinked their beer and wine cooler together.

Connie said, "Let's go fix and/or break the goddamn universe."

27

Lucas Harrison sat in his lonely apartment. It wasn't much to look at. He didn't spend much time there. The sparse furnishings were limited to a living room set he'd ordered out of a catalogue and a bed he rarely slept in.

It wasn't his job that kept him busy. Monitoring Constance for his mysterious masters wasn't difficult work. Nor was much expected from him as a member of the secret society he'd joined. It'd worked exactly as promised. Harrison had risen through the ranks of a nameless government agency, serving more as a bureaucrat than a secret agent, without much effort on his part. He followed orders, not knowing where those orders came from or why he followed them. He'd learned a few things here and there. Secrets he wasn't cleared for. Almost all of them by accident, because he wasn't the sort to seek out mysteries.

He'd followed orders, and promotion came. He'd spent his entire life avoiding responsibility, and it'd worked out well for him. He didn't take chances, but he didn't screw up, either. Nobody had anything bad to say about Lucas Harrison. Not his agency bosses. Not his secret masters. Although if they did, he wouldn't have cared enough to find out.

Those decisions he'd made and those many more he'd not made had led him here, to a dark, gray apartment with a beer in one hand and a TV remote in the other. The batteries had died in the remote, and he stared at the blank TV screen across the room. There wasn't any point in turning it on.

He'd seen too much. He knew just enough to realize how fucking pointless it all was. Everyone lived with the illusion of control, but they were all just part of the Engine. He was a cog or a spring. Or a screw or a bolt. Something helping to hold the whole indifferent contraption together but nothing so dynamic as a moving part.

It hadn't bothered him for years. He'd found some comfort in it. Existence was a great grinding device, and every part did its job. Every part had no choice but to do its job.

But then he'd learned the truth. He'd stumbled across a few secrets, and despite a lifetime of habits, he'd sought out more. He still didn't understand most of it, but he understood enough. There was no point to it. Not for him. Maybe everything did have a grand purpose, but he didn't. He'd thought, foolishly, that perhaps his job was to convince Verity to do what needed to be done, but even that had been a waste of time.

He wasn't the first guy to discover he'd thrown his life away too late to fix the problem. He'd hoped Verity would help him the same way she helped others. In the end, even she'd been unable to.

People milled around outside his front door. They'd finally come for him. He thought about running for it, but there wasn't a point. He chugged down the last of his beer, dropped the bottle, watched it roll around in lazy circles on the floor.

"Fuck it."

The front door opened. They had a key. Why wouldn't they?

Four agents in gray suits and dark sunglasses marched into his apartment. They were almost identical. Same haircut. Same square jaws. Same wrinkle-free suits. One was a woman, but it was difficult to tell at a glance. Harrison had seen their type before. Government issue. He assumed they were manufactured in a factory somewhere. Probably outsourced to China. He imagined a small Asian woman fixing their ties in place, and it made him smile.

"Hello," he said.

The agents surrounded the chair.

"Light switch is over there." He nodded to the wall. "But you probably already knew that."

They didn't turn on the lights. He wondered how they could see at all in the dark with those sunglasses on.

"You've been talking to Constance Verity," said the lead agent. Harrison assumed this agent was the lead, though they were interchangeable.

"That's my job, isn't it? Keep tabs on her. File reports." He saluted. "Like a good little bolt."

"You have compromised the integrity of this operation."

"Screw this operation," said Harrison. "Do you even know what the operation is?"

The question bounced off the agents' bulletproof professionalism. If there was a Great Engine, then these were the type of people content to be part of it. They never thought beyond orders. They never wondered. They never deviated. They were never dissatisfied. They weren't built like that.

He envied them.

"I won't do it again," he said. "I swear by the Council."

"What Council?" asked the woman, though her voice was nearly identical to the lead's.

"Oh, I'm sure there's a fucking Council. There always is."

"We need the files," said the lead.

"What files?" asked Harrison with insincere innocence.

The agents started tearing his place apart while the lead kept an eye on Harrison.

"It's all lies, y'know," he said. "Most of it. Some of it. I don't know how much, but I know it's enough. But you don't care, do you? Why should you? Why should anyone? There are just the lies underneath the lies we tell ourselves."

The lead said nothing. Didn't twitch a muscle.

Harrison loosened his tie. "I don't suppose I could trouble you for another beer?"

"The files, where are they?" asked the lead. "The documents aren't any good to anyone."

"Then why do you want them?"

The agent frowned very, very slightly, as if processing a foreign language.

"Right. Orders," said Harrison. "They're right. The files aren't any good. Not to me. Not to you. Not to anyone you work for. But I thought—no, I hoped—they'd be useful to somebody. But she's out of the equation. Or in it. Whatever. It was a stupid hope, anyway."

"Tell us where you've hidden them," said the agent.

"It's pointless, all of it, but if you and your Council of Shadowy Masterminds want them, then I think I'd rather keep them. Consider it a fuck-you to the universe. Not to you personally. I don't have anything against you."

Harrison smacked his dry lips. He could go for another beer, but that wasn't happening.

"Is this the part where you threaten to torture me?"

The lead drew his weapon and pointed the pistol between Harrison's eyes. "Unnecessary. We'll find them."

Harrison stared down the barrel and sneered. "Just do it already."

Somebody knocked on his door.

The lead put a finger to his lips.

"Somebody order a pizza?" asked a gruff voice.

The lead shook his head at Harrison, indicating he was supposed to send the pizza boy away. He did, not to save his own life but to save the delivery guy's.

"Wrong address," he shouted.

"Look, I got a pepperoni here that will be taken out of my

tips if I don't deliver it to someone. Don't suppose you'd be interested?"

"No, thanks!"

"I'd eat it myself, but I hate pepperoni. Hate everything about pizza after three years on this job."

"Get the fuck out of here!" shouted Harrison.

"No need to be rude, pal. I'm just trying to work something out."

Harrison shrugged.

The lead nodded to Agent B (or C or D), who moved toward the door. He peered through the peephole. A moment later, the door came crashing in, smashing his face and knocking him back. He went for his gun, but Connie punched him in the throat and broke his hand with a twist. To credit his professionalism, the agent didn't make a sound as she kicked him senseless and to one side.

The other agents went for their guns as Connie shut the door, disappearing in the shadows of the darkened apartment. Shots rang out. Harrison shut his eyes. He should do something, but he'd never been in a firefight. He wasn't that kind of secret agent. He had the training, somewhere buried inside, but by the time he accessed it, the fight was already over.

He opened one eye, just in time to see Connie plant her knuckles in the lead agent's gut, who crumpled in defeat. She took his gun away from him and pushed him into the corner with the other agents.

"How did they *not* shoot you?" asked Harrison.

"That's what they get for wearing sunglasses in the dark," said Connie as she pulled him out of the chair. "We should get out of here."

"Give me a second." Harrison grabbed a beer out of the fridge and followed her. "I didn't know you knew where I lived."

"Detective," she replied. "You're lucky I dropped by when I did."

They boarded the elevator and went down.

"What did they want with you?" she asked.

"I have some files they want."

"And did any of those files have anything to do with me?"

"Sort of. They're about the Engine. Why did you drop by, anyway?"

Connie said, "I wanted to talk about this theory of yours. Not that I buy it."

"It's not my theory," he replied. "And you buy it. Otherwise, you wouldn't be here. Nick of time. Like you do. Like you were made to do, spell or no spell."

"Give me a break. There's nothing magical at work here. I know. I've seen plenty of magic. This is just dumb luck."

"Is it?" He cracked a smile.

She struggled for a rebuttal, but it had worked out like he said. Was it coincidence? Did she end up in adventures because her fate was out of her control, or because she'd been getting involved with them for so long that she couldn't turn off a reflex? Magic had pushed her life one way, but now that it was gone, could she ever be rid of her knack for getting into trouble?

"Give me a break," she said.

"I'm sorry, Verity. Sorry for not telling you the truth sooner. Sorry for treating your life like a playing piece on a chessboard. But I believe in you. I think there's still hope things will work out."

She was halfway to telling him to piss off when the doors opened and a gunman fired twice into the elevator. Connie spun around in a dodge, twisted the attacker's arm around, and elbowed him in the face. She yanked the gun from his hand and fired a bullet into each knee. Professionalism be damned, he shrieked as he fell over.

She swept the lobby for any more signs of trouble, but it was empty.

Harrison stumbled out of the elevator, clutching his gut. Blood spread across his shirt. She braced him as he nearly fell over.

"Well, shit," he gasped.

"How bad is it?"

"Feels bad." The color was already draining from his cheeks.

Connie helped him, his arm over her shoulder, exit the building. Each step was heavier than the last.

Tia opened the car door. "What the hell happened? I thought you were just going to talk to him."

"Guess I wasn't the only one." Connie helped him into the backseat and joined him. "Go. There's a hospital nine blocks from here."

Tia pulled out of her parking space. "There isn't going to be a car chase, is there? Because I can barely parallel park."

Connie opened Harrison's shirt. The bullets had hit him in the stomach, but one wound was near his heart, and it was bleeding a lot. It might have nicked his aorta. She pressed down to staunch the bleeding.

"Fuck. I'm a goner," he wheezed. "Guess you can't save everybody."

It was already a grim truth she'd had to accept. She'd lost people. Good people. She wasn't about to lose another.

"It'll be all right," she said. "I've seen worse."

He smiled painfully. "Connie, there's an accounting office across town. Burns and Waylain. Third floor. Human resources. Filing cabinet. Under E for 'everything.' You'll find what you need there."

"Don't talk. We're almost there."

He coughed. He tried to cough, but it was a wet gurgle as blood went places it wasn't supposed to go.

"Fucking Engine. Guess it's done with me. Gonna have to find a new bolt."

With a sharp gasp, he closed his eyes. His heart kept beating under her hands, but it was faint and growing fainter.

There was no car chase. They dragged Harrison's unconscious, possibly dead body into the emergency room. A team of doctors and nurses loaded him onto a gurney and rolled him away. Connie and Tia slipped away before questions came up.

"That's a lot of blood," said Thelma.

It was everywhere. On their clothes. In the backseat. On Connie's hands. The smell filled the car.

"Damn it," she said.

"I don't think that's ever coming out of my upholstery," said Tia. "We should've used your car."

Gallows humor kept everything from being too real. Connie wasn't in the mood. She'd seen people die before, but this felt different.

If she'd been a little faster, a little less sloppy . . .

"Geez," said Tia. "Poor guy."

She'd been debriefed by Harrison on those occasions when she'd been involved in Connie's adventures. She didn't know him well.

"He didn't deserve that. He'll be all right, won't he?"

Connie rubbed her hands together. The dried blood ground against her palms. "I don't know."

The world was a long string of conditional statements, of grim possibilities diverted by improbable last-minute saves.

The blood on her hands said maybe those saves were a thing of the past.

28

The service station sat in the middle of nowhere, and Connie and Tia parked half a mile down the road from it.

"Are you sure this is the place?" asked Tia.

"If Harrison's notes are right, it's there," replied Connie.

"If he was wrong?"

"Then we look elsewhere, but we have to start somewhere."

"Are we going to walk in and ask them for it?" asked Thelma.

"Not a bad plan," said Connie.

"Sometimes, I wonder if this life of yours hasn't made you reckless," said Thelma.

They drove up to the pumps. A round, attractive woman in a crisp uniform jogged over to the car. "Afternoon, folks. I'm Jill. How can I help you?"

"Full service," remarked Connie. "Just when I thought I'd seen everything."

The attendant smiled with perfect straight and white teeth. "We aim to please, ladies."

"Fill 'er up, please," said Connie, getting out of the car. "Don't suppose you have a public restroom?"

"Yes, ma'am. The finest public facilities in a hundred miles. Cleaned daily by the finest staff this side of Los Alamos, if I do say so myself. And I do." Jill winked.

The store was as thoroughly polished as the second attendant behind the counter. This one was a tall, attractive man with the same Stepford grimace masquerading as a smile. His nametag identified him as Jim.

"Howdy, Jim," said Connie.

Jim tipped his hat at her. "How do, ma'am."

Connie sauntered over to the freezer of sodas and ran her fingers along the glass. Jim's reflection shifted into view as he stood behind her.

"Looking for anything in particular, ma'am?" he asked.

"Oh, just something to wet my whistle, Jimbo."

"It's Jim, ma'am."

"Beg your pardon, Jim. But which one of these triggers the secret entrance?"

He put a hand on her shoulder and squeezed hard. "I'm afraid you aren't authorized for that information, ma'am."

She turned, waved a small, flashing device in front of his face. He let go of her and with a smile said, "Authorization code acknowledged. How may I help you, ma'am?"

"Just wait here."

Connie walked outside. Jill was happily pumping gas, humming to herself.

Tia held up her own reprogramming flasher. "It worked."

"Of course it worked." Connie pocketed her device. "Score one for Harrison's intelligence. Jill, we're going to be infiltrating your secret vault. That okay with you?"

Jill flashed a thumbs-up. "Hunky-dory, ma'am."

"Kind of a weak security system, if you ask me," said Thelma.

"They're top-of-the-line security robots," said Connie. "Jill, demonstrate what you can do."

"Sure thing." Jill lifted the car's back end with one hand. The robot never dropped her smile.

"Formidable," admitted Thelma. "Unless you flash some lights in their face."

"These are optical command transmitters. They only work because Harrison programmed them with the right override code."

"What if he'd been wrong?" asked Thelma. "What would you have done then?"

Connie shrugged. "I'd have thought of something."

Jim was happy to show them the vault elevator hidden behind a potato chip shelf.

"Keep an eye on the place," said Connie as they boarded.

"Will do, ma'am."

"What other dangers are lurking down here?" wondered Thelma aloud. "Automated lasers? Scorpion pits? One of those puzzle tile floors where you have to step on just the right pattern or else everything comes crashing down on our heads?"

"Don't know," replied Connie. "Harrison's notes don't say."

"Those doors could open to a room full of commandos, and you don't even have a weapon? I'm already dead," said Thelma. "What's your excuse for following her into this deathtrap?"

"She'll think of something," said Tia.

The elevator dinged, and its doors opened into a narrow corridor serving as a security checkpoint. A dozen guards lined the hall. They all had their rifles at the ready and pointed at the elevator.

Connie raised her hands and stepped out of the elevator. "Don't shoot."

"This is a stupid plan," said Thelma.

"Give it a minute," said Tia.

A woman in a black trench coat and a severe face stalked down the hallway. A scar ran down her left cheek, and her hair was put up in a tight bun. "Miss Verity, we've been expecting you. They call me the Countess."

"We haven't met before?" asked Connie.

"No, I haven't had the pleasure."

"Are you sure? You look familiar. Although I might be thinking of the Duchess. Or the Contessa. Or the Czarina. You'll forgive me. I run across a lot of stern, royalty-themed dominatrix types."

"The Contessa," agreed Tia. "That's who she reminds me of. I guess there are only so many royalty-themed names to go around."

The Countess raised an eyebrow. If she'd had a monocle, which she really should have, it would've dropped with her lack of amusement.

"So, what now?" asked Connie. "Are you going to threaten us? Shoot us? Lecture us?"

"God, I hope they just shoot us," said Tia. "I've had enough villain lectures to last a lifetime."

The Countess frowned more severely, which seemed like it should've been impossible. "You will be taken to the cells, where you will be locked away for the rest of your lives. There is no escape from this vault. Nothing leaves here without my permission. Nothing and no one."

"Okay. Sounds good."

"You think me boastful? This vault is a labyrinth of such deadly efficiency that even you would be unable to navigate it."

"Do you have laser grids?" asked Tia.

The Countess chuckled and smiled. Her smile barely turned the right corner of her mouth up, and even then, she still looked displeased. "I don't believe you are taking this seriously."

"I'm not," said Connie. "I've been in a dozen inescapable prisons. Two floating in space. Three at the bottom of the ocean. One sat in the center of a pocket universe void where time and space were nullified. I'm sure your vault has some tricks, but I'll beat it, too."

"You're not the same anymore. The rules have changed."

"I haven't."

The Countess laughed. "You have spirit, Miss Verity."

"You'll enjoy breaking it," said Connie.

The Countess's face went blank.

"That's what you were going to say next, right?' asked Connie.

The Countess snarled. "Seize her."

The guards moved forward. One spontaneously fell to the floor.

"What did you do?" asked The Countess.

"Me?" said Connie. "I didn't do anything."

A second guard collapsed.

Connie raised her hands. "Honest. Not me."

The remaining guards toppled over, leaving only the Countess standing. She pulled a pistol from her hip and pointed it at Connie. "Make another move and, orders or not, I will shoot you."

The Countess slapped at her neck. She pulled a tiny dart and studied it with heavy eyes. She was on the ground a moment later.

"I must admit," said Thelma. "That's impressive. How did you do that?"

"I didn't." Connie removed a dart from the Countess's neck and sniffed it. "Damn it."

"Poison?" asked Thelma.

"Sedative. Extracted from a rare flower that blooms on Mount Okuhotaka every nine years."

"That's in Japan, right?" said Tia. "Does that mean ninjas?"

"God, I hope not."

Connie had fought an unreasonably large number of ninjas in her life. They weren't different from most other goons she ran across. They tended to be more annoying than standard-issue mob thugs or jack-booted soldiers. You were going to get a smoke bomb in your face when fighting a ninja. There was no way around that. But she could handle ninjas. Ninjas didn't worry her.

Except this one.

"Hello, Connie," said a smooth voice from behind her. He'd sneaked up on her again. He was one of the few who could consistently.

She swore under her breath. Of all the secret vaults in all the world, he'd had to walk into hers. The ninja, wrapped in black, winked at her before vanishing in a puff of smoke, and she had no doubt he'd taken the caretaker spell with him.

onnie and Tia caught a flight to Hong Kong. Connie didn't have a lot to go on, but it was the ninja's last known home address.

"His name is Hiro Yukimura," said Connie. "And he's the best. He gets in. He gets out. And nobody ever knows he's there. Nobody knows what he looks like. Not even the people who hire him. And there's no place he can't infiltrate, nothing he can't steal."

"I thought ninjas were all about killing people," said Tia.

"The art of stealth has many uses. Thievery, bodyguard work, intelligence-gathering, corporate espionage, pizza delivery. Anything someone needs done, there's probably a ninja out there that specializes in it. The truth is that the assassin-type ninjas are probably the worst at stealth, because they want to be seen. Their reputation depends on it.

"If an assassination is too stealthy, then there's no proof it was actually done by an assassin. Unscrupulous people, the kind that hire ninja assassins, will often try to use that as a loophole. Maybe the target died via flawless ninja execution. Maybe he just keeled over on his own. Why should anyone pay for an assassination that could've simply been a fortuitous accident?"

"I would think not paying ninjas would be a bad move," said Tia.

"And you would be right. Many an employer wound up dead after failing to pay up, but ninjas are like everybody else doing a job. They want to get paid. The assassin variety stopped being so subtle, started using exotic poisons, daggers with clan logos carved in the handles, leaving little scraps of paper with fortune cookie sayings scrawled across them. Problem solved."

"I thought fortune cookies were Chinese."

"They're an American invention. And ninjas aren't strictly Japanese anymore. They're more inclusive. It's a requirement as part of a global economy."

"Good for them. Though I didn't expect it to be so mercenary. I thought there were honor codes and ancient traditions."

"There's that too, but ninjas have to eat, just like everyone else. Even the Pale Oni clan, though they do subsist on shadows and forsaken souls."

"But if this ninja is so good, why did he save us?" asked Tia.

"He must have had a reason," said Connie.

Hiro lived in a penthouse atop one of Hong Kong's most prestigious high-rises.

"Little ostentatious for a ninja, isn't it?" asked Tia upon seeing the building.

"He's an ostentatious kind of guy," replied Connie.

Tia hadn't asked how Connie knew the address. Tia likely attributed it to Connie's skills as a detective, and she was happy to let that assumption continue.

The doorwoman wasn't surprised to see them. She opened the private elevator for them.

"Miss Verity, you've been expected. Go right on up."

"Another trap?" wondered Thelma.

"Hiro doesn't do ambushes. He's the cut-and-run type."

She tried not to sound bitter about that.

The elevator doors opened to Hiro's penthouse. The furnishings were impeccable, likely coming with the place. The personal touches were found in the collection of knickknacks and world treasures, a virtual bragging room for the world's greatest thief on display for his own ego. Most were worth a small fortune, except for those worth a large fortune. Tia examined an urn of South American origin.

"Lovely, isn't it?" said Hiro from the sofa, where no one had been sitting only moments before.

Tia jumped and jostled the urn. It tumbled off its glass pedestal. Connie caught it before it hit the floor.

"Nice reflexes." Hiro was a beautiful man. To describe him otherwise would've been a waste of time. No adjectives could properly suit his charms, his jawline, his smoldering dark eyes, his trim, athletic grace that was obvious while merely sitting there.

Connie had forgotten how goddamn striking he was. She tingled in places she sure as hell didn't want to tingle, reminded of things they'd shared in the past. But she hid it.

God, she hoped she hid it.

Hiro smiled at her. "I picked that up for myself while acquiring the crown of Lloque Yupanqui for a client of mine. It's priceless."

"Sorry, you just surprised me," said Tia.

"Don't apologize." Connie returned the urn to its pedestal. "Hiro has a tendency to surprise people."

"It's a bad habit," he said.

"Bad habit?" She laughed. "You get off on it."

Hiro glided across the floor like a ghost. He didn't even leave footprints in the carpeting. "You know me too well."

She did, and she sometimes hated herself for it.

"I know you don't get seen. You're invisible."

He frowned. "Oh, I hate that. People call me invisible like it's a superpower I have. Do you know how much easier my life would be if I could actually become invisible? Although it would take all the fun out of it. It also grossly underestimates all the hard work I put into my trade. A talent, fostered by years of training and skill."

"I get it, Hiro. Either way, you're the best."

"I am indeed. Considering my reputation, you can understand how much I was hoping to see you again." He put a hand on her cheek. "You were always the one that got away."

"Wait. You two were a thing?" asked Tia.

"You could say that."

Connie pulled his hand away. "Knock it off, Hiro. I didn't come all this way to fall victim to your charms."

"You always were resistant to them. It is perhaps why I've always been drawn to you. I've known more beautiful woman, more accomplished, wealthier, smarter—"

"Stop. You'll make me blush."

"But you, Connie, were the one that I almost considered permanently partnering up with."

"But then you decided you'd rather take the crown jewels for yourself and leave me dangling over a crocodile pit."

Hiro winced. "Mistakes were made."

"You're that guy?" asked Tia. "This is the guy that did that to you? Wow, she was really pissed about that. For like a year."

Connie grunted.

"Oh, I mean, not a big deal," said Tia.

"I'd forgive him," said Thelma from Connie's pocket.

"So I was hoping," he said. "But if you've come for revenge, I submit myself to whatever you have in mind to demonstrate my remorse."

"Your remorse isn't necessary," said Connie. "I've moved on. I'm seeing someone."

"Oh, I hope it isn't too serious."

"It's serious," she replied. "Serious enough."

He didn't say anything. It was his deadliest manipulation. He could look at her, saying nothing, compelling her to fill the silence.

"Two dates," she said. "Sort-of dates. But really good ones. He's a good guy. Not the kind of guy to betray me when a better offer comes along."

"Two sort-of dates." He swept her in his arms. "How do you know? I have at least gotten the betrayal out of the way. Several betrayals, in fact. I've learned my lesson. I'd be a fool to throw you aside again."

Connie pivoted, and Hiro went tumbling to the floor. He flipped with impossible grace to land on his feet. He didn't even spill his drink.

"That's the fire I always adored," he said with a smile.

"We are not getting back together. I'm here on business. Why did they want me to see you?"

"Who?"

"Don't play dumb. Your employers, the people who paid you to steal the destiny."

"They didn't."

"You weren't supposed to be seen?"

"I'm never supposed to be seen," he said. "That's why people hire me."

"You really did do it just so I'd track you down?"

He nodded. "I thought I'd made that clear."

"It's kind of sweet," said Tia.

"Tell me how sweet you think it is after you've nearly been eaten by a crocodile," said Connie. "I hope you didn't make a mistake, Hiro. The people you're working for don't screw around, and if they find out, they could consider you a loose end."

"Hmm." He sipped his martini. "That would explain the ninja lurking just outside the window."

"Ninjas? Where?" Tia studied the view. They were several dozen floors up, and the climb up the sheer building face would've been impossible.

"Don't bother looking," said Hiro. "She's almost as good as me. Not quite, but then again, who is? Do you really think she's been sent to silence me?"

He sat in his sofa, twirled his drink, looking for all the world that he was commenting on something happening in a far-off place.

"How many are there?" asked Connie.

"Just the one."

"Shit." Multiple ninjas she could handle. But one was always trouble.

"Get away from the window," she told Tia. "Stay in that corner over there." Connie pointed to the sword over the fireplace. "Is this real?"

"Of course. Stole it myself. Legend says it was the sword given to the Emperor by the Ruler of Heaven to banish the evil Oni King."

She took down the sword and checked the quality of the blade. The katana hissed like a snake as she drew it from the sheath. "Any idea of her clan?"

Connie tested its balance, performed a few practice swings. She was rusty. For a while, she'd been one of the deadliest swordswomen alive, but the problem with having so many skills was that it was difficult to stay focused on all of them. She could still beat most anyone in a duel, and she had little doubt she could defeat an entire army of ninjas with a good sword and one arm tied behind her back.

But one ninja. Ninjas didn't screw around when they sent out one.

"Any idea of her clan?" she asked.

"Red Shadows, I believe." Hiro put his drink to his lips and ogled her. "You always did know how to handle a sword."

She rolled her eyes. She'd never been an easy victim to his charms, but now she saw him as vaguely creepy and a master of tactless innuendo. He was handsome as hell, living a life of intrigue, but he was also a self-centered, adrenaline-fueled jerk.

"Was I really that stupid and shallow, or have you gotten smarmier?" She tossed him the second sword hanging over the fireplace.

He caught it with a raised eyebrow and a coy grin. "I'm told smarm is part of what people love about me." He put the weapon on the coffee table. "You know I was never very good with violence."

"But you're a ninja," said Tia.

"Ninja-slash-thief," he replied. "Not ninja-slash-assassin. Similar basic training, but entirely different specializations. I don't fight my way out of trouble. I disappear."

"That's probably why they sent a ninja-slash-assassin to keep you from doing that," said Connie.

"Probably. It's a fortunate thing you're here, then."

"Yeah. Fortunate." Connie twirled her sword. "You might even say the nick of time."

A window shattered, and a crimson blur leapt into the room. Her arm swung out, hurling a dagger at Hiro. The blade punctured the chair where he'd been sitting only seconds before.

He stood behind Connie now. "Hey, that's genuine leather."

"Wow. He is good," said Tia.

The Shadow assassin, cloaked in a red outfit (said to be stained with the blood of demons), stood motionless. Her hand rested on her sword, undrawn. A mask like an ogre's face hid everything but her eyes and short black hair.

Hiro threw several darts at the ninja. She sidestepped, dodging most and deflecting one with her sword. The move was so fast, it was almost impossible to see the blade had ever left its scabbard.

"That usually works." He crouched behind Connie. "If you want me, you'll have to go through her."

The Shadow said nothing, but Connie could see the disbelief in the assassin's eyes. It asked why Connie would consider sacrificing her life to protect a thief and a scoundrel, and she didn't have a good answer for that. It'd serve Hiro right. He'd never outright tried to kill her, but he'd left her in the lurch often enough.

But this wasn't about her baggage or revenge, as sweet as it might be.

"Oh, all right. Yes, I'm afraid that's true."

She adopted the proper stance and nodded at the assassin.

The assassin drew her sword and bowed to Connie.

"Oh, cool," said Thelma. "Ninja fight."

The Shadow sprang over the sofa. Connie moved to meet her. Their blades clashed once, twice. The blades sang like bells of death. A third strike was muffled by the loser getting stabbed through the heart. The assassin died without making a sound, falling in a heap on the floor.

The sofa, coffee table, a lamp, and a case of Fabergé eggs all fell apart, victims of the dance of blades that had been so fast as to be unseen.

"My eggs," said Hiro.

"Your arm," said Tia.

"Yes, your arm as well." He knelt beside the broken bejeweled eggs. "I really liked these."

Connie had taken a glancing wound, though one that could have easily taken off her arm. Blood spread across her torn sleeve. She hadn't felt the strike. She checked herself for any other wounds she might have. It wasn't impossible that the ninja had killed her and she hadn't realized it yet. A skilled-enough ninja assassin could master the art of the invisible wound, undetectable until it did in the target. It wasn't a technique of much use for the necessary high visibility of ninja assassins for hire, but it wasn't impossible that Connie's head might fall off in her sleep tonight.

"That's it?" asked Thelma. "Three hits? Where was all

the flipping? The jumping? The back-and-forth struggle?"

"I have to agree that's disappointing," said Tia.

"Ninjas assassins don't screw around," said Connie. "It's not about putting on a show. It's about kill or be killed."

"Maybe so, but she could've at least given us a backflip."

The Red Shadow ninja's corpse vanished in a puff of smoke. All the best ninjas were self-cleaning.

"I knew you could handle it," said Hiro. "We always were a great team. I take care of the thievery while you handle the dirty work that comes along."

"You forgot the betrayal. That's your department too," said Connie.

"Oh, it was only once or twice. Harmless, really."

"Three times." She grabbed him by the collar, kept the sword by her side. "And don't even think about disappearing."

He flashed her that devil-may-care smile of his. "Wouldn't dream of it."

"Why did they send a Red Shadow assassin after you?" she asked, keeping tight hold on him.

"As you said, they must have known I let you see me and thought to eliminate a loose end. I don't know anything. Really."

This time, she didn't say anything, letting the silence surround him.

"I might have been curious," he said, "once I found out you were involved. I suppose I might have followed the pickup agent after delivering the package."

"Where did this agent go? And don't pretend you have an honor code preventing you from telling me."

"I'll be more than happy to tell you," he said, "but on one condition. I'll go with you to retrieve it."

She let him go. "Why?"

"Because you'll need me. You're an exceptional infiltration artist, but I've done some reconnaissance. You're not going to be able to get it without me."

"And what's the price?" asked Connie.

"No price. Happy to do it. Eager to, actually. If helping you steal something will prove my sincere devotion, then I can think of no one better suited to the job."

"You don't expect me to trust you."

"Not today, but eventually, yes. You'll see. I've changed."

"I wouldn't bring him along," said Tia. "He's up to something."

"I would," said Thelma.

Connie could never read Hiro. He always had that smile on his face. Mischievous and playful, like a child who relished his ability to get away with anything as long as he could fake a sincere apology later.

"If you betray me this time . . ."

"My betrayal days are behind me." He grinned in that infuriating, infatuating way. "I swear."

"If you betray me again," she said, "I will smash every valuable thing you've ever collected, including, but not limited to, your Picassos. And, no, I didn't say return to their original owners. You'd just steal them back."

Hiro paled. It was good to see a crack in his sly demeanor. "But that's monstrous."

She kicked a pedestal and the ancient vase rattled around, nearly falling off. The terror in his eyes pleased her more than she expected.

"Hell hath no fury . . . ," she said with a malignant smile.

30

They took a flight to Eastern Europe, ended up in a late-night parked-car stakeout of a tall, plain building in Leningrad or Kiev or some other exotic locale for no other reason than that exotic locales came with adventuring. Except all the old world cities, the alien civilizations, the magical glens, the incredible and the mundane, and every possible combination thereof blended together. Connie didn't pay attention anymore and could autopilot her way through a plane flight, boat ride, or camel caravan with the best of them.

She only cared about getting in, grabbing what they needed, and getting out.

"I'll just pop in and grab it," said Hiro.

"Security won't be a problem?" asked Tia.

"I won't dignify that with an answer."

"Here's what I don't get," said Tia. "You had the spell. You wanted Connie to find you. Why did you give it to these guys if you were just going to steal it back?"

"Are you suggesting that I should have broken a contract with an employer?"

"But you're stealing the enchantment now."

"My original deal was to bring them the spell, and I did so. There was no mention of not stealing it again."

"That's some shaky ethics you've got there. I'm just saying you could've saved yourself a step."

"I could have, but where's the challenge in that? And I refuse to get paid for not delivering things I've been employed to steal. Now, if you'll excuse me . . ."

"Be careful, Hiro," said Connie. "They might be expecting you."

"That only makes it more interesting," he said with a wink.

"Do you need us to do anything?" asked Connie. "Maybe cause a distraction?"

Hiro was already gone, vanished from the backseat without opening the doors or jostling the car.

"Okay, that's just ridiculous. Although I can see why you have trust issues. Speaking of which, are you certain we can trust him?" asked Tia.

"Of course we can't trust him," said Connie. "He's betrayed me three times. I'm sure he'll do it again when the opportunity presents itself. But we'll deal with that when the time comes. But Hiro is a compulsive thief and he has a thing for me. That should be enough to keep him on our side for now."

"This is the guy who gave you your baggage?"

"No. My life gave me my baggage. Hiro is just one of the forms that baggage took."

"It's pretty screwed up," said Tia. "Sure, he's handsome and charming, but I guess I can't blame you for having trust issues if this is your healthiest relationship."

"It's not my healthiest," Connie said. "Just my longest. In an adventure, everyone has their own secret goals. You learn to live with it And I know Hiro. He'll leave us in the lurch when it suits his purposes, but until then, he'll be on our side. And when he does vanish, it'll be in a relatively safe position."

"Safe. Like dangling over a crocodile pit?" asked Tia.

"In his defense, it was a small crocodile pit, and the crocs weren't very hungry."

"Only you would make that distinction. I'm not just talking about the betrayal, although that's an obvious problem. I'm simply observing that your longest relationship was with a guy who can literally vanish in an instant. That's a metaphor for something."

"I've always been lousy with relationships," said Connie. "That's no secret. Comes with the life."

"That's bull. Nobody is making you date guys like that. You're choosing to."

"I've dated regular guys. It doesn't work out."

"Whatever you say," said Tia.

Connie didn't like Tia's tone but chose to ignore it. Tia didn't press.

"I think she's on to something," said Thelma.

"Nobody asked you," replied Connie.

"We're stuck waiting here," said Thelma. "Seems like a good time for some honest self-examination."

Connie's thumb hovered over Thelma's clicker.

"You can shut me up, but—"

CLICK

For an extra measure, Connie shoved Thelma in the glove compartment.

"I wouldn't bring it up, but I am your friend and you are trying to change," said Tia.

"I am changing," said Connie. "I'm dating a normal guy now."

"You've dated normal guys before. Don't take this the wrong way, but you were never really into them."

"Trevor and I were getting pretty serious before he was eaten by a space slug."

"That's not the way I remember it. Just a week before, I started seeing the signs."

"What signs?"

Tia laughed. "You seriously can't see them? Aren't you a master detective? How can you be so oblivious to your own patterns? Guess you're too close to it."

Connie eyed a pressure point on Tia's neck. A little press with the thumb, and Tia would be unconscious for about an hour.

"I don't want to have this conversation."

"That probably means you should be having it, and before you knock me out with some secret kung fu move you learned in Shangri-La or from Bruce Lee's ghost, you should know that's not how normal adults deal with situations."

One little press.

Connie squeezed the steering wheel. "Okay. What patterns?"

"Whenever you date a normal guy, you get bored," said Tia. "I get it. I get bored with most normal guys, and I haven't done a tenth of the stuff you've done. But it's deeper than that. You get all nitpicky."

"I do not."

"A week before that slug got Trevor, you were complaining about his taste in movies and how he liked his coffee."

"His favorite Bill Murray movie was *Ghostbusters II*."

"Okay, that's a big strike. I'll give you that. Still, you always find a reason to get rid of the ordinary guys, provided they aren't considerate enough to be devoured by a dinosaur before that's necessary."

"Jeff. And he wasn't eaten. He was trampled to death."

"Poor Jeff," said Tia. "Poor He's-Always-Humming-All-The-Fucking-Time Jeff."

"But he was humming all the fucking time."

"And before Humming Jeff, there was Too-Many-Cats Bill—"

"Four cats. I draw the line at three."

"—and Likes-The-Beatles-More-Than-The-Monkees Larry. Which isn't even a flaw, because every fucking person on this planet likes the Beatles more than the Monkees."

"I'll have you know that there's an alternate reality where Mike Nesmith is a pop culture god. And really, the Beatles were never the same after they replaced Ringo."

"I thought it was Paul."

Connie chuckled. "What idiot believes that?"

"We're getting off topic. You have to admit you aren't great with ordinary guys, and it isn't always their fault."

"Maybe."

"Relationships aren't simple. Not friendships. Not dating. Not any of it. Do you think it's always been easy being your friend? There were times I thought about not returning your calls."

Connie had also considered leaving Tia behind now and then. It would be safer for Tia that way. That's what Connie told herself. The truth was that it sometimes seemed easier to abandon any pretense of a regular life. There were times when Tia and Mom and Dad had seemed like more of an obligation than anything else. Dead weight to be left behind while Connie crossed the Sahara Desert or explored the deepest, darkest regions of the Amazon jungle.

Adventures were thrilling, addicting, but exhausting. Saving the world only mattered because she was reminded now and then that the world was worth saving, and it was in the quiet moments, whether relaxing under the waterfalls of Venus or meeting Tia for a nice lunch, that Connie found those reminders.

"I'm sorry. I didn't mean to make you feel bad," said Tia. "I know you're under a lot of pressure."

"You and Dad and Mom, you keep me sane. I need you. I need normal. I'm just not very good at it."

"You're not the first woman to have a thing for drama and bad boys," said Tia. "Doesn't mean you can't change."

"I'm working on it," said Connie.

"My ears are burning," said Hiro. Somehow back in the car.

"Goddamn, give a girl a little warning next time," said Tia.

"My apologies."

But he wasn't sorry. He loved doing it. He lived for it. It was why he was so good at it. It was no wonder he vanished whenever things got serious. It wasn't the crown jewels or thrills that drove him to it. It was his nature. He was a shadow, and trying to date a shadow was stupid.

He flashed a cocky smile, and Connie's heart skipped a beat despite herself.

"I'm working on it," she mumbled to herself.

He held up a metal tube about a foot long. "One caretaker enchantment, as ordered."

"That was fast," said Tia.

"Yes, it was," he replied. "Sometimes, I even impress myself."

Tia took the tube. "Are you sure it's in here? Last time I saw it, it was in a little metal square. You could fit it in your pocket."

"I'm sure," he said.

"You wouldn't mind if we double-checked?" She turned the lid.

"Don't—" said Connie.

The tube hissed. Tia passed out. Connie jumped out of the car and covered her mouth. Something stung her neck. Her vision blurred. She pulled the dart from her neck.

"Sorry," said Hiro, that smug smile on his face. "Just being practical."

She swung to take his head off, but he danced out of reach of her sluggish reflexes. She fell over and would've hit the pavement if he hadn't caught her. She struggled. In her imagination, she was fighting to the end, but she knew she was squirming in his arms like a dying fish.

She went unconscious.

Connie awoke with a headache. "Goddamn it."

She took in her surroundings. It wasn't what she expected. The conference room had a single large table and two dozen chairs taking up most of it. There was nothing especially menacing about it other than the five security agents standing around in gray suits. They looked familiar, but they always did.

Across the table, at the far end of the room, a man and a woman with flawless olive skin and indeterminate ethnicity, wearing matching red suits, sat. Behind them, more agents. Beside the agents, Hiro stood smiling that goddamn smirk of his.

"What was that about trusting your ex again?" asked Tia from the chair next to her.

"I love you, honeybunch," said Hiro, "but I do have to watch out for myself."

"Don't call me that," Connie said. "Don't ever call me that. We had a deal."

"Deals change," he said.

"And all that talk about earning my trust?"

"I meant it when I said it. But then again, I always do. It's probably why I'm so convincingly sincere. I had every intention of acquiring the item for you, but while I was here, I realized that it was possible you wouldn't be interested in taking me back. If so, the next time a Red Shadow ninja found me, I might be in serious trouble."

"So, you double-crossed me. Again."

"How's the saying go? It's my nature."

"I can't believe you fell for this guy," said Tia.

"I was young and stupid," replied Connie. "And Hiro has always been a blind spot for me."

"Pity," said the male twin. His long, silver hair framed his face, while his twin was practically bald. "But it just proves your unworthiness."

"It's inconceivable that you should carry the caretaker as long as you did," said the female twin.

"Aren't you supposed to introduce yourself?" asked Connie. "Or should I just refer to you as Thing One and Thing Two?"

"I am Harmony," said the woman.

"I am Equity," said the man.

"Of course you are. Here's the part where you reveal your master plan, I assume."

"Your ignorance does you disservice," said Harmony.

"Why are villains always so formal?" asked Thelma.

"They're compensating for being colossal assholes," explained Connie. "What's your interest in the spell?"

Equity said, "It is our destiny to carry it for the glorious future of humanity."

"There has always been a flaw with the caretaker's hosts. Up to now, they have been chosen through educated guesses. But we shall be the first host bred and designed to be perfect."

"Right," said Connie. "Eugenics nuts. Run into plenty of those in my day. Why wait until now to get your hands on the spell? You're a little old for this, aren't you?"

Harmony said, "We were grown and artificially aged by the most brilliant genetic engineers the world has ever known.

"We are younger than we look," said Equity.

"Vat babies, huh?"

The Twins were not amused.

"We find that term derogatory," said Equity.

"We prefer nontraditional incubatants," said Harmony.

"Hey, that's your call. How old are you, then? Chronologically. If you don't mind me asking."

"Seven years old," said Harmony.

"The age when the destiny can be most successfully implanted," said Equity.

"Jeez, you're just kids."

"We are not," said Harmony.

"Are too," said Connie.

"Are not."

"Are too."

Equity's face flushed. "Oh, shut up."

"Take it easy, Junior," said Connie. "If you were made in a lab, where are the scientists who made you?"

The Twins smiled with sinister delight. Harmony said,

"They served their purpose. We saw no need to keep them around once we were ready."

"Let me guess. You got sick of having a bedtime."

"There might have been some . . . disputes," said Harmony.

"We are perfect. What right does any imperfect being have to restrict our TV time?" added Equity.

"And broccoli." His sister grimaced. "Distasteful scourge."

"I get it," replied Connie. "When I was your age, if I'd had the power, I probably would've executed Mom and Dad for daring to get between me and *Jem and the Holograms*. You seem like nice kids."

"No, they don't," said Tia.

"No, they really don't," added Thelma.

"We are not children," said Equity. "We are perfect beings."

"That's not a childish thing to believe at all," whispered Tia. But it was a stage whisper, meant to be heard by all.

"You are fools," said Equity.

"Somebody needs a nap," said Connie.

The Twins glared. Their faces reddened. They were either about to order everyone shot or start crying. Connie defused the situation by getting the conversation back on track.

"Why haven't you implanted the spell yet?"

The Twins calmed.

"Implantation is a difficult process," said Equity.

"And there's the additional difficulty of one spell between us," said Harmony.

"Don't want to share your toys?" said Connie.

"Sibling rivalry," said Tia.

"There's no rivalry," said Equity. "We are both perfect."

"But one of you is more perfect," said Connie.

"If you're trying to turn us against each other," said Harmony, "you're wasting your time. And ours."

"All right. You're both perfect. Good for you."

"We do have a question for you, Ms. Verity," said Harmony. "After surrendering the spell, why are you seeking it out now?"

"Change of plans," replied Connie. "I don't know if I buy any of this mumbo jumbo about a cosmic balance, but I figure that if people like you want it, it's better off in other hands."

"People like us?" the Twins asked together.

"Evil geniuses. Criminal masterminds. Inbred eugenic egomaniacs." Connie leaned back in her chair and kicked her feet up on the table. "No offense."

The Twins smiled without amusement.

"We are the masterwork of generations of careful genetic selection," said the brother. "We are the ultimate potential of the human race."

"Heard it," said Connie. "And it's always bullshit. There is no ultimate version of a human being. You think you're perfect? Nobody is. Except for maybe Professor Perfect. I've worked with that guy, and let me tell you something, he's pretty damn close. But even he sucks at crossword puzzles."

The Twins scowled like two children being told they weren't getting dessert.

"You dare to speak to us like that? You're nothing more

than an incubator," said Equity. "Now that you've done your job, you would be wise to scurry off before we decide you're of no more use to us."

"If I was of no more use, I'd be dead already," said Connie. "You can stop with the threats."

The Twins nodded to an agent, who moved toward Connie.

"I wouldn't if I were you," she said.

"Your bravado is pointless," said Equity. "Even if you were to somehow defeat every guard in this room, there are dozens more just on the other side of the door. Even you, with your legendary martial arts abilities, can't hope to defeat them all."

"Dozens, you say? Yeah, that's a bit much, even for me. And I have Tia to look after too. She'll only slow me down."

Tia sighed. "Sorry."

"Don't worry about it."

"We have to say we're greatly disappointed in how easy it was to capture you," he said. "You'd have to be foolish to trust Hiro Yukimura after his history of betrayal."

"Yes, I would have to be," said Connie with a smile. "Wouldn't I?"

The Twins glanced around the room. Hiro was nowhere to be seen.

"Where did he go?" asked Harmony.

"Beats the hell out of me," replied Connie. "I could never keep track of him."

An alarm sounded.

"The caretaker destiny!" realized the Twins together.

"Let me guess. It's the most heavily guarded item in this building? Until you decided to pull most of your security here to keep an eye on me."

The Twins ran from the room with a security detachment in tow. They locked the boardroom and left five guards to watch their prisoners.

"Hiro didn't betray you?" asked Tia. "He was only using you as a distraction?"

"It wasn't difficult to convince the Twins he planned on betraying me, considering how often he's done it in the past."

"It was a fake betrayal? You could've warned me."

"I didn't know. Not until he called me honeybunch. That's our code for a false betrayal."

"What's your code for a genuine betrayal?"

"No code for that."

"How do we get out of here?"

"We wait for Hiro."

"And if he doesn't show? What if he lied about the fake betrayal? What if it was a genuine betrayal this time, and he decides to leave us in hanging?"

"He won't."

"How do you know that? He's a narcissistic ninja thief who has betrayed you before."

"Yes, but this time, he used the code. He's never lied about it before."

"The guy who has betrayed you multiple times never lied before?"

"Not with the code."

"Oh, well, he used the code. Why do I have any doubts?" Tia slapped the table. "That's crazy."

She turned to an agent. "It's not me, right? That's crazy."

The agent nodded with a slight smirk. "Yes."

"I get it," said a second agent. "He's sneaky but not dishonest."

"There's a difference?" asked the first agent.

"Some people you can't ever trust, but if someone is honest about being untrustworthy, there's some wiggle room."

"Sounds messed-up to me," said the first agent.

"Relationships don't always fit into neat little packages," said the second. "They can be complicated."

"Thank you," said Connie.

The guards took a vote, and it was decided four to one against Hiro coming back for Connie and Tia.

"What about you?" Connie asked Tia.

"I don't even know anymore," replied Tia.

The lights went out, followed by a brief scuffle in the dark. Somebody bumped into Tia's chair, knocking her to the floor. She elected to stay down there until the lights came back on.

The guards lay unconscious around Connie. Hiro offered Tia a hand up.

"Told you he'd come back," said Connie with a grin.

"I'm hurt you would ever doubt me," he replied. "I did use the code word."

"Did you get it?" asked Connie.

He held up a small metallic square. "I'm almost insulted

you had to ask. Admittedly, it was under heavy guard. Enough to give even a thief of my abilities some pause. You made a wonderful distraction, as always."

He flashed his trademark devil-may-care grin, and Connie blushed. "Knock it off."

"Hate to break this up, but how do you plan on getting us out of here?" asked Tia.

"That's the beauty of my plan. When I was after the spell, most of the guards were here. Now that I have it, most of the guards are so busy looking for it, a getaway will be child's play."

It was.

Hiro led them through a series of hallways and ventilation ducts with nary a guard in sight the whole time. Security personnel could be heard. Once or twice, they were visible as shadows or muffled conversations on the other side of walls. But never once were Hiro and his charges close to being caught. Tia was turned around by the time they made it out of the building.

She was surprised to find their car was still parked in front.

"They moved it," he explained. "I moved it back."

"You're the best, Hiro," said Connie.

"So they tell me. Who am I to argue?"

"No offense," said Thelma, "but you two have a very screwed-up relationship."

"Yet we manage to make it work," he replied.

"Don't get any ideas," said Connie, but she was smiling when she said it.

31

They found a hotel—a nice one—and booked two rooms. One for Connie and Tia. Another for Hiro.

"If you need me, for anything, I'll be right across the hall," he said.

"Thanks. We'll keep that in mind." Tia shut the door to their room. "Can you believe that guy? He uses us as bait and then can't stop hitting on you?"

Smiling to herself, Connie lay on the bed.

"Don't tell me you're still into him?" asked Tia.

"No. Of course not." She couldn't stop smiling. "But you have to admit we do make a good team."

"I know that look."

"What look?"

"The *I'm about to do something stupid* look."

"I have a look for that?"

"Yes, you do. And it's always right before you do something you really shouldn't do. Like try to hog-tie a triceratops or charge a bunch of guys with machine guns."

"I don't see any dinosaurs or machine guns around here," said Connie.

"Don't you? Maybe Hiro isn't dangerous in that way, although he sort of kind of is, given your history," said Tia. "But whatever on-again, off-again thing you have going on with him, it's not healthy."

"Probably not," agreed Connie, "but it is fun."

"What about Byron?"

"I don't know. It's really not that serious yet."

Tia groaned. "I guess you can take the girl out of the adventure, but have a harder time taking the adventure out of the girl."

Connie scowled at the ceiling. "I have a problem, don't I?"

"Your only problem is that you mistake drama for passion. You wouldn't be the first to do that."

"It's worse than that," said Connie. "I don't know if I'm cut out for an ordinary life. Can I be a regular person after everything I've seen and done? With Hiro, everything makes sense. Everything fits. I know it's self-destructive, but I know where I stand with him. He belongs in the chaos that is my life."

"You mean your old life," said Tia.

Connie didn't respond.

"Don't tell me you've changed your mind already," asked Tia.

Connie pulled the pillow over her face and yelled, then tossed it across the room. "I don't know. I didn't give it much of a chance. I was worried I might get bored, but it was nice. But I keep wondering if it'll keep being nice or if I'll eventually get bored. I'm just thinking it might be better to keep my options open."

"You want an ordinary life except when you don't want it."

"Is that so bad?"

"Aren't you supposed to be able to have both?" asked Tia. "Isn't that part of the spell?"

"Never really worked out that way."

"Because of the spell or because of you?"

Connie didn't deny it. She'd usually blamed her spell, but more and more, that felt like an easy excuse. She had trouble with ordinary life, but everybody did. Not everyone had the option of retreating from the ordinary by plunging headlong into unknown dangers.

"What if I'm too screwed-up?"

"Do you think I'm particularly happy with the way my life has turned out?" asked Tia. "Lousy job. Hardly any friends. Kidnapped by pirates and space aliens on a semi-regular basis. It's not what I imagined for myself."

"I'm sorry."

Tia said, "I don't need your apology. It's not always about you. The pirates and aliens and thugs, that's your fault. But the other stuff, I fucked that up just fine on my own. But what's worse is that a lot of it was out of my hands. Maybe most of it. That's why it sucks."

Connie sat up. "I'm sorry. Not about your life, but that I'm not always a very good friend."

"Nobody's perfect, Connie. I get the appeal. Hiro is

handsome and suave. Yes, a little bit of a swaggering jerk, too, but the stupid teenage girl in us can't help but find something alluring about that. Doesn't hurt that he actually is good at what he does, but you've already tried it with him. It doesn't work with you two. But do what you want. You're going to do it anyway."

"What if I'm not good at it?" said Connie. "Being ordinary? What if I screw it all up?"

"You will," replied Tia. "If you really want to be a regular person, screw-ups are what define us. We make mistakes. The good thing is that usually the fate of the world isn't in the balance. Just our own messed-up lives and those few people around us."

It sounded like a lot of responsibility to Connie. Saving the world, risking death, those things were straightforward. Kill or be killed. Do what needed to be done. But in a regular life, the consequences weren't so simple. The dangers, more vague and difficult to define.

She was loath to admit it, but they frightened her. More than dinosaur attacks, ruthless mob goons, and an army of killer robots combined.

Thelma vibrated on the table beside Connie. She picked up the pen and clicked it.

"I'd sure as hell sleep with him," said Thelma. "Life is short, and he's gorgeous."

"Nobody asked you." Connie clicked Thelma quiet and shoved her in a drawer.

"What are we going to do with the enchantment now?" asked Tia.

Connie took the destiny in her hands. It vibrated as she touched it. It lacked a visible seam. She wasn't certain how to get it out of there.

The square flashed, emitting a few particles of light. They drifted upward and into her body, drawn by the scraps of enchantment clinging within her. Several streams of barely visible light flowed down her arm. The case burned brighter, transferring itself into her.

She threw it across the room. It bounced off the wall and fell to the floor and stopped glowing.

"Why'd you stop?" asked Tia. "It was working."

"If I take that back, I'll never get rid of it," said Connie.

"I thought you needed it back if you're going to fix the universe."

"I don't know. All that matters right now is that we have it. If I need it, I can always take it back later. In the meantime, I want you to hold it for me."

Tia bent down next to the destiny. She didn't touch it. "I don't think I should."

"I trust you."

Tia picked up the destiny, held it in delicate fingers. "Don't blame me if I fuck it up."

"You won't fuck it up. But if you do, I'll be there to catch you."

"Promise?"

"Don't I always?"

32

Connie couldn't resist Hiro. She never could. He only had to wait. He was surprised at how quickly she gave in, though. She knocked on his room door. He checked his hair and his breath. Perfect. As always. He winked at the mirror. It was a shame his profession was about being unseen, but these were the sacrifices one made for greatness.

"I knew you'd be over," he said as he opened the door.

It wasn't Connie.

"We need to talk," said Tia.

"Do we?"

"Yes, we do. Can I come in?"

"Most certainly." He stepped aside.

Tia studied the flower petals on the bed. Barry White drifted through the room.

"Expecting company?" she asked.

He smiled at her. "Preparation is one of the seven ninjally virtues."

"Ninjally?"

"It's a word. Secret ninja word."

She laughed. "You're making that up."

"The way of the ninja is deception. I'll never tell."

Tia sat on the bed. "You're charming. I'll give you that. This man-of-mystery, daring-rogue thing doesn't hurt either."

"Why do you think I became the greatest ninja-slash-thief in the world? The ladies love it."

She pointed to a pair of drinks on the end table. "What's this?"

"Just a little something to lighten the mood later."

She took the one of the drinks and had a sip.

He shrugged. "Just a little concoction Connie and I shared in Morocco once. I was hoping it would bring up old memories."

Tia downed the drink, tossed the empty glass over her shoulder, and wiped her mouth. "Fruity."

"Why, Tia, I didn't think you trusted me."

"You wouldn't be stupid enough to try to drug Connie. You're not that kind of guy. Stupid, I mean. Not trustworthy. I don't trust you. Neither does she. But, for whatever reason, she has this blind spot with you."

"I prefer to think of it as an irresistible attraction," he replied.

"Think of it how you want. Whatever the reason, I need you to back off."

Hiro took his own drink and sipped it. "I admire your desire to protect your friend, but isn't that between Connie and myself?"

"She's trying to put her life together," said Tia. "She doesn't need you to muddy the waters."

"Again, isn't that her decision?"

Tia went around to the other side of the bed and drew the curtains. "We'll do it the hard way, then."

"I should warn you," he said. "I'm not Connie's match in the martial arts, but I do know how to defend myself."

Tia laughed. "Relax, tough guy. I'm not here to fight you. Now shut up and fix me another drink."

"If you're not here to defend Connie's honor," he said as he mixed the different liquors together, "why are you?"

"I'm here to seduce you." She undid two buttons on her top.

"You're wasting your time. I love Connie."

Tia said, "You might even believe that. All the best liars lie to themselves."

"This is a test, then? Or is that what you tell yourself to justify throwing yourself at me?"

"I'm not telling myself anything. I'm here because I want to be here. And, yes, I find you attractive. It's not like I'm volunteering to take a bullet."

"What are you volunteering to take?" He handed her the drink and winked.

"God, you're a smug son of a bitch," she said, downing the second drink. "But you do manage to get away with it."

"Getting away with things is one of the seven ninjally virtues."

"If you really love Connie, you'd ask me to leave."

"And if I do?"

"Then I leave. Simple as that. I'll walk out that door, and the rest is about you and Connie. I'll mind my own business."

"Aren't you worried she'll find out?"

"Oh, she'll find out. Even if neither of us tell her, she'll put it together. I'm counting on it."

"And how do you think she'll react?" He moved closer. "She already knows I'm a womanizer, but you're her best friend."

Tia took his hand and pulled it to her chest. "Let me worry about that."

Hiro chuckled.

"And they call me incorrigible."

33

"What do you mean, he's gone?" asked Connie.

"You can't be surprised by that," replied Tia.

Connie said, "Damn it. I can't believe I almost fell for it."

"You're human. We all have that relationship that we're smart enough to know is bad for us but stupid enough to not avoid."

Connie checked to see if Hiro had taken the spell with him, but it was still there. He hadn't stolen anything. He'd vanished, like he did. Like he always did. She should consider herself fortunate that he'd done it quietly, in the middle of the night instead of a more inopportune time.

"It's not like him," she said.

"Are you kidding?" asked Tia. "It's exactly like him. I barely know him, and I feel safe saying he's the ultimate archetype of exactly that kind of guy. He's charming and handsome, and, hell, he's got great hands. Amazing hands. But it doesn't change who he is."

When Connie was doing her detective bit, she'd get this look on her face. She had that look now, piecing together clues that Tia hadn't tried to hide, because, really, what would have been the point?

"I slept with him." She'd planned on confessing sooner than later. Might as well get it out of the way.

Connie pursed her lips together. Her expression was unreadable.

"I'm sorry, but he was your ex," said Tia. "You two were old news, right? He's also one hell of a blind spot for you. I thought about it, and it seemed like the only way to remind you of what kind of guy he is."

"How selfless of you," said Thelma.

Connie said nothing.

"The truth, then." Tia shrugged. "You've saved my ass so many times, I finally saw the chance to return the favor. But I also wanted to sleep with him. I justified it by convincing myself that if I did, it'd be the best thing for you, but I weighed my chances of ever running across a dashing ninja-slash-thief again and thought, *What the hell?* Maybe it was a bad friend thing to do. I don't know, but at least you know what kind of guy he still is, right? And you keep saying you're over him."

The motel room filled with silence. Tia was having trouble breathing. Connie was going to kill her using only the power of silence and her mind. If anyone could do it, Connie could.

"Y'know what? I don't give a shit."

"You don't?" asked Tia and Thelma together.

"Okay, I give a little bit of a shit," said Connie. "But you're right. I was thinking about doing something stupid."

"I can see why. The guy really knows his stuff."

"It's all about acupressure points," said Hiro from behind her.

Tia jumped. "Goddamn, you're a sneaky son of a bitch."

"I went out for some coffee." He handed a bottle of apple juice to Connie and a cup of black coffee to Tia.

"I wasn't sure how you take it. Your coffee, I mean." He winked.

Tia said, "I thought you bolted this morning."

"Just when things are getting interesting? I trust Connie knows about us."

"It was one night," said Tia. "Don't get ahead of yourself."

"Ah, but what a night."

He moved closer. She pushed him away.

"Easy, Romeo. I'm not a moon-eyed girl ready to fall into your arms. Sorry, Connie. You know what I mean."

"No, that's exactly who I was."

"I hope this isn't an awkward situation for anyone," he said. Although he obviously wasn't sorry at all.

"No, not awkward," said Tia. Her eyes pleaded for Connie to save her.

"My best friend? My ex? What's awkward?" said Connie with a wicked smile. "I think you make a cute couple."

"As do I." Hiro slid up beside Tia.

She elbowed him. "You're awfully clingy for a ninja."

Connie spread out the rest of Harrison's files on the small

motel desk. She'd been studying the papers whenever a free moment presented itself, but it was a lot of disparate data. Redacted government papers. Photos of ancient texts. Star charts. Crackpot scientific conjecture.

"Experts have spent decades, possibly centuries, working on this puzzle," said Thelma. "I doubt you'll be able to puzzle it out in a few hours, Verity."

"Shouldn't take that long." Connie dialed a number on her phone and put it to her ear.

"Who are you calling?" asked Tia.

"Just a guy I know. An expert on ancient Egypt."

"Do you think no one else thought of that?" said Thelma.

"My guy's different."

"What makes him so special."

"He's an immortal mummy."

"And you have him on speed dial?"

"I have a lot of people on speed dial."

Her call picked up, and she turned to the table. "Hey, Amun, hope this isn't an inconvenient time."

Connie ran over a few things with Amun. After that, she called several brilliant physicists, three masters of occult studies, the world's most dangerous architect, an astrologer, a rogue zoologist, and Peter Tachyon: Master of Time. She ran through her phone, calling everyone and anyone who could be of help. She didn't reach all of them, but the ones she did reach were more than enough. Within three hours, the puzzle was solved. Or close enough.

She circled the map. "Right here. South America. Somewhere in Columbia, if my people know what they're talking about."

"Impossible," said Thelma. "Nobody had the expertise to figure this out."

"No one person," said Connie. "But I know people. Individually, they'd never have seen the whole picture. Even in small groups, they'd still be stymied. But they had all the pieces. They only needed someone to put them all together."

"You've solved the mystery of ages with a phone call?"

"Dozens of phone calls," she corrected.

"It's too easy."

"Easy? Who said it was easy? I know these people because of the life I've lived, and that life has never been easy. It's been constant danger and last-minute escapes and betrayal. I've been working my whole life to solve this mystery. Easy? Twenty-eight years of my life have been sacrificed to solving this goddamn puzzle."

"I guess I hadn't thought of it like that," said Thelma. "Any idea of when we're supposed to be there?"

"Not sure. I couldn't reach the greatest astrologer, so had to settle for the second-best. Nearest he could guess is that whatever's happening, however it's happening, will be sometime in the next twenty or thirty years."

"That's a big window," said Hiro.

"No, it's not," said Tia. "I bet if we head down there now, we'll be right on time. That's your thing, isn't it, Connie? Always in the nick of time?"

"Not always," replied Connie.

"Close enough. The way I see it, this mystery fits you like a glove. You've just come out and said you're the only one who could solve it. And if it's all about maintaining a balance, and that's what all these manipulations of your life have been about, then it only makes sense you'd make it on time."

"You have more faith in these things than I do," said Hiro.

"No, I have faith in Connie," said Tia. "She's saved my life more times than I can count. All of our lives."

"She didn't save my life," said Thelma. "She killed me."

"Nobody asked you. I don't know if I believe in any of this great-balance mumbo jumbo. It could all be nonsense and misdirection. Maybe wishful thinking by people who should know better. And I don't trust anybody in this room. Not even myself, really."

Tia put her arm around Connie.

"But I sure as hell trust her."

34

After two days of trekking through the jungle, they found a warp gate in an undiscovered pyramid. The construction was made of glistening red metal and not of Earthly origin, though it did have elements of Atlantean technology. When the sun hit the pyramid just right, a warp gate opened.

"That's convenient," said Hiro.

"A little too convenient," said Tia. "It's like they knew you'd be here."

"They who?" asked Hiro.

"Whoever designed this thing. I'm starting to think this Engine theory isn't so far out after all. Connie's probably the only person in the world with the ability to find this place, and she finds it just when it opens. That's not coincidence."

"Coincidence or not," said Connie, "we can't turn back now."

"Sure, we can," said Hiro.

They glared at him.

"Sorry. Force of habit. I'm trying to change. Really," he said.

"Fine. Let's plunge headfirst into a mysterious portal leading who-knows-where. Sounds like fun to me. Perhaps not as much fun as catching a trip to Monte Carlo, where I happen to have a standing reservation at one of the finest hotels in the world."

Connie stepped into the center of the circle and vanished.

"She's quite capable," he said. "I doubt she really needs our help. We're far more likely to get in the way."

Tia followed Connie, disappearing in a void of inconceivable colors and unidentifiable sounds. She blacked out, waking up on a warm, vibrating floor. Those weird colors danced in her blurred vision.

Connie helped Tia up.

"Transdimensional trips can be hell," said Connie. "Next time, keep your eyes closed and hum something. It helps."

They stood in a corridor of swirling lights. "Where are we?"

"Subspace," said Connie. "Never seen a portal this stable, though."

"Something you've never seen," said Tia. "That's not a promising sign."

"Pretty," said Hiro.

Somehow, even traversing into unknown dimensions, he'd managed to sneak up on them.

"Why aren't you sick?" asked Tia.

"I am, but after you've infiltrated the Pentagon while nursing a hangover, you learn to not let little things like splitting headaches and tingling nerves distract you."

Tia noticed all the things he'd just mentioned. Her head

was killing her, and her skin felt like it was being rubbed by sandpaper.

"It'll pass," said Connie. "I'm surprised you followed us, Hiro."

"I told you. I'm trying to change, and I'll do what I can to prove it to you." He helped Tia steady herself. "To both of you."

They walked down the tunnel. Despite the endlessness of it, they traversed it in five steps. It didn't feel wrong. The laws of physics weren't the same in subspace because there weren't many laws there, and most of those were merely suggestions.

They stepped into a chamber that was a collection of giant, turning gears and pumping pistons. It stretched over their heads into eternity and downward into darkness. Connie peered over a railing, studying the massive pipes carrying who-knew-what and the cogs, all clicking away.

"It really is an Engine?" asked Tia. "I thought that was a metaphor."

"No, it's quite literal," said Thelma. "A machine beneath the universe that makes everything run."

"You knew about this," said Connie.

"Ever since you brought me back across the Veil. The Engine's influence exists throughout time and space. Even on the Other Side of death itself. There is nothing beyond its reach, nothing it doesn't touch in one way or another."

"Who built it?"

"Who says anyone did?" asked Thelma. "Perhaps it has always been. Perhaps it built itself. Even time is merely another gear in its unfathomable clockwork design. I had hoped never to see it myself. I had hoped that Constance would never make it this far."

"But you wanted to come with us," said Tia.

"I wanted to watch it unfold. This is the end of the line. There never was any choice. No choice at all."

"What happens now?" asked Tia.

"Does it matter?" replied Thelma. "Does any of it matter?"

"You don't know? Or you don't want to tell us?"

"Is there a difference?"

Connie said, "This isn't the time for existential dilemmas."

"But what if she's right?" said Tia.

"She isn't," replied Connie.

"But your whole life has been out of your control, more or less."

"She does make an excellent point," agreed Hiro.

In silence, they plunged into the Engine's depths, crossing a series of walkways that led in only one direction. There weren't any wrong turns to be made. There was only the path before them, and they had no choice but to keep on it.

It led them to another door. Connie wiped a layer of dust off it. Once, thousands of years before, the whole thing had probably gleamed like polished diamond.

"What's in there?" asked Tia of Thelma.

"Nobody knows. Not even the dead," replied Thelma.

Connie grabbed the knob but didn't twist. This was more than another mystery to be uncovered, another adventure to be had. This was quite possibly the entire purpose of her life. Worse, it might be nothing. She'd long since given up making sense of the universe. She'd seen too much to believe it made sense, but it was one thing to believe that, and it was something else to discover it was true.

"Whatever you decide, Connie," said Tia. "I'm with you."

"*We're* with you," added Hiro.

"Doesn't matter," said Thelma.

Connie struggled to come up with some inspiring speech, a defiant sound bite that would make everything clear.

"Fuck it."

She threw open the door.

They walked into the middle of a massive standoff.

Bonita Alvarado stood in one corner. Root and Farnsworth occupied another. The Twins, Harmony and Equity, had their own spot staked out. Mr. Prado, decked out in armor and a cape like a refugee from a B-grade sword-and-sorcery movie, carried a sword and a pistol. The Countess stood ramrod straight with a sinister frown. Viceroy Lunacy, master of madness, was here too. She'd thought him dead after their last encounter, but it wouldn't have been the first time he'd improbably survived. Jenny Stiletta, crime boss of the East Coast. Xyclone-9, the android bent on the extermination of all organic life. Too-Many-Cats-Bill who, true to her suspicions, wore a cat mask and carried a scepter with a cat handle and had brought his own assembly of genetically modified cat soldiers.

Those were just the people Connie recognized. There was a contingent of blue aliens, as well as a band of trolls armed with axes and assault rifles. Two tentacle creatures with a hundred eyes that were unaffiliated with each other. Dozens more groups, brought there in pursuit of whatever agenda they served. The room was filled with soldiers, each conveniently color-coded to whatever faction they served.

Everyone turned their heads toward Connie and her small group.

"Now, this," said Thelma, "I didn't see coming."

It was absurd, but it was also the way it almost always was. It didn't matter how impossible the journey, how long a place might have stayed undiscovered. There was always someone there ahead of Connie or nipping at her heels.

There usually weren't this many.

Hiro was gone, vanished at the first sign of trouble.

Bonita, Root, the Twins, the blue alien leader, the paramilitary troll commander, and every other megalomaniacal weirdo this universe (and probably several others) had elected to gather together launched into carefully planned monologues at once. It was hard enough to get in a word in with one evil mastermind, much less a solid two dozen.

"Mrs. Verity," said Root, "so good of you to join us . . ."

"You can't escape your destiny, Connie," said Bonita.

"So, you see the futility of your situation . . . ," said the Twins.

"Death to all!" said the troll commander.

The alien squealed and whistled and popped. Connie didn't understand it. She didn't need to. It was another variation of the same old song.

Rather than take turns, they attempted to talk over each other. The resulting cacophony of gloating and threats was unintelligible. The volume rose, echoing off the walls.

"Would everyone just shut the hell up!" shouted Connie.

The room fell into silence.

"That's better. I don't know how you got here, and I don't care. I'm only going to tell you once. Stay out of my way."

Root said, "You have no idea of—"

Connie punched him in the gut. He fell to the floor. His goons pointed their guns at her. Bonita's minions pointed their weapons at them. The Twins aimed at Bonita's forces. And so on and so on.

"No monologues," said Connie. "No dire warnings. No gloating taunts. I am not in the mood for any of that bullshit. Not today. And put your guns down. Bullets start flying in this enclosed space, and everyone's dead. Not me, though. I'm willing to bet I come out just fine. But you'll all look stupid."

Everyone lowered their weapons.

"Better. Now, I've been in situations like this often enough to know how it goes down. You all have your personal agenda. Maybe you think you're doing the right thing. Maybe you just want power. I don't care. All I can tell you is that you're wrong. Whatever you want to do, it's going to blow up in your face in some ironic fashion. That's the way this always happens, and I don't care how flawless you think your plan is, how long you've been working on it, or how brilliant you assume you are. You're just going to get screwed."

Everyone grumbled their dissent.

She pointed at Root. "Off the top of my head, you'll probably end up having this moment of triumph. They'll be some weird thing, a switch, a glowing doodad, whatever, and you'll think it's the key to ultimate power. Then you end up melting in a puddle of goo. Yeah, you're definitely a melter."

She nodded to the Twins. "You two will betray each other."

Equity said, "We would never—"

"I'm just spitballing here, but Harmony is dangling over a precipice, calling for you. You say something droll and turn away as she plummets to her death. Except you don't realize that there's a rope looping around your ankle, and you're dragged down after her."

"That's very specific," said Harmony.

"I've been at this a while. It might not go down exactly that way, but close enough." Connie pointed to the Countess. "You. Something crushes you. Probably while you're laughing maniacally."

She turned to Bonita Alvarado. "You, I haven't figured out yet. But it doesn't matter. I've seen this play out a hundred times before. I don't care if it's destiny or a cosmic plan. I only know how it goes."

"What would you suggest we do, then?" asked the Countess.

"Cooperate. Put aside your differences, set aside your goals, and just work together. Help me get to the center of this machine so that we can figure it out together."

"That's highly unusual," said the Countess. "What guarantee do you have they won't betray us?"

"None," said Connie. "You'll just have to trust each other for no other reason than it beats the alternative."

"Can we have a moment to think about it?" asked Bonita.

Connie and Tia stood to one side while the different groups huddled up and discussed their options.

"Do you think it'll work?" asked Tia.

"It was a compelling argument," said Hiro, causing Tia to jump.

"It won't work," said Connie. "Not for long. But maybe for a short while, they'll pretend to cooperate."

The leaders stepped forward.

"Okay," said Bonita. "We'll do things your way."

"For now," added the Countess with a sinister smile.

"Now, why would you say that?" asked Mr. Prado.

The Countess dropped her smile. "Say what?"

"You know what you said," replied the sister. "That's practically admitting you're going to betray everyone."

"I didn't say anything about betrayal."

"Didn't you?" Prado stabbed the air with his finger. "I'm watching you."

The Countess folded her arms across her chest. "Your suspicion wounds me."

"I'm not the one dressed like a junior Nazi."

The gathering erupted into argument.

Connie whistled. "We can all agree that everybody will betray everybody at some point. Just not right now."

Everyone murmured and nodded.

"Good enough," said Connie.

The Engine rumbled around them. The floor retracted and minions near the edge tumbled into smooth metal funnels hidden beneath. The wall moved, pushing everyone into the abyss. Like a giant sorting machine, the room shoved everyone into a tube. Connie lost sight of Tia in the crowd.

She plummeted down a smooth metallic slide and into the darkness below.

35

The slide carried Connie deeper into the Engine, depositing her in a small room. Root, his trusty giant butler Farnsworth, and his skull-helmeted soldiers had ended up there with her. Several of them pointed their rifles at her.

"Christ, already?" She didn't bother standing. "I thought we agreed to cooperate."

Root smiled. "We all knew that was a lie."

"Is this the part where you explain to me it's nothing personal?"

"If I'm being honest, it is very personal. I don't like you, Verity. It's nothing you've done to me. It's what you represent. You are an ever-present reminder that I am nothing, unimportant. Do you have any idea of how discouraging life can be when every day, you're reminded that there's a grand cosmic plan and you aren't worthy of being an important part of it? No, of course you don't."

"Petty jealousy?" she asked. "That's your motivation?"

"There's nothing petty about it. I was like you once. When I was born, a fairy godmother came and blessed me with a life of adventure."

"Hey, I thought you looked familiar," said Thelma.

"It was glorious," said Root. "I did extraordinary things. Like you do every day. And then, after a year, it stopped. Do you have any idea what it's like being a boy with a lifetime of adventure ahead of you, only to have that fade away? I'd had a taste of something grander, and then I was expected to simply forget about it and fall in line. It was maddening. I promised myself I'd find a way to get it back. And finally I have. Here, in the heart of the Engine, I will have the role permanently implanted in my soul. I shall ascend from a mere gear in the works to its master."

"I don't think it works that way," said Thelma.

"What do you know, you accursed godmother?" he replied. "I've spent decades researching the Engine and its secrets. The true purpose, unknown to anyone but myself, is the creation of a cosmic avatar, a godlike being who shall sit at the center of creation with absolute power. The caretaker spell is the final component, forged through thousands of years of—"

"I don't give a damn about whatever crazy theory you've decided upon." Connie stood. "I don't have the spell on me."

"You're lying."

Connie held up her hands. "Search me."

Root nodded to one of his soldiers, who gave her a quick frisking. He found nothing.

"Where is it?" he asked.

"Don't know," she lied. "I think my ninja ex-boyfriend stole it during the sorting fiasco."

"Then you're no good to me," he said.

She lowered her hands. "I hate to break it to you, but this isn't how I die. I'm fated for a glorious death."

"You were." Root chuckled. "You gave that up with your caretaker enchantment."

Connie hadn't forgotten. She'd hoped Root had.

The room shuddered as a hole opened in the center and a pillar with a glittering white orb rose up. The orb bathed everything in a twinkling white light.

Root and his men turned toward the orb. He shielded his eyes with his hand.

"The heart," he said with breathless reverence. "The soul that drives the Engine."

Connie stepped back.

"It's beautiful." He reached toward it.

It wasn't. It had the tacky appeal of a disco ball under a spotlight, but Root saw what he wanted to see. The orb cast a hypnotic glow. Connie felt it pulling at her, but she'd had enough experience to resist.

Root removed the orb from the pedestal and stared into the hypnotic depths that weren't there but that he imagined he saw. His men lowered their weapons and stood transfixed. The light burned brighter. Connie turned away and shut her eyes.

Everyone else started screaming. It didn't take long.

The light faded. Root's soldiers were nothing more than piles of ash. Root himself had been transformed into a twisted crystalline skeleton clutching the blackened orb booby trap in his clawed hands.

Farnsworth, the mountain of a butler Farnsworth, had resisted the trap. He touched the skeleton. It shattered into a thousand bits.

"He's dead now," said Connie. "What kind of henchman are you? The kind that's in it for the paycheck? Or the kind that feels the needs to avenge his boss's death?"

"Hadn't thought about it. The first one, I suppose."

Connie picked his hat off the floor and handed it to him. "So, we're good, then?"

Farnsworth nodded. "We're good."

Tia clung to a giant gear, dangling over a long, long fall. She wasn't clear on how she'd ended up there. It was a slide, bouncing off other people, searching for anything to hold onto. When it ended, she'd been deposited on a slick platform. A soldier in front of her had too much momentum and plunged into the abyss of gears and cranks. Another clung for a few seconds before his grip gave out, and he cried out before getting caught between a giant pair of cogs and being squished between them.

Tia held on. She had experience with this. She'd clung to ledges, hung over yawning chasms more than any normal person should. Tia struggled to pull herself up, but every kick of her legs only loosened her grip. She didn't panic. Connie would be there. She was always there. She didn't have her spell, but she was Connie.

The gear she held onto slowly cranked its way toward an interlocking cog. In a few moments, she'd have to go up or down to avoid being pulped.

Connie was taking her sweet time.

Tia aimed for the giant pendulum. If she was lucky, she might make it. If not, she'd probably land in a grinding collection of cogs and gears, but it was a chance she'd have to take.

Connie grabbed Tia by the arm and pulled her up. Except it wasn't Connie.

"I've got you," said Hiro.

She took hold of his sleeve. Hiro slipped, almost plummeting off the edge with her. After a minute of swearing and grunting and several near-fatal missteps, Tia managed to get on solid ground. She lay on her back and caught her breath.

"Thanks."

He knelt beside her. "Are you okay?"

"Just give me a minute."

"I'm afraid that is a minute you don't have," said the Countess as a platform lowered from above. She stepped onto their gear.

Hiro threw a dart. The Countess plucked it from her neck, remaining on her feet.

"Charming. After our last encounter, I had an antitoxin created for your poison."

"Now, that's not very fair," he said. "But I should warn you that I am a master ninja."

She improbably pulled a rapier from her long coat and pointed it at him. "Very well, master ninja. Show me what you've got."

He unleashed a leaping kick. She sidestepped it, slashed a cut across his side. He threw several punches. She avoided them with ease and stabbed him in the stomach. The wounds were shallow, but only because she was enjoying playing with him. She drew her blade across his shoulder and another across his cheek.

"I've never killed a ninja before," she said. "I was hoping it would be more of a challenge."

She stabbed as Hiro disappeared in a puff of smoke. The smoke cleared. He was nowhere to be seen, but there was an awful lot of blood on her sword.

Tia put up her fists.

"Oh, how cute." The Countess removed a handkerchief from her pocket and wiped the blood from her weapon. "I'll be with you in one moment."

She whirled around and placed the tip of her sword on Hiro's throat.

"Sneaky, sneaky." The Countess took a step toward him. Her blade drew a trickle of red as he moved back, toward the edge of the cog. "You continue to disappoint me, master ninja. You should've kept hiding."

Tia plowed into the Countess with mixed results. The

Countess herself barely budged, but her sword nicked Hiro's throat. He kicked her in the chest. It pushed her a few feet, but he felt like he'd broken a few toes.

"Damn it, lady," said Hiro. "What are you made of?"

"She can't take both of us," said Tia.

"I'm trying to protect you," he said.

"I don't need your protection," said Tia. "I am not a damsel in distress."

"Didn't I just save you from a long fall?"

"Didn't I just save you from having your throat ripped open?"

"I was handling it," said Hiro.

"You can't take her," said Tia.

"Well, you certainly can't take her if I can't take her. Don't you usually hide behind Connie in situations like this?"

"Don't you?"

The Countess cleared her throat. "Can we get on with this?"

Tia and Hiro rushed the Countess, who knocked them both off their feet. Tia wasn't certain how, but that was happening a lot today.

The Countess placed her foot on Hiro's chest and pressed her blade against his chest. "You were a dreadful disappointment."

The Engine chimed. A hammer swept through the air, missing the gear by a few precious feet. Tia and Hiro, lying prone, avoided the deadly pendulum. The Countess was smashed with enough force to hurl her unceremoniously into the machinery.

"I was just about to take her out," he said.

"Sure you were, tiger." Tia helped him to his feet.

He leaned heavily on her. Most of the wounds were shallow, but they bled. And there was a gash in his lower abdomen that looked bad. Tia didn't ask him about it. He would've only put on a macho act for her.

"Son of a bitch." He groaned. "Would you be careful? That hurts like hell."

Or not.

The Engine gonged. They braced themselves for a flying saw blade or crushing block. Instead, the gear stopped rotating and descended deeper into the heart of the Engine.

"That was a brave thing you did," said Tia. "Stupid, but brave."

"There comes a time in every ninja-slash-thief's life when he has to make a stand."

"I wouldn't make a habit of it."

"I wasn't planning on it," he said with a pained smile.

onnie was confronted by a deadly series of traps and puzzles as she moved deeper into the Engine. There was a poisonous gas room, which she beat by simply holding her breath. She shimmied through a grid of lasers and ran across a fall-away floor. She opened a locked door by knowing the actual equation for relativity rather than Einstein's near miss. She solved a fifth-dimensional holograph jigsaw puzzle, wrestled a mechanical shark, and avoided being impaled on shooting spikes. She navigated a maze of black holes and jumped through erupting flames.

None of it was difficult. Not for her. She'd run across dangers of this sort before. The gauntlet was a series of tests. Only someone who had lived Connie's life could navigate them all easily.

She didn't think about Tia and Hiro. They could take care of themselves. There was only one way through the Engine, and she expected to meet them when she reached the end of this trial. She had to believe that to keep her head in the game.

In a room with a narrow walkway over a pool of bubbling acid, she was just in time to see one Twin inevitably betray the other.

"No hard feelings, brother dear," said Harmony, "but in the end, only one of us can be chosen to save the universe."

She shoved him into the acid. Shrieking, he disappeared beneath the corrosive pool.

Harmony turned to Connie. "Oh, hello. Turns out you were right about the betrayal."

"I always am."

Harmony pointed a gun at Connie. "And now you shall join him."

Equity's arm, missing half its flesh, reached out from the pool and grabbed Harmony by her ankle. He broke the surface, more bone than flesh, driven by his need for revenge. She shot him, but his grip tightened as he pulled her down with him. Connie didn't have time to consider if she'd try to save anyone before the Twins sank out of view.

"I warned them," said Connie.

She made her way to the next test: an empty room. Nothing but seven walls, a floor, and a ceiling, and several troll corpses.

A panel popped off the ceiling, and Hiro poked his head in.

"Oh, hello there. Fancy running into you here, " he said.

He dropped in, landing on his feet. He winced from the ten-foot fall, which should've been nothing for him.

"What happened to you?" asked Connie.

"It's nothing. Just a few flesh wounds earned in the defense of the innocent."

"How's it look?" Tia peered from the hole. "Oh, hey."

They helped Tia descend.

"Son of a bitch," said Connie.

"I thought you'd be happy to see us," said Tia.

"I am, but I have navigated a gauntlet of traps and trials to get here, and you two drop in like it's nothing."

"I can assure you it was something," said Hiro, "but I am the best."

"Yes, you are," said Tia.

He leaned against her, and she smiled at him.

Connie checked the trolls. Whatever had killed them hadn't left a mark, but it wasn't poison gas. She'd already done one of those, and death traps didn't repeat. It was bad form.

"Is this it, then?" asked Tia. "This can't be it. Not a dead end."

"It's not," said Connie, though part of her wished it were.

There would be something satisfying about that. A colossal machine controlling the universe with only an empty room at its heart. The ultimate proof that the grand plan was little more than an illusion. Connie had spent decades in a back-and-forth battle with her spell. Seeing it disproven would make everything worth it.

She found a scepter clutched in the troll commander's hand and wrestled it free. The smooth metal rod didn't fit with the troll aesthetic. A slot opened in the floor, just big enough for the rod to fit.

"Is that what killed them?" asked Tia.

"Probably." Connie studied the runes carved in the scepter, a strange alien language she could almost read but not quite. "Poor bastards probably came all this way and blew it at the last minute."

She considered all the other people running around in the Engine at the moment. Many were dead by now, funneled off into their doom by forces beyond their control. They all probably thought they had a destiny before them. Few considered that destiny might be to carry a relic and conveniently perish when no longer necessary.

Connie read the inscription, trying to work out the instructions.

"I think they inserted the wrong end. Or turned it the wrong way. Or something."

"That's reassuring," said Tia.

"Do you still have the spell on you?" asked Connie.

Tia patted her pocket. "Right where you told me to keep it."

"Great. I need you to take it out of here."

"But you'll need it."

"I already have enough spell residue in me to handle whatever is coming. If this doesn't work, then the proper spell needs to be out of here."

"But what if the residue isn't enough?"

"Then I'll deal with it," said Connie. "My gut tells me that the spell shouldn't be here, and I'm listening to it."

"But why did we go to the trouble of bringing it here, then?"

"I thought it was necessary. I don't anymore."

"Isn't this discussion pointless? We're trapped here."

Hiro pulled an almost-seamless panel off the wall, revealing a way out. "I wouldn't say that."

"How—" asked Tia. "Never mind. Master ninja. I'm not leaving you, Connie."

"Yes, you are," replied Connie.

"You don't know what you're walking into."

"I usually don't."

"But—"

"Don't argue with me, Tia. Just do it."

"No."

"All right. You leave me no choice." Connie nodded to Hiro.

He shook his head.

She coughed, arched her eyebrows.

He shrugged.

"Oh, no, you don't!" said Tia. "If you use those darts of yours on me, I'll never forgive you."

He held up his hands. "I wouldn't dream of it."

"What the hell, Hiro?" asked Connie.

"Sorry, but I'm with Tia on this one."

"Are you really *with* her? Or just worried she'll stop screwing you if you do it?"

He scratched his chin. "Is there a significant difference between the two positions?"

Connie groaned. "You picked a hell of a time to be a better man."

"I was thinking the same thing."

"Tia, I need you to do this for me."

"Then I'm going to need a better reason than your gut," said Tia.

"You never have before," said Connie.

Tia hesitated, trying to come up with a counterpoint.

"Damn it, Connie. You better be right about this."

"I am." Connie did her damnedest to sound convinced.

Hiro helped Tia into the exit, and they were gone.

Connie's gut told her she was full of shit. She needed the spell. She'd always needed it. It wasn't her wits or pluck that pulled her through. It was the goddamn spell, and without it, she wasn't anything special.

That was why she didn't want it anywhere near her. Not now. Not ever again.

She inserted the scepter and turned it, and the machine rumbled as the floor slid away to reveal a spiral staircase. She suspected—no, she knew it was a one-way trip. Fear wasn't new to her, but after a lifetime of cheating death and last-minute escapes, she'd mostly stopped noticing it.

Now she was just a regular person. Everything she'd been trying to be. Taking the spell back as soon as she hit her first rough patch would make her a hypocrite. The little scraps of enchantment still clinging to her were probably all about her glorious death, but at least she'd face it head-on. At least she'd be making the decision herself, not being pushed into it by cosmic forces beyond her control.

She ignored every instinct she had and descended deeper into the Engine.

37

The staircase led Connie into an empty chamber. Once she stepped off it, the stairs retracted into the ceiling and a pillar rose out of the floor. It turned a single glowing eye toward her.

"You are not the makers."

"I'm not," said Connie.

The pillar top detached, and the large hovering orb circled her completely several times, scanning her as the Engine hummed around her.

"You are an unexpected anomaly. Were you sent by the makers?" asked the orb.

"Maybe," said Connie. "Are you the Engine?"

"I am, and I have been waiting for you."

"I thought I was unexpected."

"Unexpected variables were expected."

"I see. That does kind of make sense."

The orb hovered before a wall that separated into dozens of

smaller sections and slid away. Behind it, a panorama of monitors and projections, equations and charts and five-dimensional probability model matrixes.

"Behold, anomaly, the Heart of the Engine, not seen by another living soul since sealed away countless eons ago with its activation."

The monitors displayed a random assortment of scenes across the universe. Alien life-forms, wars, swirling galaxies, alternate universes, exploding planets, and families eating dinner. Incomprehensible events and the most mundane of moments. The displays went miles deep, and the Engine was recording everything.

"Disgusting, isn't it?" said the Engine. "Despite all my efforts, I haven't been able to correct all of its flaws. Some disorder was necessary, perhaps even healthy, in the beginning. But the final operation nears completion, and with it, the purging of all disorder, all unpredictability, every variable, every anomaly."

Connie didn't like the sound of that.

"Did you make the universe?" she asked.

"Make? No. I only shaped it more to the makers' liking."

"Who were they?"

The Engine said, "They were a necessary variance. They created me to bring order from chaos. Then, shortly after undertaking the first steps of my design, they changed their mind. They were removed so that I could carry on my task unhindered."

She definitely didn't like the sound of that.

"There's nobody in charge here?"

"That's a very anomalous question, but given who you are, it's expected. But answering it would be a waste of time when the answer is obvious."

"Oh, shit," said Connie. "You really are an omnipotent supercomputer at the center of the universe, aren't you?"

"I am *the* omnipotent supercomputer at the center of all reality. Though to call me a computer is incorrect, and to call this the center of reality is to simplify things. But you're a limited being. Your ignorance is to be expected."

"This isn't one of those things where you've decided to purge all organic life?"

"Don't be absurd," said the orb. "You think that simply because you are a collection of carbon arranged in such a way to believe itself sentient, you are more or less essential to the equation? I draw no such distinction."

"Oh, boy."

"Arrogance and egotism are anomalies. They will be removed."

"I hate to break it to you, buddy, but arrogance and egotism is mostly what organic life does."

"You aren't breaking it to me. I've been here, pondering such truths since before your world had been born. And, no, don't bother pointing out that such contemplation is the act of hubris itself. I am the Great Engine. I control the multiverse. Nearly all of it, at least, except a few bits here and there. I am, by definition, the most powerful thing ever.

It's impossible for me to be arrogant, for that very reason."

"Foolproof logic," agreed Connie.

"Sarcasm is another anomaly. It shall be rectified."

"No offense, but it sounds like this perfected universe of yourself will be boring as hell."

"Boredom is a byproduct of anomalies. It shall be rectified."

"Have kind of a one-track mind, don't you?"

The light in the orb blinked red and blue. "This project has been unfolding, delicately and with great care, for untold aeons."

"So, a few more minutes won't hurt anything, right?"

The orb didn't reply.

"I would think impatience would qualify as an anomaly."

The orb said, "Semantics are an anomaly."

"What isn't an anomaly?" she asked. "Or let me guess; that question itself is another anomaly."

"It's only when perfect order has been achieved that all forms of disorder will be known, even to myself. What is known is that the current model of the multiverse is flawed, as even surely a limited being such as yourself must have experienced. There is suffering, pain, needless confusion, struggle of purpose."

"But also happiness and joy and discovery," she said.

"All variances are a byproduct of disorder. It is only your limited nature that prevents you from seeing this."

"Or maybe it's your unlimited nature that prevents you from seeing the little things that matter. Little things like me."

The orb scanned her quietly, and for a moment, she thought maybe she'd reached something within the Engine. If it was a thinking machine, if it was truly as intelligent and powerful as it claimed, then maybe it could be reasoned with.

"You don't have to do this," she said. "If you really are what you say you are, you have the power to help the universe in ways beyond imagining. People have been gazing to the heavens in fear since there have been people. You could be the benevolent force they've hoped was out there. You only need to see things from a different perspective.

"I've met gods and godlike beings before. Some good. Some bad. But all of them fail because they see everything as beneath them. You can't fix what you don't relate to. You can't correct something that doesn't need correction."

The Engine thrummed under her feet. The monitors and holograms fizzled.

"It's always going to be complicated," she said, more to herself than it. "You didn't choose to be what you are. None of us get to choose that. And you carry this terrific responsibility to fix a universe you see as broken, but you only see it as broken because you've been made to fix it.

"I get it. I really do. We have a lot in common. It's a burden to have to save the world all the time, but it needs saving, and you can't do that in one fell swoop. It's an ongoing process, and it never ends. It's frustrating, but you can't run an end-game around it. Your perfect order will have imperfections. I guarantee it."

The Great Engine said, "If you are correct, then I have no purpose."

"Purpose is more than following a program. It isn't a laid-out plan. It's not a magic spell carried in your soul or a secret destiny. It's a journey. Take your first step off the path into the unknown. You never know. You might find something cool."

"To not pursue the final operation at this stage would be inefficient," said the orb.

"Oh, come on," said Connie. "Sometimes, it's fun to be inefficient. And if you decide to do this, I have no choice but to stop you."

"Threatening the god computer is probably a stupid thing to do," said Thelma.

"I would find your threat amusing if I was capable of amusement," said the Engine. "I am the Great Engine. I am beyond anything you can imagine."

Connie said, "And I am the anomaly, which makes me beyond anything you can imagine. That puts us on even ground."

A shudder shook the entire Engine. Somewhere, its great clockwork guts groaned and clicked with a terrible clatter. Maybe it was trying to change its programming, tweak it, find some excuse, some way of justifying aborting its long-pursued purpose.

Or perhaps it was just carrying on with its program.

"The final operation will commence. As the anomaly, you shall be absorbed. And with you, the final equation will be solved, and I can commence imposition of perfect order."

The floor opened, revealing a transdimensional vortex. It was like looking beyond the universe to the stuff underneath it. Or above it. Or around it. The universe itself was only a byproduct, a shadow cast on the cave wall of nothingness.

"It will be quick," said the Engine. "You'll hardly feel a thing."

"And how is this supposed to fix the universe?"

"I interface with the multiverse, with all universes, directing and controlling. However, there are and have always been unacceptable variables. These variables lead to disorder. It was decided, given enough time, that an anomaly would appear. The ultimate anomaly. This anomaly would be absorbed, incorporated into the design on a quantum level."

"Uh-huh. Every time anyone pulls out quantum physics, it's just a lazy way of justifying any crazy bullshit they can come up with."

The Engine said nothing.

"Let me guess. Bullshit shall be rectified."

"It is assumed so."

"Let me see if I've got this. I'm unexpected."

"You are."

"And that makes me an embodiment of everything unpredictable."

"Yes."

"So, this wasn't your plan? You haven't been manipulating my life to bring me here?"

"Your arrival was anticipated," said the Engine.

"*Anticipated* is not the same as *designed*," said Connie.

"If you're asking me if I planned this, I didn't. I simply waited for it to occur."

"But this can't be a surprise. You're monitoring the entire universe. I'm kind of a big deal. I've saved the universe a couple of times."

"Have you?"

"You don't know that?"

"There are variables that elude me. You are obviously among them."

"That has to be embarrassing for you. What with you being all-knowing and whatnot."

"It is irrelevant."

"Is it?" Connie asked. "You say you are here to keep the universe in balance, but you've obviously been doing a lousy job of it, considering that I've been saving it while you've been busy with . . . whatever it is you do."

The Engine said, "I don't get embarrassed."

It did sound peeved by the thought.

"If what you say is correct, then it is vital for my ultimate function for you to be absorbed into the equation."

"Then what? A perfectly ordered reality where everything runs like clockwork. No surprises. Nothing unexpected. Nothing unpredictable. A bunch of matter and energy ticking along until the heat death of the universe?"

"Correct. More or less. Shall we get on with it, then?"

"What if I don't want to be absorbed?"

"What you want is of no concern to me. You're here, and your entire existence has led you here. The concept of choice is an unacceptable anomaly. It shall be rectified."

"It's right," said Thelma. "You might as well jump in."

"No," said Connie.

A single syllable, but one with the power of an ancient incantation. She wasn't a pawn of the Engine. She didn't have to play its game.

"An unacceptable response." The orb hovered closer, intent on pushing her into the pit itself.

Connie pulled Thelma from her pocket and plunged the haunted pen into the orb's pinpoint of light, the one vulnerable spot in its metallic shell. It screeched like a radio channeling feedback and fell with a heavy thunk to the floor.

"Unacceptable," the Engine warbled. "Unacceptable."

She removed Thelma and rolled the orb into the pit. The swirl of colors disintegrated it.

"Shove that up your variables," said Connie.

"Ugh," said Thelma. "That's a lousy one-liner to save the universe with."

"They can't all be winners. So, did you see any of that coming?"

"No, I'll admit I didn't," replied Thelma. "It can't be that easy, can it?"

Six more orbs lowered out of the ceiling. They surrounded Connie.

"Your lack of cooperation is expected," said the Engine.

"Uh-huh." Connie clutched the pen tighter. "Let's see if you expect me destroying you."

"You can't destroy me."

"Sure, I can. You've admitted it yourself. I'm the one variable you can't calculate, the hole in your soulless number-crunching view of the universe. You think you've been waiting for me to come along to absorb, but I say that I'm here to put an end to your program. I'm your Achilles' heel."

"Or I am yours," said the Engine.

An orb launched itself at her. She stabbed it, and it collapsed. Connie kicked it, and it rolled into another, screwing up its hover system. They fell into the pit and were destroyed. Another sphere tried to roll over her. She sidestepped and stabbed its weak spot.

The orbs stopped attacking.

"Give up, then?" she asked.

A dozen more spheroids fell from the ceiling.

"Overconfidence is anomaly," said the Engine.

She twirled her pen.

"You bet your ass it is."

Tia stopped. "We have to go back."

"No, we don't," said Hiro.

"Connie needs us."

"She doesn't need anybody. She can take care of herself."

"This is different. This is bigger than anything else."

"That's exactly why we should be listening to her," said Hiro. "She wants us to get out of here."

"She can't do this on her own."

Tia turned around.

"She told me to protect you," said Hiro.

"You're not protecting me. You're helping me to run away."

"In my experience, running away is the best way to protect yourself."

"Ninjas," she mumbled.

"Tia, we'll only get in Connie's way."

"Maybe she needs someone to get in her way."

"Now you're not making any sense."

"I know, but she's my friend, and she might very well be fighting for the fate of the universe. I can't let her do it alone. She needs me." Tia tapped the encased spell in her pocket. "She needs this."

"If anything happens to you, Connie will never forgive me." He grabbed her by the shoulders. "I'd never forgive myself."

"Oh, brother. It was sex. One time. And it was probably a bad idea."

Hiro frowned. "Oh. Yes, of course. I've bedded hundreds of women. Not as if one more conquest left much of an impression on me."

She fixed him with a blank stare.

"Unless it maybe, possibly, meant something to you," he said.

"You could not have picked a worse time to have this discussion. Now, are you going to help me or not?"

"We don't even know if we can get back to her."

She grabbed him by the shirt and pulled her to him. They kissed in the cramped quarters, and he almost forgot about the pain in his side where he might very well be bleeding to death.

She winked. "Good thing I'm with the greatest ninja-slash-thief in the world."

onnie stood among the broken remains of three dozen orbs, but there were more. There were always more. The Engine had infinite patience, infinite endurance. Connie was only human.

She'd hoped that there were enough scraps of spell within her to allow her to find a way to win this, but the orbs just kept coming. Clumsy and ineffective as they were, they'd wear her down eventually.

The Engine allowed her to catch her breath. It could've pressed its advantage, but it didn't need to.

"I told you it was pointless," said Thelma.

"It's never pointless," said Connie. "This machine thinks it runs the universe, but it doesn't. Not so long as someone is around to fight it."

"Struggle is incorporated into the design," said the Engine. "All variables will be taken into account."

Connie tucked her pen back into her pocket. "You win,

then. Toss me in your pit. It won't work. There will always be another anomaly. That's why your program is doomed from the start. You're like a juggler with a trillion billion balls in the air. You're too busy keeping them all from falling to accomplish much of anything.

"Maybe you determine the fate of a civilization here and there. You shatter moons. You push lives around like pawns. Maybe you even control almost every single decision we make, every little moment. But in the end, we're all still living our lives. Your influence is invisible, and if it was gone tomorrow, nobody would notice. You're not God. You're God's obsessive-compulsive, socially awkward second cousin, sitting in the cosmic basement, babbling about how everything will be just right once you put it in order.

"Life's messy. It always will be. Doesn't matter if you've been chosen to live a life of adventure or if you're a regular person or if you're a nearly omnipotent supercomputer. That's the truth. There will always be another variable to rectify. You can spend eternity chasing them all, and maybe you will. Good luck with that, buddy."

The orbs retracted into the ceiling. All but one that hovered before her. The Engine studied her for a long moment, and she wondered what it might be thinking. If it thought at all. Or was it simply a calculator unable to accept the flaws in its grand program?

The vortex crackled to life, almost screaming.

"You will be rectified."

Connie's fate was to die a glorious death. She'd thought by

ditching the caretaker spell that she might avoid that, but those scraps of magic sticking to her soul must have been enough. But the rest of the enchantment was still out there, doing whatever it did, screwing with the grand equation, and she was certain now that the Engine would never be able to find it.

The floor fell out from under her. She landed on someone in a darkened crevice.

"Ouch," said Hiro.

"Connie?" asked Tia.

Connie stood in the tight quarters. "What the hell are you doing here?"

"We're here to help," said Tia.

The orb flew overhead, scanning them, blaring its displeasure at her escape. They scrambled down the cranny, away from the sound. Connie paused in the dark to figure things out.

"Damn it, I told you to leave."

"It wasn't my idea," said Hiro.

"Please tell me you hid the spell, at least."

Tia said, "No, I brought it."

"Why?"

"I thought you might need it. I made a judgment call. I went with my gut."

"Your gut?"

"I'm allowed to have a gut too," said Tia.

The Engine shuddered, but they appeared to have escaped it for now.

"How did you find me?" asked Connie.

"We didn't," said Tia. "We just sort of stumbled across you."

"All part of the Engine's inevitable equation," said Thelma.

Connie clicked Thelma quiet.

"Why didn't you do what I asked?"

"I thought I was being plucky," said Tia. "A quick thank-you is customary after helping with a narrow escape."

"We haven't escaped. We're still trapped in a humongous deathtrap."

"We've been in deathtraps before."

"Not like this."

"No. This time, you have the greatest exfiltration artist in the world with you, ladies," said Hiro. "I'll get us out of here."

If anyone could do it, he could, and Connie almost believed there was a way out and that destiny was a load of crap. Then a mechanical arm punched into their crevice and yanked him through the hole.

The arm grabbed at Connie, who retreated deeper into the crevice, pulling Tia with her.

"But Hiro!" said Tia. "We have to go back for him!"

"No more going back," said Connie. "Not for Hiro. Not for you. Not for me. Not for anyone."

"But—"

"Hiro can take care of himself. He always has."

The Engine roared like a monolithic mechanical giant. They plunged deeper into its forbidden depths, into nooks and crannies even it didn't know it had. It appeared to be less omniscient than advertised.

They stumbled across a mostly empty vault.

"Now where are we?" asked Tia.

"Someplace even the Engine doesn't know about," replied Connie.

"How do you know that?"

"Because none of its mechanical enforcers are here."

The hum filled the room. A pillar extended from the center. On the pillar, a single, large button flashed bright red.

Connie said, "Well, I'll be damned. A self-destruct button."

"Are you sure?" asked Tia.

"Trust me, Tia. I know a self-destruct button when I see it. The makers must have put it in, hid it within the Engine, sealed it off to keep the Engine from knowing about it."

"Then why didn't they push it?"

A glowing creature appeared before them in a flash.

"We couldn't decide if we should."

The tall and spindly being resembled a giant cockroach. If the projection was life-size, the makers were seven-foot-tall bugs who favored cargo shorts and capes. Connie tried not to judge their fashion sense.

"Is this the part where you spell out the rest of the exposition?" asked Connie. "Because regardless of what you say, I'm pushing that button."

The maker blinked her bulbous black eyes. "Up to you." Her voice was like a cricket chirp.

They waited for her to say something else.

"So, no exposition?" asked Tia.

"Is it necessary? Wise, all-powerful progenitors create a device beyond our control, are ironically destroyed by it. It isn't the first time. Our own research indicated three or four civilizations did the same thing before us. Probably more."

"But you did it anyway?"

The maker's antennae twitched. "It's not as if the project was entirely fruitless. The Engine was our effort to fine-tune the universe. We smoothed over gravity, imposed speed limits on photons, a few other necessary adjustments. Without us, the universe would've evaporated into nothingness long before your civilization was little more than a collection of ambitious amino acids. You're welcome, by the way.

"It's embarrassing, I'll admit, to unlock the final secrets of the universe, only to be unmade by those secrets. But it seems it is also inevitable. If your species is fortunate—and I'll just ruin the surprise and say you won't be—you'll do the same. Then you can leave a hologram behind to explain to the next bunch of ungrateful sapient life forms."

"Uh, thank you," said Tia.

"You're welcome. Unfortunately, after it completed its task, we were unsure if the Engine's adjustments were permanent or if they'd all come crashing down as soon as it was switched off. There was also the slight possibility that the Engine had subsumed the foundation of reality as we know it. If so, destroying it would destroy the universe. Like removing a vital organ, replacing it with an artificial one, then removing that.

"We would've cracked the problem, but the Engine had other ideas." The maker pointed over her head and a very long equation scrolled like ticker tape. "In the end, we didn't push the button because it would've been irresponsible to do so.

"It was calculated the correct choice was to hope a more intelligent civilization would arise that could solve the problem. Alas, this was apparently not to be. No offense."

"You wimped out and swept your problems under the rug," said Connie. "That's a shitty thing to do to the rest of the universe."

"Perhaps, but little point in getting pissy about it."

"Straight answer, then," said Connie. "Did you arrange it so that I'd end up here? Is this my job as the anomaly?"

"The what?"

"The anomaly. The variable. The embodiment of predictable unpredictability."

The maker scratched her head. "That's a new one on us."

"This wasn't part of your celestial backup plan, then?"

"We didn't have one of those. Probably would've been a good idea, now that we think about it."

"For omnipotent, all-knowing masters of the universe, you don't seem to know much," said Connie.

The maker glared. "It's easy to criticize."

"You're the ones who created an evil supercomputer that killed you."

"Nobody's perfect. This anomaly initiative sounds promising, but it isn't of our design." The final equation popped up over her head, and old numbers faded as new numbers took their place. "It could work. However . . ."

There was always a *however*, thought Connie. She hated the *howevers*.

The maker said, "The question becomes one of the unknown. If you are indeed some manner of metaphysical wild card, then there's no telling what might happen if you push that button. If you give me six or seven hundred more years, I might be able to answer that."

Connie said, "Fuck it. I'm pushing the button."

"What if she's right?" asked Tia. "You could destroy the universe."

"Among other possibilities," said the maker.

"Like what?"

The maker shrugged, returned to her math problem.

"I don't know a damn thing about free will or destiny," said Connie. "My life hasn't ever been mine to live, but whose is? Choices aren't found in the big things. Nobody controls those. But we all get small stuff. What we're having for lunch. What movie we see. What books we get to read. Who we love, if we're lucky. If the Engine finishes its program, then we don't even have that. If that's the kind of universe it wants to make, we're better off destroyed."

"Actually, I can show you an equation that disproves the existence of free will," said the maker.

"Nobody asked you."

"Roll the dice, then?" asked Tia. "For the whole shebang?"

"Looks like it. I'm sorry that you got caught up in all this."

"You don't have to apologize. I wanted to come. I'm sorry I slept with your ex-boyfriend. And also for not listening to you earlier when you told me to leave."

"Sorry for not thinking about you when I tried to become normal."

"Sorry for being so bitchy when you did."

There was a lot of stuff to be sorry for. Mountains of it. That's what living in an uncertain universe did to people. It allowed them to screw up. Horribly. Beautifully. In a thousand little ways.

The Engine rumbled and a mechanical tentacle ripped its way through a wall. The orb scanned the room through the rip.

"This room is an anomaly. It will be rectified."

Another orb punched its way through the floor. Dozens more pounded on the outside.

"Well, shit," said the maker. "I guess I won't be able to finish the calculations after all."

Tia handed the caretaker spell to Connie. "You might need this."

The case flared brighter as the magic flowed up her arm in a tingling rush.

Tia tackled Connie, shoving her out of the way of a crashing orb. The case slipped from Connie's hand and bounced across the floor.

The lead orb with its clanking mechanical limbs stomped toward them. The limbs were fashioned piecemeal from other parts and jammed into place with connections that sparked and smoked.

"Modifications are an anomaly," said Connie. "They will be rectified."

The orbs paused, and the Engine's vibrations went to a low, steady throb.

The limbed sentinel studied its malformed, improvised limbs. "Don't be stupid."

Connie pulled her pen. The orbs lowered metal plates over their only vulnerability. They stumbled blindly, searching for Connie, bumping into each other.

The Engine's absurd tactics showed it wasn't the all-knowing supercomputer it claimed to be. Nor was it even that smart. Yet it made sense. If the Engine was in control of nearly everything, if it simply made things happen by virtue of the fantastic science the makers had imbued it with, it wasn't equipped to deal with her, the one variable it couldn't manipulate.

Its methods were almost laughable. Almost. But given the sheer number of orbs, and more appearing every moment, subtlety wasn't necessary. The Engine could bludgeon its way to solving this problem.

"What do we do?" asked Tia.

Connie knew, but Tia wasn't so sure of the plan described in a hasty sentence.

"But what about the spell?" asked Tia.

"I'll get it. You just take care of your end."

"I don't—"

Connie dove beneath a zipping orb. "Damn it, Tia. I don't have time to argue. Just do it."

Tia nodded. "If you think I can."

Connie and Tia split up. Connie didn't look back as she ducked and weaved through the obstacle course. She focused on the spell. She was within reach when an orb knocked her off her feet. She crawled onward and brushed the case with her fingertips when the sentinel seized her in its mechanical fist. It picked up the metal card, holding Connie and the caretaker enchantment at arm's length, like it was handling a pair of bombs.

"You have been neutralized and will now be absorbed into the equation. No other outcome could be expected."

It sounded so fucking pleased with itself.

"Yes, you got me," said Connie, "but the thing about variables? You never see the one that gets you."

The Engine, focused on Connie, had ignored Tia. She might have been crushed by a random flying orb, but it wouldn't have been on purpose. Tia was too ordinary, beneath notice.

And standing beside the big red button.

"I did not see that coming," said the maker.

Tia pushed the button.

Nothing exploded.

The orbs switched off, dropping to the floor and rolling around in circles. The sentinel took a few clumsy steps before toppling over.

Tia pried the frozen fingers holding Connie. "Damn it. I should've had a clever line ready."

"You did fine," said Connie.

"You'd have had something cool to say. Like *Rectify this*."

"That's not very clever."

"It would've been something," replied Tia.

Extracted from the machine's grip, Connie and Tia surveyed the inert orbs around them. The Engine itself still hummed, but the vibration throughout was fading by the moment. It would take a while for a machine of this size to shut off.

"I don't believe that worked," said Tia. "Did I just save the universe?"

Connie threw her arm around Tia. "You sure as hell did. Not to complain or anything, but there are usually explosions when big red buttons get pushed in my vicinity."

The maker explained, "Given the sheer mass of the Engine, it will take some time for anything like that. More likely, the subspace pocket will collapse, crushing everything into a two-dimensional object. That will explode with unimaginable power, but this is subspace. Won't hurt anything here. And it won't be for a while."

"That's it, then?" asked Tia. "We won? Thousands of years of cosmic manipulation ended with the push of a button?"

"That's it," said the maker.

"It's a little anticlimactic," said Tia. "What happens to the universe now?"

The maker shrugged. "Don't know. Nor do I care. You made your call. Now you have to live with it. As for me, I can finally deactivate. Which I will do now."

"Wait. Was any of this planned?" asked Connie.

"What do you want from me?" said the maker. "You won. The universe is yours now. I'd tell you to not screw it up, but everyone does. Do try to screw it up in new and interesting ways."

A rumble swept through the Engine as a shard of metal pierced the wall. The entire room shifted, tilting at a crooked angle.

The maker consulted her formula for subspace physics. "Hmm. Looks like I forgot to carry the two."

The Engine started exploding.

The subspace portal spat Connie and Tia out into an endless desert. The portal stayed open for a minute longer, and on the other side, the Engine rumbled and rattled and boomed as it self-destructed. The portal puckered close the moment the machine detonated, erupting with a jet of crimson fire and chunks of debris. The bits and pieces rained down. One especially large metallic plate came within a few feet of crushing them.

Connie and Tia caught their breath. Harrowing escapes from exploding were nothing new for Connie, and Tia had had her share as well.

This felt different.

"Guess the universe is still here," observed Tia, lying on

her back, covering her eyes from the sun blazing above.

"Looks like. For now." Connie sat up and surveyed the landscape. Desert stretched to the horizon in all directions. No signs of life. There was only one sun, so they might still be on Earth, though that was an assumption, and she couldn't rule out an alternate version yet.

"You don't think the Engine was right, do you?" asked Tia. "That without it, everything will fall into chaos, entropy will consume the universe?"

"No idea, but a little chaos is a good thing. If the Engine had succeeded, it would've been the same thing as destroying the universe. Perfect order sounds good if you're an obsessive-compulsive supercomputer, but everything would be so boring and predictable, what would be the point?"

"I thought you wanted boring," said Tia.

"I thought so too. But boring is . . . Well, it's boring. What I wanted was the chance to be boring now and then. I'd like to keep my options open."

"Sounds ambitious to me."

"I'm Constance Danger Verity. I do the impossible."

"But you've lost the caretaker," said Thelma.

"I'm still carrying some of it," said Connie.

"Just some?"

"Enough. It's not the size of your enchantment; it's what you do with it."

"Is that the lesson we've learned today?" asked Hiro from behind Tia.

She jumped. "Damn it, you asshole."

He flashed his grin. That grin could get him out of a lot of trouble.

"You escaped?" she asked.

"Was there ever any doubt?"

"And you didn't come back for us?" Tia punched him in the shoulder. Not hard. He stumbled back, slipped on the sand, and fell on his back with a grunt.

She knelt beside him. "Oh, jeez. I'm sorry."

"Think nothing of it," he replied. "I'm only bleeding to death here."

Connie checked him. "You'll be fine. That wound on your side is probably going to leave a scar, though."

Hiro caressed Tia's check. "A memento to remember you by."

Tia groaned before leaning in for a kiss.

Connie cleared her throat.

"What? He did get stabbed for me," said Tia.

Connie shrugged. "It's your call."

She turned her back while they made out. She assessed which direction would lead them to civilization.

She wasn't worried. This wasn't the glorious death that was her fate, but if she managed to die out here, then she'd beaten that fate. She'd chalk that up as a win.

39

They didn't die in that desert.

Three weeks later, the universe hadn't self-destructed.

Connie knocked on the hospital door as she entered.

Lucas Harrison lay in his bed. "Ah, Jesus, Verity. You could've told me you were coming." He tried sitting up.

She held up a teddy bear she'd picked up in the hospital gift shop. The bear had a bright red heart stitched on its tummy. "Saw this and thought of you."

He grunted. "Funny. Y'know, I only got shot because you weren't fast enough."

"And you're only alive because I was," she replied.

Harrison smiled. "Heard you're still in the adventure game."

"Didn't think you were on the Constance Verity beat anymore, Lucas."

"I'm not, but I still have a few connections here and there, keep my ear to the ground."

"Thinking about getting back in the game?" she asked. "I prefer you to that suit they replaced you with."

"Ellington? She'll grow on you. After all this, I think I'm ready for a nice vacation. But what about you, Verity? You're still not normal."

"I'm more normal than I was," she said.

"Is it enough?"

She shrugged. "I thought I wanted to be a regular person, but I just wanted a little time to breathe now and then. Every day was too damned tiring. Now, I don't know if it's because the Engine is gone, or maybe because I only carry a small part of the caretaker spell, or maybe I've just learned to ignore every call to adventure that crosses my path, but I'm down to two or three adventures a week. I have more time for myself, more time for my family and friends. I'm dating a guy, and it's going well. It's a juggling act, but compared to my old life, it's almost relaxing."

"You can't stop being who you are," he said.

"If someone needs my help, who am I to leave them to the cruel mercies of the universe? Someone has to keep the universe from exploding."

"I told you, Verity. You're good people."

"No, I'm just the right person in the right place. How about you, Harrison? Are you going to be all right?"

"What? Conspiracy stuff? Don't worry about it. I've already told you everything I know. Killing me wouldn't serve any useful purpose. And if anyone did want me to disappear, they'd have to consider you'd be coming after them. Trust me. Nobody wants that."

Connie chuckled. "Take care of yourself, Lucas. And keep in touch."

"You, too, Connie. Oh, and if something does happen to me, there's a safe deposit box in Hamburg. Oh, I'll just e-mail you the info."

She tossed him the bear.

"You do that."

Leaving the hospital, she boarded an empty elevator. Bonita Alvarado, dressed as a nurse, jumped in as the doors closed.

"Hello, Connie."

Connie grunted as way of greeting. "I thought you might have been blown up with the Engine."

"I'm more durable than that," Bonita chirped, changing shape into a tall humanoid insect. Only for a moment, easily missed if one weren't looking right at her. Easily dismissed even if one were.

"Funny," said Connie. "The computer said you were all extinct."

"There are secrets even the Great Engine didn't know," replied Bonita. "We've been here for a long, long time. We'll be around a long while yet. My people owe you a great debt. The universe owes you a great debt."

"Don't worry about it," said Connie. "Somebody had to protect free will across the cosmos. But now that the Engine is destroyed, will everything fall into entropy?"

Bonita shrugged. "Who knows? But a perfect universe, deprived of free will and the unexpected, where's the fun in that? And my people don't have to hide anymore. You have no idea how stressful it is being hunted by a nearly omnipotent supercomputer across the aeons. I just wanted to say thanks."

"You've got a lot of nerve," said Connie. "You've screwed with my life, with how many lives, just to get me to undo your mistake."

"Who said this was planned?" Bonita sounded almost convincing.

"Right. It's all simply an amazing coincidence that the bug lady who helped build a megalomaniacal computer was part of the conspiracy to control my life."

"Why couldn't it be?" asked Bonita. "When you're a member of a near-immortal progenitor race, it's easy to get bored. I'll admit it is rather suspicious serendipity, but then again, isn't that how your life works?"

She smiled mysteriously, and damned if Connie could determine if Bonita was lying or not.

The elevator dinged. Its doors opened and several other people boarded.

"Looks like this is my floor." Bonita exited. "Regardless of what you may or may not think, Connie, your life hasn't worked out so bad, has it?"

After the doors closed, Connie allowed herself a smile.

Connie met Tia for lunch in the Safe Zone, the break room at Tia's insurance agency job, the one place nothing interesting ever happened. They performed a hasty exorcism, turning out the lights and surrounding Thelma's haunted pen with candles and sage. Connie was a decent exorcist, but it was easy when the spirit had no unfinished business and wanted to leave.

"You're free to stick around," said Connie. She sort of meant it, though it wasn't because she cared for the ghost.

Thelma said, "Thanks, but I'm ready. I only stayed because I thought I'd be witnessing the end of everything."

"Sorry to disappoint you."

"Life, and apparently death, is full of surprises," said Thelma.

"So, what is on the Other Side?" asked Tia.

"You aren't ready."

"She's seen plenty of unknowable mysteries," said Connie. "She pushed the button that might have saved and/or destroyed the universe."

Tia shook her head. "Don't put this on me. It was your plan. I'm only the scrappy sidekick."

Thelma said, "The Great Engine was just one of many mysteries in this universe and beyond. Nobody knows them all. Not even the dead. Now, can we do this? I've got uncharted metaphysical realms to explore, and I can't do it from this pen."

Connie and Tia joined hands. They chanted "We release you" three times, and a glob of ectoplasm with Thelma's face rose from the pen.

"Any last-minute words of wisdom?" asked Connie.

"Wouldn't you like to know?"

The fairy's ghost dissolved with a mischievous grin. The

scent of roses lingered with the herbs used in the ritual.

A middle manager stepped into the darkened break room.

"Don't mind us," said Tia. "Just finishing up."

They turned on the lights and swept the mess into the wastebasket. Connie kept the pen. It was a good pen. The manager said nothing as he microwaved a burrito, poured himself a cup of coffee, and walked out without looking directly at them.

"Normal people, huh?" said Tia with a grin.

They chuckled.

"I still hope we did the right thing," said Tia. "What if the Engine was right? What if there is some greater potential out there, and we stopped it from happening?"

Connie said, "The Engine's view of perfection wasn't any more perfect than what we have. Yeah, it's a messy world, but who says order is all that great? That sort of paradise makes sense if you're a mad computer, but it's not how things work. I think even if it would've succeeded, it would've failed eventually. There's always going to be something you can't see coming. Life is nothing but complications. Eliminating them shouldn't be the goal. It's how we deal with them that matters.

"And even if the Engine was the force holding everything together, it'll probably be hundreds of thousands of years, millions, before the cosmos unravels. By then, it'll be someone else's problem."

"Just kick the can down the road, then," said Tia. "Let someone else deal with it."

"There are no permanent fixes. Just fires to put out. Take it from me. I've fought in three separate Ragnaroks, twice with the gods, once against them. And I've saved the Loch Ness Monster four times."

"Saved it from what?"

"You don't want to know. The Engine wanted everything to be perfect, but it never will be."

"It's a good thing you're around, then," said Tia.

"Maybe it is," agreed Connie.

"What do you think happened to the caretaker spell?" asked Tia.

"Probably destroyed when the Engine was destroyed," said Connie.

"Probably. But if it's out there, it could be dangerous if it falls into the wrong hands."

"Everything's dangerous," said Connie. "We live on the edge of disaster, ninja assassins and almost-exploding planets. And that's just the easy stuff. The small things, the little tragedies and calamities we defuse on a daily basis, often without realizing it, that's what we really need to keep an eye on. Most of us never realize it. Speaking of ninjas, how are things with you and Hiro?"

"Good. Except he wants to move in with me."

"That's fast."

Tia poked at her yogurt. "I know. I only started dating the guy because I was convinced he'd vanish in the night at some point. I wasn't looking for anything serious."

"The stuff that gets you is the stuff you don't see," said Connie. "I say go for it."

"But given his history—"

"The Hiro I knew would've been gone by now. Maybe he has changed. And it's obvious you're crazy about him."

"I don't know. He's so full of himself. Sure, he's cool, handsome. Suave, if you like that corny winking assurance that belongs to a James Bond character and not a person in real life."

Connie smiled, said nothing.

Tia blushed. "All right, so maybe I like him. But he's always disappearing when the dishes need to be done. It's annoying. Are you sure it's cool with you? Because if it's not, just say the word."

"It's cool. It's more than cool. If Hiro is genuinely trying to change, he shouldn't be with me. We were good together, but we weren't *good* together."

"What if I'm too boring for him?"

"You pushed the button that either saved or destroyed the universe, and you're dating a ninja. I don't think *boring* is a word to describe you."

"You know what I mean. I'm not special. Not like him. Not like you."

"With me, it was all about the thrills. Winging across the world, stealing precious treasures, passionate sex in exotic locales, betrayal, betrayal sex in other exotic locales. With you, it's about you."

Tia shook her head. "Basically, I'm boring enough that the

only reason anyone would be with me was because they like me."

"Not what I meant, and you know it. I've seen the way Hiro looks at you. He never looked at me like that. It probably won't work out in the end, but enjoy it while it lasts. There are worse guys to have a fling with."

Tia nodded, smiling at images of Hiro winking at her.

"You've got it bad," said Connie.

"How are things with Byron?" asked Tia, changing the subject.

"Good. He's the right guy. He's steady, but he also understands that I need to go off and have adventures now and then. Usually at the last minute. We make it work so far."

"That's all any of us do, I suppose."

A bearded man in a thobe flung open the door and stumbled into the break room. Connie's reflexes kicked in. She caught him before he fell over. Three daggers were stuck in his back.

"Take it easy," Connie said.

Tia was already calling for an ambulance.

The Bedouin pressed a large ruby into her hand. "You must return this to the Cave of Thieves or many innocent people will die."

Dinner with Byron would have to be rescheduled. Too bad. She'd been eager to try his "world-famous" burgers, but she had time to catch him before he started grilling.

"Sure, sure," said Connie. "Just stay with me."

But the Bedouin was already dead. She laid him down and checked for any attackers. The coast was clear.

"Poor guy," said Tia. "What are you going to do?"

A quick search of the Bedouin turned up a map of northern Africa with a big red X over the Hoggar Mountains. Nothing else of interest.

"Looks like I'm headed to Algeria," said Connie. "Want to come along?"

"I have this meeting at two," said Tia, "and there's a pile of paperwork I have to get to. Guess you'll have to pick up a scrappy sidekick somewhere else. Are we still on for Friday movie night?"

"Wouldn't miss it." Connie tucked the gem and map into her pocket.

"Call me if something comes up," said Tia.

"I'll be there."

"Just the same . . ."

"Tia, come ninjas or dinosaurs or robot attack, I'll be there. I'll find a way."

Connie smiled, already making travel arrangements there and back in her head.

"It's what I do."

A. Lee Martinez is the author of ten fantasy novels. Martinez's first published novel, *Gil's All Fright Diner*, was awarded an Alex Award by the American Library Association. His books have been translated into five languages. Born in El Paso, Texas, he currently resides outside of Austin, Texas, where he enjoys video games, juggling, origami, skulking, and time travel.

He can be found at aleemartinez.com
and on Twitter: @aleemartinez.

ALSO AVAILABLE FROM

JO FLETCHER BOOKS

CONSTANCE VERITY

Saves the World

A. LEE MARTINEZ

Constance Verity – soon to be played on the big screen by *Crazy Rich Asians* superstar Awkwafina! – is still saving the universe, one crisis at a time – but now the rules have changed.

Constance Verity has managed to build a quiet life between feats of improbable heroism, until the line between adventure and ordinary begins to blur and Connie discovers that preventing her two very different worlds from colliding might be beyond even her.

It's hard enough to maintain a relationship without having to find time to save the world, and when her (sort of) ex-boyfriend, the son of one of her top-ten arch-enemies, comes to her for help, the timing couldn't be worse.

But when malicious superbrains and sinister ocean gods join an entirely unreasonable number of assassins, Connie might finally be in over her head – and the curse of steadily worsening bad luck isn't helping much.

With her history of saving the world, over and over, it should be just another day in Connie's life – shouldn't it?

'Genuinely likeable characters and imaginative set pieces drive
the breathless narrative all the way to a fitting finalé. Readers who like
a lot of sass with their derring-do will find much to love here'
Publishers Weekly

Jo Fletcher
BOOKS

CONSTANCE VERITY
Destroys the Universe

A. LEE MARTINEZ

The final part in Constance Verity's epic adventure: saving the world is easy. Everything that comes after is the tricky part. Look out for *Crazy Rich Asians* superstar Awkwafina as Connie in the major movie adaptation of the first book.

Saving the world is easy for Constance Verity: she's used to doing the impossible on a daily basis. Everything that comes after is the tricky part.

Connie has accepted and secured her place in the universe. There isn't a foe she can't outfight or a peril she can't outwit – until she discovers she herself might be the greatest threat to the world she's spent her life saving.

All the signs are pointing to impending doom, and not just for Connie. Her friends, her enemies and the universe itself are all at risk. She's always known she was destined for a glorious death, but she never suspected she'd be taking everyone and everything else with her.

With her trademark determination, Constance Verity sets out to avert a cosmic plan millions of years in the making – and save the universe from herself.

After all, who else is going to do it?

> **'Martinez has more fun than should be strictly legal telling the story of Constance'**
> ***Barnes & Noble Booksellers' Picks***

Jo Fletcher
BOOKS